Kissing Bailey was like ~~a~~ **drug. Benjamin's head** ~~dizzied and~~ **his heart quickened the moment his lips met hers. She tasted of cinnamon and coffee and sweet hot desire.**

He deepened the kiss by dipping his tongue in to dance with hers. She tightened her arms around his neck and pressed herself closer to him, making him half-wild with his own heightened desire for her.

He reminded himself that he didn't want to get in too deep with her, but it was hard to remember that when she filled his arms and her mouth was so hot and so hungry against his own.

What he wanted to do right now was to take her into his bedroom. He wanted to strip her naked and then make slow, sweet love to her. However, he still had his wits together enough to know he couldn't let that happen. That definitely wouldn't be fair to her.

He cared about her enough not to sleep with her and then dump her. With that in mind, he finally pulled away from her.

Dear Reader,

Growing up in the Midwest, thunderstorms are just a force of nature to be dealt with. Sometimes they can be nothing more than distant rumblings in the sky and a patter of welcomed rain at the window. Other times they are tornado-breeding monsters that put people and property in imminent danger.

I've always wondered, in my sick little writer's mind, how frightening it would be to wake up during a thunderstorm and realize there's a stranger in your home. How horrible would it be to only see the intruder during the lightning flashes and not be able to hear them due to the thunder overhead.

Stalker in the Storm is about a woman who is being stalked by an unknown person. There was a time in my life when I was stalked by an ex-boyfriend. Wherever I went, I would see his car and I knew he was watching me. Even when I went out on dates, when my date took me home, I would see my ex-boyfriend's car parked just down the street. Thankfully, it only lasted for a little while and then he stopped.

Still, it was a creepy feeling that hopefully I brought to this book. Storms...stalkers...and secrets—I hope you enjoy reading *Stalker in the Storm*.

Happy reading!

Carla Cassidy

STALKER IN
THE STORM

CARLA CASSIDY

HARLEQUIN
ROMANTIC
SUSPENSE

HARLEQUIN®
ROMANTIC SUSPENSE™

Recycling programs
for this product may
not exist in your area.

ISBN-13: 978-1-335-59411-2

Stalker in the Storm

Copyright © 2024 by Carla Bracale

Harlequin Enterprises ULC
22 Adelaide St. West, 41st Floor
Toronto, Ontario M5H 4E3, Canada
www.Harlequin.com

MIX
Paper | Supporting
responsible forestry
FSC® C021394

Printed in Lithuania

Carla Cassidy is an award-winning, *New York Times* bestselling author who has written over 170 books, including 150 for Harlequin. She has won the Centennial Award from Romance Writers of America. Most recently she won the 2019 Write Touch Readers' Award for her Harlequin Intrigue title *Desperate Strangers*. Carla believes the only thing better than curling up with a good book is sitting down at the computer with a good story to write.

Books by Carla Cassidy

Harlequin Romantic Suspense

The Scarecrow Murders

Killer in the Heartland
Guarding a Forbidden Love
The Cowboy Next Door
Stalker in the Storm

Cowboys of Holiday Ranch

Sheltered by the Cowboy
Guardian Cowboy
Cowboy Defender
Cowboy's Vow to Protect
The Cowboy's Targeted Bride
The Last Cowboy Standing

Visit the Author Profile page
at Harlequin.com for more titles.

This book is dedicated to my friend and inspiration—
my mother.

Chapter 1

Bailey Troy roared down Main Street, aware of the minutes ticking by far too quickly. She was late to open her business, the Sassy Nail Salon. One of her first customers of the day was Letta Lee, head of the women's gardening club and number-one gossip and mean witch of Millsville, Kansas.

She and some of her cronies would make Bailey's life an absolute living hell if Letta had to wait ten minutes or so to get her butt into the salon chair to get her nails done. With this thought in mind, Bailey stepped on the gas.

The late September air caressed her face, reminding her of how much she loved her sporty red convertible. Her big, round sunglasses reduced the bright sun's glare and it was nearly impossible for the breeze to mess up her short, spiky hair.

She was almost to the salon when she heard a siren coming from someplace behind her. Looking in her rearview mirror, she couldn't see what kind of an emergency vehicle it might be. She should pull over to the curb, but instead she hit the gas once again, thinking she could stay well ahead of it.

The Sassy Nail Salon was just to her left and she whirled into the lot and parked, pleased to see that Letta Lee's car wasn't there yet. Hopefully, Bailey would have time to get inside and set things up for the older woman before she showed up.

Her pleasure was short-lived as a patrol car pulled in just behind her, the siren blaring and the lights on top swirling in a red-and-blue blur.

"Crap," she murmured under her breath. She couldn't tell who was in the patrol car, but she hoped it wasn't Officer Joel Penn. He could be a real jerk, and she knew she'd never be able to talk him out of a speeding ticket. The siren stopped its shrieking and the lights quit spinning.

She watched in her side-view mirror as the door opened and Officer Benjamin Cooper stepped out. Her heart immediately took on an accelerated beat. His blond hair sparkled in the sunshine as he approached her car.

She'd had a mad crush on the man forever, but he'd never made a move for her to think he might want to date her. He'd certainly dated most of the other women in town and rumor had it he was now seeing Celeste Winthrop, a very thirsty, attractive divorcée.

His blue uniform shirt stretched taut across his broad shoulders and his dark blue slacks fit nicely on his long legs. His holster was slung around his narrow hips and Bailey felt half-breathless just looking at him.

"Bailey," he said, his deep voice somber as he reached her driver window. He pulled down his sunglasses, exposing his beautiful, long-lashed blue eyes. He glared at her sternly. "You want to tell me what's the hurry?"

"Oh, Officer Cooper, was I speeding?" she asked innocently. "I'm sorry, I guess I might have been going a little bit over the speed limit."

"Nineteen miles over the speed limit isn't a little bit," he replied.

She looked at him in genuine surprise. Jeez, she hadn't realized just how fast she'd been going. "License and registration," he said.

"Are you really going to give me a ticket?" she asked miserably, and to make her misery worse, at that moment Letta Lee pulled in and parked.

"Bailey, this isn't the first time I've seen you speeding down Main Street. One of these days you're going to kill yourself or somebody else," Benjamin said.

"Please—please don't ticket me. I'm so sorry and I'll definitely do better in the future. I was running late this morning. I overslept and then I forgot to put a pod in my coffee machine, so I got nothing but a cup of hot water, and I had Letta Lee as my first client of the day and she can be such a pain and..." She was babbling and she couldn't seem to help herself. Not only did she not want a ticket, but she also always felt ridiculously nervous around him.

"I got it," he replied with a hint of sympathy in his voice. "Okay, Bailey, I'll let you go this time, but the next time I see you roaring down the street, I promise you're going to get a ticket." He pushed his sunglasses back up. "Now, go tend to Letta Lee before she calls 911 for having to wait on you."

"Thank you, thank you," she replied with relief. "I swear I'll do better in the future."

"I'll be watching you, Bailey," he replied. "Now, have a good day."

As he headed back to his car, she got out of hers. She'd never had much actual contact with Benjamin and it upset her that the brief exchange she'd had with him had been about her speeding. Why couldn't he have pulled her over to ask her out on a date?

What made things even worse was Letta Lee was standing by the salon's front door, tapping her foot with obvious impatience. The thin, older woman was clad in a light blue pantsuit and her short white hair was perfectly coiffed. She looked like a sweet old lady, but her personality was anything but sweet.

"I must say, it's quite an embarrassment for me to be doing business where the police show up," Letta said as Bailey unlocked the front door. "I hope that isn't going to be a regular thing here."

"The police were here because I was speeding to get here on time so you wouldn't have to wait on me," Bailey replied.

"And yet here I am, waiting on you," Letta said with an audible indignant sniff.

Bailey swallowed a deep sigh and ushered the older woman inside. Ten minutes later Letta had her feet soaking in a bowl of warm, scented water and Bailey began to take off her old maroon fingernail polish.

"How are things going with the gardening club?" Bailey asked in an attempt to make some pleasant small talk.

"Really well. We're getting things all ready to have a nice display at the fall festival," Letta replied.

The fall festival in Millsville was a big deal. All the businesses closed for two days and there were booths to buy goods, cooking contests and a full carnival for everyone to enjoy. The festival was in a week and already there was a thrum of excitement in the town.

Lord knew they all needed something to look forward to after the two heinous murders that had taken place recently. Bailey didn't even want to think about them, but thoughts of the murders now played in her mind. The first one had occurred almost two months ago. The victim, a nice young woman named Cindy Perry had been stabbed to death and then made into a human scarecrow and stood up in a corn field.

The second victim had been Sandy Blackstone. She had also been stabbed and made into a scarecrow then stood up in the backyard of the bakery. Thinking about the murders always gave Bailey the shivers.

As she painted first Letta's fingernails and then gave her a pedicure and painted her toenails, the two continued to talk about the festival. By the time she was finished with Letta, Jaime Davenport and Naomi Crawford came into the shop. The two women worked for Bailey. Naomi worked full-time and Jaime part-time. Within minutes of their arrival, the busy Saturday began.

It was just after seven that evening when she finally closed up shop. She was exhausted and grateful that the salon was closed the next day and on Monday. She intended to use her "weekend" to thoroughly clean her house. She had a feeling the next week would be crazy busy as most of the women would want their nails all done for the festival next Friday and Saturday.

She got into her car and once inside she headed home. Home was a two-story house just off Main Street. She'd bought the place two years before and loved being a homeowner.

Before that she had been living with her mother in the small ranch house where she was born. As much as she loved her mother, they often butted heads. It had been important to Bailey to build her own life and live by her own rules. She'd wanted to set down roots and live on her own terms, so owning a house had been important to her.

As she drove, she kept her speed within the legal limit and continued to look in her rearview mirror to make sure she wasn't followed by anyone.

When she reached the attractive Wedgwood blue house with the white shutters, she parked in the driveway. Her garage was filled with salon supplies and was completely disorganized, making it impossible for her to park inside there right now.

She entered by the front door and beelined into the kitchen, where she set her purse on the counter and then opened the fridge to see what she was going to eat for dinner.

Her kitchen was painted a bright yellow and she had large colorful roosters hanging on one wall. She loved the airy, cheerful room. She'd chosen a round glass-topped table and red accents popped around the room.

She pulled out a bowl of chicken salad she'd made the night before and made a sandwich with it, then added potato chips to the plate and grabbed a soda.

She had just sat down to eat when her cell phone rang. She looked at the caller identification, swallowed a deep sigh and then answered. "Hi, Mom."

"Bailey, I'd like you to come over tomorrow and help me clean out the spare room." Angela Troy was a strong woman who had raised Bailey as a single parent. Bailey had spent most of her life trying to win her mother's love and approval, and at thirty-four years old she felt as if she had yet to gain it.

"What time do you have in mind?" Bailey asked, even though the last thing she wanted to do on her day off was work in her mother's spare room.

"Around noon, but don't expect me to make lunch for you. Eat before you come," Angela instructed. "I heard that the police were at your place of business this morning." There was more than a touch of displeasure in her tone.

"Don't worry, Mom, it was nothing serious," Bailey assured her.

"I do worry about you, Bailey. You do realize you are the physical type for the Scarecrow Killer. I would feel so much better if you were married or at least had a serious boyfriend and you didn't live all alone."

Bailey rolled her eyes. This was a common diatribe from her mother. "Mom, it's hard to get married or have a serious boyfriend when you aren't even dating anyone."

"What was wrong with Howard Kendall? He's a nice-looking man who has a good job at the bank and he was absolutely crazy about you."

"But I wasn't crazy about him," Bailey replied. Howard Kendall was a nice man she'd dated several times, but he hadn't given her butterflies or sparks. Even if he had, Bailey had a rule—she only dated a man three times or so and then she was done with him.

"You aren't getting any younger, Bailey. Surely you do realize your biological clock is definitely ticking faster now," Angela continued. "I'm ready for some grandchildren."

"Okay, Mom. On that note, I'll just see you tomorrow," Bailey replied.

The two said their goodbyes, and as Bailey ate, her thoughts weren't on her mother, but focused on Officer Benjamin Cooper. He definitely gave her butterflies in the pit of her stomach each time she was around him. If she was anyplace that she might talk to him, she became a tongue-twisted fool. It was no wonder he'd never asked her out.

She finished eating, then put her plate in the dishwasher

and headed to her bedroom upstairs. Her bedroom was definitely her safe haven. Decorated in hot pink and black, it was both contemporary and stylish.

Not only did the room boast a king-size bed and a large smart television, but it also had an en suite bathroom done in the same pink-and-black color scheme.

After a quick shower, she pulled on her comfy nightgown and then crawled into bed. She turned on her television and found a program she enjoyed watching, but her thoughts were scattered and made concentrating on the show difficult.

As much as she would love to date Benjamin, she knew marriage was probably not in her future. And she'd made peace with that. But there were times when she got lonely and wished she had a special man in her life. There were times when she wished she could be normal.

When she thought about her conversation with her mother, there was one thing that threatened to walk shivers up and down her spine. The Scarecrow Killer. The man had already killed two women, but the worst part was what he had done to their bodies.

He'd dressed up each of them in frayed jeans and a flannel shirt, then put them on poles as if they were scarecrows. Their mouths had been sewn shut with thick black thread and their eyes had been missing.

The whole town had been on edge since the murders had occurred. It was obvious there was a sick, vicious serial killer at work in the small town of Millsville, Kansas. And her mother had been right: with Bailey's blond hair and blue eyes, she fit the Scarecrow Killer's victim profile.

The next day at precisely noon, Bailey pulled up to the farmhouse where she'd been raised. It was a small, two-bedroom place painted white with black shutters. Her mother rented out ten acres to the farmer next door, since she had never been interested in farming and it had been an easy way for her to make a little extra money.

Rather, Angela had worked as a secretary for the mayor, Buddy Lyons, for years and had finally retired from that position last year.

"Mom," Bailey yelled as she stepped through the front door and into the living room. The living room had a burgundy sofa and a matching floral chair. Bailey didn't remember there ever being different furniture in the room. New furniture had never been in her single mother's budget.

"I'm back here." Her mother's voice rang out from down the hallway.

Bailey headed back to the bedroom that had been hers while growing up, but the minute Bailey had gotten her own place, the bedroom had become the catch-all spare storage room.

Angela was in the process of pulling boxes off the closet shelf and placing them on the twin bed. "Bailey, I'm glad you're here. A lot of this is your stuff and I want you to take it all with you today. I'm not a storage unit and I'm going to need this space for my own things."

Angela Troy was an attractive woman with short ash-blond hair and pale blue eyes. Even though it had only been her and Bailey, her mother had never really fostered a close relationship with her daughter. Of course, she'd had to work hard to support the two of them, and then when she was home from work, she was often too tired to have time for Bailey.

For the next few hours, Bailey carried boxes and bags to her car, and then helped her mother get the room reorganized with new craft items Angela had bought for herself.

"I think I'll really enjoy getting to know how to make jewelry," Angela said.

"That's great, Mom," Bailey replied. "I'd be proud to wear anything you made."

Angela looked pointedly at Bailey's oversize, dangling bright yellow earrings. "I don't think you'll be interested in wearing any of my jewelry. It's going to be quite subdued and tasteful."

Bailey stifled a deep sigh. This was Angela at her best, throwing out little jabs to undermine Bailey's confidence. But Bailey was used to it and it quickly rolled off her back.

It was nearly four o'clock when the two sat at the kitchen table and her mother poured them each a glass of iced tea. "Thank you for all your help today," Angela said. "How are things going at the salon?"

"Good. I'm expecting a really busy week ahead as most of the ladies in town will want their nails done before the festival," Bailey replied.

"Yes, I have an appointment on Thursday to come in and see Jaime," Angela responded.

"Mom, I've told you a million times just to call me and I'll come over and do your nails." Bailey took a big drink of the cold tea.

"It's all right, dear. I know how busy you stay and I would much rather you spend your spare time dating. So has anyone asked you out lately?"

"Howard is still calling me, although I've been firm in telling him that I'm not going out with him again. Then last night after I talked to you, Ethan Dourty called to see if I wanted to grab a cup of coffee with him tomorrow morning at the café."

"I certainly hope you're going. Ethan seems like a fine

man, and with him owning his own insurance company I'm sure he's solid financially," Angela replied.

"I'm going," Bailey said. Ethan wasn't the man she was most interested in, but Benjamin certainly wasn't making any moves on her.

The truth of the matter was that Bailey was lonely. She'd been particularly lonely since her best friend, Lizzy Maxwell, had hooked up with the love of her life, Joe Masterson. While she was thrilled that Lizzy had found her one true love, that left Bailey uncomfortable playing the role of third wheel whenever she visited with Lizzy.

"You know, Bailey, you're very picky when it comes to men. You only see them a few times and then you find something wrong with them," Angela said.

"I can't help it that they aren't right for me," Bailey answered.

"You have to compromise, Bailey. You're never going to find a husband that way."

"Then maybe I'll never find a husband," Bailey replied airily.

"Don't be ridiculous," Angela said. "You need a husband. You don't want to go through life all alone like I have. If your father had been a real man and had stepped up to the plate when I found out I was pregnant with you, then my life would have been much better and so much easier. I should have married one of the nice men who dated me when you were young."

"But from what you've told me in the past, you weren't in love with any of them."

Angela made a scoffing noise. "I've come to believe love isn't all that important. If you're compatible and share common goals and respect each other, then that's enough to make a good marriage and you should remember that, Bailey."

"I'll keep that in mind," Bailey replied. "And now, if you're finished with me, I think I'll head on home."

"All right, dear. I'll see you in the salon on Thursday." The two women stood up from the table and headed for the front door.

"Then I'll see you Thursday," Bailey said, and minutes later she was in her car and headed home.

She always found spending time with her mother completely exhausting and today had been no different. She realized Angela expected her to get married and pop out a couple of kids, but Bailey knew that wasn't in her future.

The next morning at ten o'clock, she walked into the café to meet Ethan. The Millsville Café was a popular place in town. Inside, the walls were vibrant with color, and three of them were decorated with huge paintings. The first held golden bales of hay with bright red roosters. The second was a yellow cornfield with three silos and the final wall was farmland in patterns of browns, greens and golds.

It was definitely a place for friends and families to meet neighbors and enjoy a good, reasonably priced meal. There were booths along both walls and a row of tables and chairs down the middle. The place was packed with the Monday morning crowd. Ethan rose and waved to her from one of the two-tops.

He was a nice-looking guy with light brown hair and hazel eyes. She knew he was well-liked and respected in the town, and she wished he gave her butterflies like Benjamin did. But even if he did, she knew there would be no future for them.

Most men her age would be looking to start a family, and Bailey just wasn't ready for that.

You're not right. You're the most selfish woman I've ever met. You're not normal.

The deep male voice echoed in her head, a voice from her distant past. She quickly shoved away the memory. The last thing she wanted was for that voice to start playing around and around in her mind.

"Hi, Bailey," Ethan said with a wide smile as she joined him at the table. He was dressed in a pair of jeans and a short-sleeved white button-down shirt.

"Hi, Ethan." She sat in the chair across from his. "Thank you so much for asking me out for this morning." It would be nice if she and Ethan could just be friends. It would be nice to have a male friend who just wanted to spend time with her and wanted nothing more.

"No problem." He sank back down in his chair. "I know I said we'd meet for coffee, but if you'd like some breakfast or an early lunch, feel free to order whatever you want."

"Thanks, but coffee is fine," she replied.

"I just thought it would be nice to get to know you a little better. We sometimes run into each other on the street or at a town function, but I've never really gotten an opportunity to sit down and talk with you."

At that moment, Regina Waltz, a waitress, appeared next to the table to take their orders.

"I'd just like a coffee," Bailey said.

"I'll take the same, but I'd also like one of those big cinnamon rolls," Ethan said and then looked at Bailey. "Are you sure you don't want something else?"

She smiled at him. "No thanks, coffee is good for me."

Within minutes they had been served and Regina left

their table. "I figured with both of us being business own-ers, we'd have a lot in common," Ethan said.

"I'm sure we do," she agreed. "I don't know about you, but my business keeps me very busy."

"Yeah, I have to hustle quite a bit to keep mine grow-ing." He smiled at her once again. "So tell me about Bailey Troy. Why isn't a beautiful, smart woman like you not mar-ried yet?"

"I guess I just haven't found that special man yet," she replied. "And I could ask the same thing about you. Why isn't a handsome, smart man like you not married?"

"I guess I haven't found the right woman yet," he replied with another smile. "I've been so focused on my business that I've neglected my love life, but I'm ready now to relax some on the business end of things and get more social."

For the next forty-five minutes or so, the two visited and got to know each other a little better. He seemed like a nice man and she found him easy to talk to. They talked about the difficulties and joys of owning a business and how much they enjoyed living in the small town.

"I was wondering if you'd like to go with me to the festival next Saturday," he said as she got ready to leave.

"Oh, I'm so sorry, Ethan, but I'm working at the fes-tival. I'm offering all the kids under sixteen a free nail painting," she replied.

"Wow, that's really nice, Bailey," he said.

"I just thought it would be fun. We're also doing five-dollar face paintings, too, however Naomi Crawford is in charge of that."

"Maybe we could get together sometime after the fes-tival," he suggested.

"Sure, just give me a call," Bailey replied. "And now,

it's time for me to get out of here. Thank you so much for the coffee and good conversation and I'll talk to you soon."

Minutes later, as Bailey drove home, a wave of depression swept over her. There was no question that she was often lonely, and she filled that loneliness by dating men who really meant nothing to her.

Even though her mother thought it was because she was too picky, that simply wasn't the case. Bailey was just trying to protect herself and anyone she might date. She didn't want feelings to get too deep on either end because she knew she was a bad choice as a wife and mother.

You're not right. You're the most selfish woman I've ever met. Again, those words from her past haunted her. As much as she didn't want to believe them, she knew Adam had been correct about her, and that was why she would never have a serious relationship after him.

It had been ten years since she'd dated Adam Merriweather, and still, he had a profound effect on her. When she'd told him what she saw as her future, he'd told her how selfish and sick she was.

Thankfully, it was soon after they broke up that he had moved out of town. It was nice that she didn't have to worry about bumping into him around town. Even though she'd put that relationship far behind her, his parting words to her still haunted her and stabbed her in her very soul.

The rest of her evening she cleaned house and did laundry to prepare for the busy workweek ahead. Tuesday morning, she got up and dressed in a pink dress that was one of her favorites with its cinched waist and flirty skirt. She added pink-and-white polka-dotted earrings and white sandals.

By the time she left her house, she felt ready to take on

the world. It was a beautiful sunny day without a cloud in the sky. She was careful to watch her speed as she drove and then she pulled up and parked in front of the salon.

Ten years ago, right after her relationship with Adam was finished, she had decided to go to nail school and she had opened the business eight years ago.

She had begged, borrowed and tapped into every credit line she could get to buy the building, all the equipment and then get the business up and running. There had been no other nail salon in town and almost immediately the place had been a huge success. That very first year she had turned a profit and she was very proud of what she'd built here.

The building was the perfect size for the salon. She had five pedicure chairs and four manicure stations. There was a nice restroom for the guests and a back room for the employees to take their breaks or eat lunch.

The outside was painted black with hot pink trim. Large pink lettering announced it to be the Sassy Nail Salon. She loved every inch of it.

She got out of her car and walked up to the front door. She frowned as the doorknob turned easily in her hand. Had she been in such a hurry to leave on Saturday night that she'd forgotten to lock it up when she'd left? If so, it wasn't the first time it had happened. She reminded herself she had to be more careful in the future as she pushed open the front door.

Bailey took a step inside, flipped on all the lights and then she saw her. "She" sat in one of the salon chairs. She was clad in frayed blue jeans and a red plaid shirt.

A straw hat rode her head at a cocky angle. Her mouth was sewn shut with thick black thread and her eyes were missing. Even with everything that had been done to her,

Bailey immediately recognized her as Megan Lathrop, a young blonde who worked as a nurse at the hospital.

She was a horrific sight. As Bailey stared at her, the back of her throat closed up as cold chills raced up and down her spine.

Help. Oh, God, Bailey needed to get help. As her mind worked to process the fact that the Scarecrow Killer had struck again and there was a dead woman in her salon, her hand fumbled in her purse to grab her cell phone. As she punched in the emergency number, she tried desperately to stifle her screams.

Chapter 2

Officer Benjamin Cooper sped up to the nail shop, parked and then jumped out of his car. He shoved open the door to the salon and Bailey immediately flew into his arms. She sobbed into the front of his chest as her entire body shook with deep tremors.

He stared over Bailey's shoulder and gazed at the lifeless body that sat in one of her pedicure chairs. It… She was a terrible sight. Dammit, he'd hoped there wouldn't be another one. He'd hoped like hell they would be able to catch the killer before he could take another victim.

Despite what had been done to her, he recognized her as Megan Lathrop, a cute blonde with big blue eyes—eyes that were now missing. The whole salon smelled of death and he hoped like hell they would be able to get some clues with this one that would lead them to the killer.

"D-do you s-see her?" Bailey asked between choked sobs. "Oh B-Benjamin, why wa-was she left here? Wh-why is she here?"

Benjamin guided the sobbing woman outside the salon and to the bench that sat in front of the place. The last thing he wanted was for her to contaminate the scene any more than she already had. As she sank down, he sat next to her and put an arm around her slender shoulders. He'd stay with her until other officers showed up. She weakly leaned into his side.

"Wh-why here?" she asked again. "Wh-why was she l-left in my salon?"

"Bailey, we don't know why they are left where they are," he said softly. As sorry as he was for Megan, he was just grateful that Bailey hadn't been the victim.

This murder confirmed for sure that the killer had a penchant for blondes with blue eyes. Bailey was highly visible whether she was racing around in her red convertible or walking down the street in one of her stylish outfits. Benjamin was incredibly drawn to her and that was why he had always stayed away from her.

Now that they were outside and he was sitting so close to her, he could smell her scent. It was the very attractive fragrance of fresh florals and mysterious spices.

"Wh-who is this m-monster?" Bailey continued to cry as her entire body trembled against his.

"I wish we knew. Can I ask you some questions, Bailey? Can you tell me exactly what happened when you arrived here this morning? Did you see anyone lingering around the salon?"

She shook her head. "No…nobody, but the front door was unlocked this morning when I got here. But sometimes I forget to lock up after myself. I just assumed I'd forgotten to lock up when I finished up here on Saturday night." She released a deep sigh and melted farther into the side of him.

"So you didn't see anything or anyone unusual before you walked into the salon?" Benjamin asked.

"No…nothing. It was just a normal day," she replied and then began to cry once again. "I can't b-believe she was just—just sitting there. It's so—so horrible. She looked so h-horrible."

At that moment, Chief of Police Dallas Calloway pulled in with his sirens blaring and his lights whirling. He turned off both the sirens and the lights and then quickly got out of his car. He was followed by two more police vehicles, which held officers Joel Penn and Darryl O'Conner.

"You good out here?" Dallas asked Benjamin.

Benjamin nodded, and Dallas and the other men entered the building. "I—I just can't believe this is happening," Bailey said. She looked up at him with her big, beautiful blue eyes. "Who would do this to poor Megan? She was such a sweet young woman. And what does he do with their eyes? Oh, God, why does he take their eyes?"

"I wish we had all the answers," he replied.

She began to weep all over again and Benjamin pulled her closer and awkwardly patted her back in an effort to comfort her. Under ordinary circumstances, he would have enjoyed having her in his arms. She was petite and fit perfectly against him. But these weren't ordinary circumstances. Another heinous murder had occurred and he was sure it had been horrendous for Bailey to walk into her salon and find a dead woman in one of her chairs.

They remained sitting there for several long moments and once again she got herself under control. Dallas stepped out of the door and greeted her softly.

"You might as well go on home, Bailey. Your salon is going to be closed for the next day or two while we process the crime scene," he said.

They all paused as the coroner pulled up in his black hearse. Josiah Mills was probably ten years past retirement age, but according to him, he had no desire to retire anytime soon.

He got out of the hearse along with Gary Walters, his

thirtysomething assistant. "Bastard got another one, eh?" Josiah said as he approached them.

"That's right, although this one is a little different in that she's sitting rather than standing somewhere outside," Dallas replied.

"Let's go see what we've got," Josiah said somberly.

Dallas ushered in Josiah and Gary, and then indicated to Benjamin that he wanted him inside, as well. Benjamin stood and cast a sympathetic smile toward Bailey. "Go home, Bailey. Or better yet, go to your mother's place or go sit with a friend. I know you've been through a terrible shock and right now you need to be with somebody who can comfort you."

"I was finding you very comforting," she replied with a shuddering sigh.

"I'm sorry, but I need to get to work now. I need to help process the scene, so hopefully we can catch this guy."

"Okay, maybe you could check in on me later today?" she asked anxiously as she stood.

A faint breeze caught the bottom of her pretty pink dress and sent it ruffling all around her shapely legs. "Sure, I'll try to stop by your place later tonight," he replied. "Now, get home or get someplace safe."

At thirty-seven years old, he wasn't looking for marriage or even a long-term relationship and that's exactly why he kept his distance from Bailey, because he suspected if he had a little bit of her, he'd want way more.

It was just after nine that night when he pulled into Bailey's driveway. He was absolutely exhausted, with more work to come before the night was over. Dallas had given some of the men thirty minutes or so to get something to eat and then return to the salon, as they intended on working through the night.

Instead of getting anything to eat, Benjamin had first headed directly to Bailey's house. He'd kind of promised he'd check in on her this evening. He got out of his car and walked toward her house, where light spilled out of several of her windows, letting him know she was still up.

He knocked on her door and she immediately answered. She was dressed in a pair of gray jogging pants and a gray-and-turquoise T-shirt. Her makeup was minimal and her eyes were slightly red and swollen as if she'd spent most of the day crying.

"Oh, Benjamin, I'm so glad you came by," she said as she opened the door wider to allow him entry. She gestured him toward the sofa and he sat down. The room looked exactly like he'd expected it to—contemporary and colorful with bright pink and yellow throw pillows on the sleek black sofa. There was also a bookcase holding books and knick-knacks. "Would you like something to drink?" she asked.

"No thanks, I'm fine. The real question is how are you doing?"

She sank down in the chair facing the sofa and shook her head. "To be honest, I don't know how I'm doing. One minute I think I'm doing just fine and then I think about poor Megan again and I totally lose it."

Even now her beautiful blue eyes filled with the shimmer of impending tears. "I mean, I'd heard about the women who were killed before, but hearing about it and seeing it up close and personal are two very different things." She swiped at her eyes.

"I'm so sorry you had to see that, Bailey," he replied. "But keep in mind that it had nothing to do with you."

"It's hard not to think that it has something to do with me. I mean, out of all the places in town, why did the killer choose my salon? Is the killer somebody I know? Did I somehow make him mad at me?" She searched his face.

"Bailey, you shouldn't be thinking that way at all. If we've learned anything from the first two murders, it was that the places where the bodies were found were totally random and we're sure that's the case with this last one."

"I just wish he would have randomed someplace else," she replied dryly.

"The bad news is that we'll have your salon closed for tomorrow, but the good news is hopefully on Thursday you'll be able to open up for business again," he said. "We're working as long and as fast as we can to see that will happen. And now, I need to get out of here. I need to grab a burger and then get back to work at the salon." He stood from the sofa.

She rose, as well. "I really appreciate you stopping by to check on me," she said as they walked toward her front door.

"Just take tomorrow to rest up because I'm sure you'll be really busy on Thursday," he said as they reached the front door.

"Or I won't be busy at all because nobody will want to get their nails done in a place where a scarecrow body was found."

Benjamin released a small burst of laughter. "Surely you know the women in this town better than that. They'll be beating each other over the head with their purses in order to get a chair in the infamous salon."

She offered him a small smile. "You're probably right about that," she agreed. She then leaned forward and into his arms. It was unexpected and he had no other choice than to put his arms around her.

Once again, he noticed her scent, one that drew him in. Her body fit perfectly against his own, and for a moment he wanted to hold on to her forever. Which is exactly why he stepped back away from her.

"Take care, Bailey, and I'm sure we'll see each other around town."

"Thank you again for stopping by to check on me," she replied.

As he walked back toward his car, he tried not to think too much about the woman he had just left. She'd always appeared so strong and full of a zest for life as she went about her business in town.

But the woman he had just left had appeared anything but strong. She'd been achingly vulnerable and all alone. He knew she'd been dating Howard Kendall for a while, but that lately she hadn't been seeing anyone.

So who held Bailey Troy when she was afraid? Who comforted her through a long night? Why was she still alone? She was beyond pretty and appeared very successful, so why was she not married with kids?

And why in the hell was he sitting in her driveway and contemplating these things about her?

Benjamin was back in the salon at six thirty the next morning despite the fact that they had worked until after one the night before. The only officer there before him was Dallas. Not only was Dallas Benjamin's boss, but the two men were also close friends.

With his dark, curly hair and gray eyes, Dallas had always been a favorite among the ladies in town. But since the first murder had occurred, it had been obvious his love life was the very last thing on his mind.

"Hey, man," he greeted Dallas as he stepped inside the salon.

"Hey, Benjamin," Dallas replied and sighed heavily.

"That sigh sounded very tired," Benjamin observed.

"Yeah, I'm sure all the men are going to be tired today, but I want to get this all processed so we can give it back to Bailey as soon as possible. I also had trouble going to sleep when I finally did get home," Dallas admitted. "I was really so hoping we wouldn't have another murder and then I was hoping we'd get more than a damned button as potential evidence."

The day before, when they had been collecting evidence, they'd found a button at the foot of the chair where Megan's body had been sitting.

But they weren't sure if the small light blue button had come off their killer or off one of the many women who visited the salon. However, it looked like a man's shirt button and it had a bit of Megan's blood on it. So it had either been there before, or they were all hoping it had been accidentally lost by the killer during the placement of Megan's body.

"That's more than we've gotten at any of the other murder scenes," Benjamin replied.

The first woman who had been murdered was Cindy Perry, who had worked as a waitress at the café. The second had been Sandy Blackstone, who had worked as a teller at the bank.

There had been no clues left behind at either of those scenes, nothing to present any kind of a lead in those two cases. However, both women had been blond with blue eyes.

"He's stayed with the same pattern of picking blond-haired women with blue eyes," Benjamin observed.

"Yeah, that definitely seems to be his go-to for a victim," Dallas replied. "So far, this bastard isn't making any mistakes and I have a sick feeling that he isn't just going to go away. This is the most public place that he's left a body, which to me means he's getting far more brazen, and I feel so damned helpless."

Cindy's body had been found in Lucas Maddox's cornfield. Lucas was a local farmer and he had been quickly cleared of the crime. Sandy Blackstone's body had been found standing in the backyard of the Sweet Tooth Bakery. They didn't have a clue as to why those two places were chosen to leave the bodies.

"Dallas, everyone knows how hard you've been working on these murder cases," Benjamin said.

"All of us have been working hard," Dallas replied. "I swear I don't know what we're missing," he said in obvious frustration. "But we have to be missing something."

"I can't imagine what it is. We've interviewed everyone close to the victims several times and we've gone over the crime scenes with a fine-tooth comb. We just don't have anything to go on in identifying a suspect."

"And it doesn't look like this one is going to give us anything to go on, either, except a damn button that is too ordinary to give us much at all. Still, like I said to all the men yesterday, I want that button kept from the public."

"I agree. It's the one thing we have that might identify the killer. But if he finds out we have it, he'll sew on another button or get rid of the shirt it might have come off of," Benjamin said.

"I wish we knew what kind of a time line this creep is on."

If the Scarecrow Killer wasn't enough, three weeks ago they had dealt with a serial killer the press in New York City had dubbed the Nighttime Creeper.

It had been discovered that a new ranch owner, Clint Kincaid, was actually in the witness protection program. His real name was Joe Masterson and he had been the star witness against Wayne Lee Gossage, a man who had raped and killed at least six women, including Masterson's wife, in New York City. Joe had walked in while the crime against his wife was being committed and was able to identify the killer and see that he was put away for the rest of Gossage's life.

Because Gossage had made vile threats to Joe and his little daughter when he'd been sentenced, it was agreed that it was best if Joe entered the program and disappeared. He'd moved here to start a new life, but it was a life interrupted as Gossage had escaped from prison and had come after Joe by kidnapping Joe's young daughter and Lizzy Maxwell, the neighbor he'd fallen in love with.

Thankfully, in the end Gossage had been rearrested and sent back to prison, and Joe, Lizzy and little Emily were safe to resume their normal lives.

For several days, the Nighttime Creeper had been in the headlines of the local paper and had used up all the resources of the police department, but now it was over with a happy ending.

In fact, Lizzy and Joe were now planning their wedding and the paper was running stories about the upcoming fall festival. But this morning, once again the headlines had been all about the Scarecrow Killer and this latest murder.

At that moment two other officers arrived, and close on their heels were two more, and the work in the salon began again. They reswept the floors, paying special attention around the chair where the victim had been found.

The actual entry had been through the back door, where the cheap lock had been jimmied open. They checked the parking lot in the back of the building, around the back doorway and down the hallway where they assumed Megan had been carried inside.

They fingerprinted every surface they could and tried to ignore the lookie-loos who stood at the large front window staring in.

As they worked, they threw out different scenarios about motive. It was one of the things that was completely missing with regard to these murders. Maybe if they could figure out the motive, a potential suspect would surface.

"Maybe a blond-haired, blue-eyed woman broke his heart and so now he's killing her over and over again," Joel Penn said.

"That doesn't explain his trussing them up like scarecrows," Darryl O'Conner replied.

"There is absolutely nothing in my wheelhouse to figure out a motive for that," Ross Davenport said with disgust. "I mean, why sew their mouths closed and what in the hell does he do with their eyes?"

"It's so damned creepy," Darryl replied.

Benjamin listened to the others discussing the case and the only thing he kept thinking about was Bailey's sparkling blond hair and bright blue eyes.

She would make a perfect victim. She lived alone and was often out and about on her own. She didn't appear to have many friends, and even if she did, they weren't joining her when she was out shopping or whatever.

It had been after the second murder that Dallas had

called for a town meeting, where he'd warned all the women to travel in pairs. Most of them had taken his advice for a week or two after that murder, but many of them had now gone back to their usual ways. Hopefully, this murder would remind them of just how deadly it could be to be out by themselves.

They had no idea why the killer picked his victims and they didn't know how he got them into his control. It appeared he just picked them up off the street, as there was nothing at the victims' houses that indicated a struggle of any kind. They also didn't know where he actually killed them and dressed them up. It was someplace different from where he staged them as scarecrows.

They also had been unable to find the source of the frayed jeans and straw hats and flannel shirts. Where was the man getting them all from? There were so many things they just didn't know about this killer.

What they did know was the cause of death in each case was knife wounds to the chest. There had also been a high level of valium in the victims' systems and needle marks in Cindy's arm and Sandy's thigh. Thank God, according to the coroner, the women were dead before their mouths were sewn shut and their eyes were taken out. Josiah believed that a sharp, delicate scalpel had been used to remove the eyes.

Toward the end of the day, the talk turned more personal among the men. "How's Amelia?" Joel asked Ross. "The wedding is only a few weeks away, right? Are you starting to get the jitters yet?"

Ross laughed. "No—no jitters—but I've never been so happy that my fiancée has black hair and dark brown eyes."

"Don't think that keeps her safe from this creep," Dallas

warned. "At any time in the future, this guy could change the victimology and start going after dark-haired women."

"That's a scary thought," Darryl replied.

"It's something we all need to keep in mind," Dallas replied.

"Hey, Benjamin, are you still seeing Celeste?" Joel asked.

"Yeah, but not for too much longer," Benjamin replied.

"You breaking it off with her?" Darryl asked.

"Nah, she's going to break if off with me," Benjamin responded. "The next time I see her I intend to tell her that I'm not the marrying type and we all know more than anything Celeste wants to be married again. She'll drop me like a hot potato and move on to the next available man."

"Don't you want to keep dating her?" Joel asked.

"I'm over it. To be honest, I find her rather, uh—"

"Shallow," Dallas said, interrupting Benjamin as the others laughed. "Personally, I don't know why you started dating her in the first place."

Benjamin knew the answer. It had been loneliness and she had just happened to be in the right place at the right time. But he was ready to stop seeing her. It was the best thing to do. He never intended to get married and so it was wrong of him to keep seeing her and leading her on.

Besides, lately he couldn't get a certain woman off his mind. He had a feeling that Bailey would be a lot of fun on a date. Lord knew with everything that was going on in his professional life, he could use a little fun in his personal life.

The officers continued with small talk for a few more minutes, but then it was back to business. It was around four o'clock when Bailey showed up at the front door.

As usual, she looked stylish in a neon green blouse and a pair of black slacks that hugged her shapely legs perfectly.

Big neon green-and-black earrings hung from her ears and accented her gamin features.

Dallas opened the door and allowed her to step inside. Benjamin saw her gaze shoot directly to the chair where Megan had been found and her beautiful eyes darkened. "Uh, I was just wondering if I'm going to be able to open in the morning," she said.

"Yeah, we're pretty much done in here," Dallas said. "We'll finish up the last of things by this evening and it should be fine for you to open back up again in the morning."

"Okay, thanks," she replied. She turned to go back out and Benjamin quickly walked out with her.

"Bailey, how are you doing today?" he asked.

She offered him a small smile. "A little better than yesterday. It will be good to get back to work, although it's going to be hard at the same time."

"I understand," he replied. "You'll be just fine and the more distance you get from all this, the better you'll be. You're a strong woman, Bailey."

"Maybe not as strong as some people think I am," she admitted.

"No matter how strong you appear, you definitely worry me," he replied.

She looked up at him in surprise. "How do I worry you?"

"Bailey, you're always alone when you're out running the streets," he said. "And you have to know by now that you're the killer's type."

"I do know that, but there isn't much I can do about it."

"I just hope you stay aware of your surroundings whenever you're out. Don't let anyone get too close to you. Remember that this killer is somebody we probably all know, somebody you might think is perfectly harmless."

"If you're trying to freak me out, it's definitely working," she replied dryly.

"I want you to be freaked out if that's what it takes to keep you safe."

She smiled at him once again. "Thanks, Benjamin."

"I was also wondering if Friday night after the fair closes up if you'd like to have a quick drink with me at the Farmer's Club."

Once again, she looked at him in surprise. He felt a bit of surprise himself, as he hadn't intended to ask her out... until he just had.

"I would love to," she replied. "Thanks so much for asking."

"How about I give you a call sometime tomorrow and we can firm up the plans."

"Sounds great to me," she agreed. "Then I'll talk to you tomorrow." He watched her as she headed back down the sidewalk. What had he just done and why was he suddenly looking forward to Friday night?

Chapter 3

It felt so wrong that Bailey could feel this kind of hard-core giddiness, especially given the fact that she was still traumatized by finding Megan's body in her salon. That trauma still weighed heavy in her heart and probably would for some time to come. But she couldn't help the happiness that danced inside her and filled her heart as she raced down the highway toward her best friend's house. Only Lizzy would know how absolutely monumental it was that Benjamin had finally asked her out.

The fall festival closed at ten on Friday night and then on Saturday it was open until midnight. There were two bars in Millsville.

Murphy's was a large place that was popular with the singles in town. It was loud and raucous and the bar to go to for a night of drinking and dancing.

The Farmer's Club was much smaller and more popular with the older people in town. It was more conducive to conversations and she was thrilled to be going there with Benjamin. She couldn't wait to get the opportunity to get to know him a little better.

When she reached Lizzy's farmhouse, she went past it to the place next door. It always shocked her a little to see the

For Sale sign in front of Lizzy's place, but Lizzy now lived next door with Joe and his five-year-old daughter, Emily.

She pulled up in front of Joe's place, parked and then raced for the front door. She knocked and Joe answered. He was a nice-looking guy with dark hair and blue eyes. "Hey, Bailey," he said with a warm smile.

"Hi, Joe. I was wondering if I could grab Lizzy for a quick little girl talk."

He opened the door wider to allow her inside. "She's in the kitchen."

"Thanks." Bailey beelined to the kitchen, where Lizzy stood at the island cutting up vegetables. Little Emily was on a step stool next to her.

Lizzy was a pretty woman with shoulder-length blond hair and blue eyes. She and Bailey had been best friends since their early high school days. While Lizzy was also the Scarecrow Killer's type, Bailey didn't worry about her friend too much as she had Joe to protect her.

"Well, doesn't this look like fun," Bailey said.

"What a nice surprise," Lizzy said with a big grin. "I wasn't expecting to see you today."

Bailey had spent some time here with Lizzy the afternoon that Megan had been found in the salon. Lizzy had cried with her and consoled her the way a good friend would.

"Yeah, I'm not staying for long," Bailey replied.

"Hey, Emily, why don't you come on into the living room with me and we'll color a picture together," Joe said.

Bailey flashed him a grateful look as the little girl got down from her step stool. "Okay, Daddy. I love to color with you. 'Bye, Bailey."

"Goodbye, sweetie," Bailey replied.

A moment later the two women were all alone in the

kitchen. "How are you doing?" Lizzy asked as she put down her knife and looked closely at Bailey.

"To be honest, I'm kind of all over the place," Bailey admitted. "I'm still freaked out and sad over Megan's death and her body being in the salon. At least tomorrow I can open the salon again, but it somehow doesn't seem right to continue business as usual."

"It will be good for the entire town to get back to business as usual," Lizzy replied. "We can't give this killer any more oxygen than he's already getting."

"Easier said than done," Bailey said. "However, I came to share some good news for a change."

"Share away." Lizzy offered her another smile.

"Guess who asked me out to the Farmer's Club Friday night after the festival closes."

"I can't imagine."

"Officer Benjamin Cooper," Bailey replied.

"For real?" Lizzy's eyes widened. Only Lizzy had known what a mad crush Bailey had had on Benjamin.

"For real," Bailey confirmed as another wave of joy swept through her.

"Oh, Bailey, I'm so happy for you." Lizzy gave her a quick hug.

"Thanks, I can't wait to spend a little quality time with him and get to know him better."

"So, is he going to be like all the others you've dated?"

Bailey looked at Lizzy curiously. "What do you mean?"

"Does he get the same three-date maximum that everyone else you've dated has gotten?" Lizzy eyed her pointedly.

Bailey released a slightly uncomfortable laugh. "I don't have a maximum number of times I see somebody. I can't help it if after two or three dates I realize the person I'm seeing isn't right for me. Anyway, I can't wait until Friday night."

"I'm so happy for you, Bailey, and I hope he turns out to be the man you've always imagined him to be. I hope he meets all your expectations."

"Thanks, Lizzy. I just had to come by and tell you that he asked me out. And now I'll get out of your hair so you can finish up your dinner preparations."

"You want to stay and eat with us?" Lizzy offered. "You know I always make plenty."

"Thanks for the offer, but I think I'll just head on back home with a quick stop at Big Jolly's. I've been yearning for a double cheeseburger from there." Big Jolly's was a hamburger drive-through joint on Main Street that, as far as Bailey was concerned, made the best burgers and fries in the world.

"Bailey, I hope you're being safe," Lizzy said somberly.

"I try to be," Bailey replied, knowing Lizzy was talking about the Scarecrow Killer. "Hopefully Dallas and Benjamin and the rest of law enforcement will catch him before he can strike again."

"We can all pray that will happen, but in the meantime, I worry about you."

"Don't worry. I can take good care of myself," Bailey assured her. That made three people who were worried about her. "And on that note, I'm out of here."

The next day flew by as the salon was packed with women who had appointments along with plenty of walk-ins who had missed their appointments on the two days that the salon had been closed.

All of them wanted to know what chair Megan had been found in and exactly what she'd looked like. Bailey refused to give out any information about the dead woman, making some of the women get a little testy with her, but she didn't want to talk about the murder and she certainly didn't want to point out the murder chair.

She and Jaime and Naomi stayed until a little after nine that night to make sure all the clients were taken care of. She fell into bed almost as soon as she got home, exhausted by the long day she'd had.

It was just after ten o'clock on Friday morning when she headed to the fairgrounds. The big festival was taking place in what had once been a rodeo area. However, the big rodeos no longer came to Millsville, so the massive grounds with an old grandstand were dormant and unused except for special events like this.

She was dressed in a good pair of jeans and a bright royal blue blouse that hugged her body and showed off the blueness of her eyes. She had to dress knowing that there would probably be no time to change between working the fair and going out with Benjamin after the fair.

A nervous flutter shot off in the pit of her stomach as she thought of her date that night with the very hot police officer. She couldn't even believe it was really happening. She'd wanted to go out with him for what felt like years. It was just too bad it had taken a terrible tragedy like a horrendous murder for it to finally happen.

The fairgrounds came into sight. The carnival had already set up with a Ferris wheel rising up in the sky, along with a variety of other rides.

It was a perfect day to spend outside. The sun was bright overhead and there wasn't a cloud in the sky. The temperature forecast was for a pleasant eighty to eighty-four degrees, with just a faint breeze that was refreshing.

As she entered the actual grounds, she drove up and down the aisles of tents that the town provided, looking for the one she'd been assigned to. She finally found it and pulled behind it to park. Her location was absolutely perfect.

She was smack-dab in the center of the aisle and across from her was a hot-dog stand next to a fried-ice-cream-and-dessert place. Those two places would draw a lot of traffic and hopefully some of that would trickle over to her tent.

She was not only offering free nail painting to anyone under sixteen years old, but she had also brought plenty of new products to sell to any adults who needed polish and such.

For the next twenty minutes or so, she worked to unload her car. Folding tables and chairs were set up inside. She walked back outside to get a table for her display of nail bottles for sale. She finally leaned against the side of her car for a moment to take a break.

RJ Morgan popped out of his tent next door. RJ was the tattoo artist in town. He was a big bald man and his muscled arms were covered in bold tattoos. He carried himself rather aggressively and most people in town steered clear of him.

"Hey, baby doll, need any help?" he hollered over to her.

"Thanks, but I think I've got it all," she replied. "Are you actually going to be tattooing people today?"

"That's the plan. Why don't you come on over here and let me give you that sweet little butterfly tattoo we talked about doing on your neck?"

She laughed. "You talked about that, not me."

"You definitely have a beautiful neck, Bailey."

She laughed again. "And you, RJ, have a gift for flirting." She pushed herself off her car. "Now I've got to get back busy."

"You know, Bailey, I wouldn't mind us going out to-gether again," RJ said.

"We had our time dating, RJ, and things just didn't work out between us. I just think it's best if we remain good friends."

"I suppose you're right," he replied. "But you'll call me if you ever change your mind and want to go out with me again?"

She laughed yet again. "I promise you'll be the first person I call." She opened her trunk to retrieve the last of her items.

As she worked to arrange things inside the tent, her thoughts remained on the buff, bald man next door. She had gone out on a couple of dates with him and had discovered that beneath his big muscles and wild tattoos, he was really a sweet guy. However, the minute he started talking about wanting to get married and have a houseful of children, she was out.

By that time, Naomi had arrived. She was a pretty woman with long dark hair that cascaded down past her shoulders and brown eyes that snapped with liveliness. She was petite like Bailey, and had been married for five years to her high school sweetheart. "Are you ready for this?" Bailey asked as Naomi dragged in two chairs.

"Actually, I'm really looking forward to it. It should be lots of fun," she replied.

For the next half an hour, they got things in place and Bailey decorated the interior with pink-and-white boas and gold-and-silver crowns, turning it from a mere tent to a magical place for little girls.

Naomi had rented a canister of helium so they blew up dozens of pink and white balloons that now danced across the ceiling, adding to the fanciful aura. They also hung a bouquet of the balloons at their tent's entrance to catch peoples' eyes.

When they were finished, they each set up a chair in the front of the tent and watched others scurrying around to get ready for the noon opening.

The air now smelled of cooking hot dogs and hearty chili. There were also the scents of popcorn and cotton candy, and of fried Twinkies and funnel cake. It all smelled absolutely delicious. Colorful flags and banners hung on many of the tents, announcing the business being offered inside.

They knew when the festival officially opened, as people began to surge down the aisles. Children screamed with enthusiasm and parents urged them to slow down. The air of excitement grew, and within minutes Naomi was painting the face of a six-year-old while Bailey painted the nails of her seven-year-old sister.

The afternoon flew by. Their tent stayed busy with girls coming in and out. It was about six that evening when there was a lull in the traffic.

"You want to get us something to eat?" Bailey asked Naomi.

"Definitely, I'm starving," she replied.

Bailey pulled some money out of her purse and handed it to Naomi. "Dinner is on me. If you could just get me a hot dog and some funnel cake, then I'll be a happy camper."

"Okay, what do you want on your hot dog?"

"Mustard and relish," Bailey replied.

A moment later Bailey was once again alone in the tent. She sat out front. The crowd seemed to be a younger one now, with lots of teens and fewer little kids in the mix. However, she would remain open until the very end of closing in case a young girl came along and wanted her fingernails painted. After all, they were all future clients.

She saw him coming up the aisle and her heart began to beat a quickened rhythm. Officer Benjamin Cooper. He looked tall and handsome in his police uniform. He also looked like a man who owned the space around him. There was a command to him that definitely drew her in.

A slow grin curved his lips as he approached her—a grin that made her heart speed up even more. "Hey, handsome. Want your fingernails painted?" she said to him when he stopped in front of her tent.

He laughed. "No thanks, I doubt if you have my color. Are we still on for tonight?"

"As far as I'm concerned, we are," she replied.

"Great. Why don't I show up here at ten and I can help you load up for the night," he offered.

"Oh, you don't need to do that. All we're loading up is the nail polish and face paint. We're leaving the chairs and tables here."

"You do realize the security overnight is going to be pretty minimal," he said.

She smiled up at him. "If somebody wants to steal a card table or folding chairs, then they must need them more than me. Besides, I'm really not too worried about a theft."

"Then why don't I just meet you at the Farmer's Club as soon as you can get away after closing time."

"That sounds good," she agreed. "I'll see you then."

As he ambled away, her heart continued to beat wildly in her chest. Lordy, he looked as good going as he had coming. His broad back tapered down to what appeared to be a nice, firm bottom. Physically, he appeared to be the perfect specimen of a man.

She couldn't wait until ten o'clock. It would be so great if he really did live up to the kind of man she thought he was, aside from his physical attributes. Hopefully, she discovered they both wanted the same out of life.

Oh, it would be wonderful if he turned out to be the one for her. She could easily imagine their life together. He would continue his job and she would continue to work the salon. But there would be time for traveling and exploring new things together. There would be years of laughter and love with him. Yes, it would be absolutely wonderful if he turned out to be the special man for her. At that moment, Naomi returned with their food, pulling her out of her wistfulness. They ate and then sat in front of the tent once again.

Within an hour, the sun had begun to set and the lights on the rides pierced the encroaching darkness. Everything looked magical with the colorful illumination. There were only a few girls who came in for nail work and face painting.

It was a few minutes before ten when they began to pack up everything. Once again, her heartbeat had picked up speed in the sweet anticipation of spending some quality time with Benjamin.

It was then she found it—a single red rose. It was on the ground just inside the entrance and there was a small note attached to it. She stared at it for a long moment before picking it up. She wasn't sure why, but she didn't have a good feeling about this.

She finally reached down and picked it up off the ground. "'Bailey, I love you,'" she said, reading the note aloud.

"Oh, Bailey, that's so romantic," Naomi said as she tucked a strand of her long dark hair behind her ear. "Do you know who it's from?"

Benjamin certainly didn't seem like the type of man to leave this for her before their very first date. This also wasn't the kind of thing RJ would do.

"I don't have any idea," she replied. It didn't feel romantic. It felt creepy and the creepiness continued when minutes later she headed from the tent to her car.

As she unlocked the car door, she looked all around. The hairs on the nape of her neck stood up as she couldn't shake the feeling that somebody was watching her. Still, she didn't see anyone to give her pause, or to explain the creepy feeling.

She couldn't help the fear that filled her and chilled her blood. A dead person had been left in her salon and now she'd gotten a creepy gift from somebody. Who had left the rose for her? She just hoped she wasn't being sized up to be the next Scarecrow victim.

Benjamin arrived first at the small bar. Before he'd left the fairgrounds, he had dipped into one of the restrooms and had changed out of his uniform. He now wore a pair of jeans and a light blue pullover.

He went inside the bar and grabbed a booth, and fought against a wave of nerves. He sat down and wondered what in the hell he was doing here.

He'd always stayed his distance from Bailey because instinctively he knew he would like her. Whenever he saw her, aside from her tears over Megan, she was always smiling. There was a pep in her step that spoke of gusto for life and he found it very attractive.

He'd broken things off with Celeste on Thursday night and she had not taken it well. She'd cried and called him every name in the book and then had finally hung up on him.

The one thing that had pushed him into asking Bailey out was the fact that she seemed so all alone. She'd gone through a terrible trauma with seemingly nobody by her side. He knew she had a mother, but he suspected the two weren't very close. He found himself wanting to help her through these dark days.

He figured if she wanted, he'd see her a couple of times and by then the trauma in the nail salon would be behind her. When the time felt right and she appeared strong enough to not need anyone anymore, then he'd break things off with her.

Then he saw her. She stood just inside the front door of the fairly busy bar and looked around. Even after working all day, she appeared refreshed and beautiful.

He stood and waved to her. He could tell the moment she saw him—a wide smile curved her lips and she hurried toward him. A deep warmth filled his chest. God, she had such a beautiful smile.

"Hi," she greeted him and slid into the booth seat facing his.

"Hi yourself," he said in return and sank back into his seat. "Did you get everything squared away at the fair?"

"I did—it's all ready to unload once again in the morning," she replied.

Bright blue was definitely a good color on her and the blouse showcased her slender waist and full breasts. Her jeans hugged her long legs and slender hips and big blue earrings danced from her ears.

"Tomorrow is definitely going to be a long and crazy day, especially with all the contests going on in the afternoon," he said.

She smiled. "All I know is Letta Lee better win the best-apple-pie baking contest or there will be hell to pay."

He laughed. "You've got that right. I don't think she's ever lost."

"I don't remember her ever losing," Bailey replied.

At that moment, Ranger Simmons, the owner of the Farmer's Club, stepped up to the side of their booth. "Hey, Benjamin… Bailey. I see the two of you survived the first day of the fair." Ranger was an older man who was liked by everyone in town.

"Yeah, we live to fight another day," Benjamin replied.

"What can I get you two to drink?" Ranger looked at Bailey first.

"I'll take a gin and tonic with a couple of twists of lime," she said. "Light on the gin," she added.

"And I'll just take a beer. Whatever you have on tap is fine with me," Benjamin said.

"Got it. I'll be right back with those." Ranger moved away from them.

"Bailey, how are you really doing?" Benjamin asked her when the two of them were alone once again.

"I have my good moments and I still have some bad ones," she admitted.

"Do you have a good support system? Is your mother there for you?" he asked curiously.

She released what sounded like a dry laugh. "Angela Troy is a tough cookie and I'm not sure she knows how to be there for me."

"I'm so sorry to hear that," he replied.

"Are you close to your parents?" she asked.

"Very. In fact, I usually have dinner with them and my sister and her family every Sunday, which is one of my days off." He almost felt bad saying this, given her position with her mother.

"Your sister comes into the salon from time to time to get her nails done. She's always been very nice."

Benjamin smiled. "Yeah, Lori is all-around a great person, although there was a time I would have gladly paid somebody to kidnap her." He laughed as Bailey widened her eyes. "She was the definition of a pesky little sister, always bugging me and wanting to hang out with me and my friends. I love her dearly, but there were times growing up when she was definitely a pain in my side."

Bailey smiled. "You don't know how lucky you are to have a sibling. I would have loved to have a brother or a sister. In fact, for about a year when I was around eight years old, I pretended I had a twin sister. I made my mother set a place for her at every meal and kiss her good-night when we went to bed."

"Here we go," Ranger said as he came back to their booth. He placed the gin and tonic in front of Bailey and a cold mug of beer before Benjamin.

"Thanks, Ranger," Benjamin said.

"Enjoy." He once again left the side of the booth.

"So what happened to your sister?" he asked, picking up the conversation where it had left off.

"Oh, it was all very tragic. She was struck by a speeding car going by our house. The driver of the car didn't even stop." Her blue eyes were lively as she spun her tale and he found himself drawn toward her.

"And I'm sure her funeral was completely over-the-top," he said.

"Totally," she replied. "I decorated the whole backyard with everything black I could find in the house and I wrote a long eulogy about how much she was loved, and then poof, she was gone."

"To be replaced by more present friends, I hope." He took a drink of his beer.

"Definitely, but it was in high school when I met my very best friend for life, Lizzy Maxwell."

"I got to know her and Joe when she was kidnapped by the creep who came after Joe," he said.

"I've never been so afraid for anyone as I was for her and little Emily when they were missing." Bailey took a drink of her gin and tonic and then continued, "Thankfully it all ended on a happy note."

"Thankfully," he agreed.

For the next hour, they got to know each other better. He was surprised by how many things they had in common. They both liked old rock and roll and crime suspense shows. Their favorite type of food was burgers and fries with an occasional steak or pizza thrown in.

She had a terrific sense of humor—one that vibed with his own—and the more time he spent with her, the more he liked her. Then there was the fact that he found her very physically attractive.

He could lose himself in the depths of her bright blue eyes. As she talked, he found himself wondering how she would kiss and what her lips would taste like.

Despite his overall attraction to her, he just wanted to see her a few times, until she got some distance from the horror in her nail shop. At least that was what he kept telling himself.

"This has been really nice," she said when their drinks were almost gone.

"It has been," he agreed.

Her eyes darkened a bit. "It's nice to talk to somebody who understands what I've been through, somebody who is a bit sympathetic."

He couldn't help himself. He reached across the table and covered one of her small hands with his bigger one. "It will pass, Bailey. It will eventually get better." He withdrew his hand as she smiled warmly at him.

"I know. It helps to keep busy. The festival couldn't have come at a better time. And speaking of the festival, I'd better get out of here before it gets any later."

"Yeah, the day starts early tomorrow and it's going to be a long one," he agreed. He waved to Ranger for the tab and once he'd paid, he and Bailey walked out of the bar together.

The moon was high up in the sky and spilled down silvery strands that caressed her pretty features. He could once again smell the enticing fragrance of her perfume as he walked her to her car.

They reached the driver side of her vehicle and she turned and smiled up at him. "Thank you, Benjamin. I really enjoyed spending this time with you and getting to know you a little better."

"I enjoyed it, too. In fact, I was wondering if you'd like to have dinner with me at the café on Sunday—that's given nothing comes up with work to stop me."

"I'd love to have dinner with you," she replied. "And, of course, I would understand if your work interferes. But don't you usually eat with your family on Sundays?"

He smiled. "I'm allowed to skip a Sunday with them to have dinner with a pretty woman. How about I pick you up around five on Sunday?"

"That sounds perfect and, in the meantime, I'll probably see you at the fair tomorrow," she said. "Can I ask you one question about the Scarecrow Killer?"

He looked at her in surprise. "Sure, but I'll warn you there are some things I can't talk about."

"I was just wondering if he left little gifts for the women he intended to kill." Her eyes were now somber and filled with what looked like a touch of apprehension.

"Not that I'm aware of," he replied. "Is there something I need to know about, Bailey?"

She hesitated a moment and then shook her head. "No, it's fine. I'll just see you tomorrow."

He watched her drive away from the parking lot and then headed toward his car, which was parked nearby. He couldn't imagine why she had asked him about gifts from the Scarecrow Killer, but it certainly made him wonder what was going on in her life?

He'd definitely ask her more questions about it on Sunday and he didn't even want to think about how much he anticipated spending more time with her even though he knew there would be no happy ending for him with her.

He was back in the headlines again and he couldn't be prouder. Scarecrow Killer Strikes Again, the headline of the paper had read. For the last couple of days, he'd dominated the news.

How many nightmares was he in? Whose dreams did he haunt at night? All the people in town who had never paid any attention to him before were definitely paying attention to him now.

He leaned back in his chair and looked around his basement with a sense of contentment. He still had plenty of the frayed jeans and flannel shirts in all sizes. He had the poles for when he wanted to use them to tie the victims to in order to stand them up wherever he decided to leave them.

It was amazing what could be bought on the internet and he'd planned this for years, ordering the supplies here and there that would make his dreams come true.

Scarecrows.

He definitely knew what it felt like to be one and there had been nobody to save him when he was young. He remembered it all—standing in a hot field...thirsty and with legs aching. He remembered begging for it to stop, but it hadn't. Oh, yes, he remembered.

His gaze finally landed on the shelf that held three large jugs with the eyeballs floating inside. They weren't right. They'd looked right before he'd taken them, but he realized now they weren't quite right. They weren't *hers*.

He tore his gaze away from them and instead looked again at all the supplies he had. Even though it had only been a couple of days since his last scarecrow, the hunger was back inside him. The hunger was back and the crows cawed loudly in his head.

It all roared inside him and he knew it wouldn't be long before he made the headlines once again and inspired more fear in the hearts of every single person in town.

Chapter 4

"What color would you like me to paint on your pretty little nails?" Bailey asked a nine-year-old girl the next morning. "As you can see, I have lots of colors to pick from."

The girl frowned and looked at all the nail polishes on display. It was as if this was the most important decision she would ever make in her life. She then smiled up at Bailey. "I want pink."

Of course, she wanted pink. Almost all the little girls who had come in for nail polish had chosen pink. Thankfully, Bailey had brought extra bottles of that color, suspecting this would be the case.

"Are you having fun so far? Have you ridden any of the rides yet?" Bailey asked.

"We rode the carousel. I sat on a big white horse with flowers painted all over it. It was beautiful," the girl replied. "I wanna ride the Ferris wheel but my mom is scared of heights so I don't know if we'll ride it or not. I'm gonna try to talk her into it."

So went the day…pink polish and carnival rides. Both Bailey and Naomi were kept busy until about two o'clock in the afternoon, when there was a lull in traffic and Bailey knew the winners of the various contests were being announced at the grandstand.

It was during the lull when Benjamin walked up to their tent. "Bailey… Naomi, how's your day going?" he asked with the smile that threatened to melt Bailey's insides.

He was so handsome with his strong brow and straight nose. His lower jaw was also strong and well-defined and his lips held just enough curl to make them sensual and very kissable. Despite the light blond of his hair, his blue eyes were surrounded by thick, dark lashes. He rocked the police uniform he wore and as far as she was concerned, he was easily the best-looking guy in town.

"Very busy. This is the first real break we've had all day. What about you? How is your day going?" she asked.

"Not too bad. I've had to arrest two men for drunk and disorderly and then I chased after a teenager who stole an older woman's purse and that's been the highlights of my day so far."

"Sounds way more exciting than listening to young girls gossiping about their schoolmates," she replied.

He laughed. "Ah, future women of Millsville in the making."

"Yes, and I already know who is likely to become mini Letta Lees in the future. By the way, have you heard—did she win the apple-pie contest?"

"No, she didn't. Mabel Treadway won and Letta came in second."

"Oh, there will definitely be hell to pay over that. Even though Mabel is Letta's best friend, Letta is going to find a way to punish Mabel for a while," Bailey said with a small laugh. "If I was Mabel, I would not want to be at the next gardening club meeting."

He returned her laugh. "You've got that right."

"Any other wins from the grandstand that were surprising?" she asked.

"Not really, but I was glad to see that our mayor presented an honorary award to Elijah Simpson for running the food bank out of his basement," he replied.

"Oh, I'm so happy to hear that. Elijah is a wonderfully kind man and he makes sure the people who are in need in town get the ingredients they need to have a home-cooked meal." Elijah was an older man who ran his food bank on donations. As the economy had gotten tighter, there were more and more families than ever depending on him and his kindness and hard work.

"Well, I'd better get back to my beat," Benjamin said. "I just thought I'd stop by to check in on you."

"Thanks, I appreciate it," Bailey said.

"Have a good rest of the day," Naomi said to him.

"Thanks, Naomi," he replied and then looked at Bailey once again. "And I'll see you tomorrow evening."

She smiled. "I'm looking forward to it."

"That man is totally crazy about you," Naomi said once Benjamin was out of earshot.

"How do you know that?" Bailey asked as she worked to suppress happy shivers.

"Just the way he looks at you. I'm telling you he likes you a lot."

"So far I like him a lot, too," Bailey admitted.

Minutes later Bailey was once again painting little nails and talking about the carnival with bright-eyed little girls. By the end of the day, she was absolutely exhausted. It was after one when she finally got home and crashed into bed.

She slept sinfully late the next morning and then spent the day cleaning up her house and unpacking the fair items from her car. At four, she took a shower and got ready for her date with Benjamin.

Forty-five minutes later she looked at herself in the floor-length mirror that was on the back of her closet door. Her skinny black jeans fit her perfectly and the red blouse was one of her favorites. Big black-and-red earrings completed her outfit. Her makeup was light and she looked casually chic—perfect for dinner at the café.

At four forty-five she sank down on her sofa to await Benjamin's arrival. Nerves jumped around in the pit of her stomach and her chest was tight with anticipation.

Aside from the time spent patrolling the fair, she knew he and the other law-enforcement officers had been working hard to identify and catch the Scarecrow Killer. A shiver walked up her back as she thought about the person who had now killed three women.

What in God's name went on in his head when he made them into human scarecrows? Why was he doing it? She couldn't imagine what darkness must be inside him, a darkness that sane people couldn't begin to understand. She just hoped he got arrested soon, before another woman was murdered. She really hoped that the rose left in her tent at the fair hadn't been left by the Scarecrow Killer.

She jumped as a knock sounded at her door. She got up and answered. It was Benjamin, looking totally hot in a pair of jeans and a blue button-up shirt that enhanced the blond of his hair and the gorgeous blue color of his eyes.

"Hi," she greeted him.

"Hi, yourself," he replied with a smile. "Are you ready to go?"

"Just let me grab my purse and I'm ready."

A few moments later she was in the passenger seat of his car. His personal car was a nice dark blue sedan.

"Are you hungry?" he asked as he backed out of her driveway.

"Definitely," she replied.

"How has your day been?" He turned onto the road that would take them to the café on Main Street.

"Quiet. I slept obscenely late this morning and then did some chores and unloaded my car, and now I'm here."

He slid a quick glance toward her. "And I'm glad you're here."

A warm glow filled her. "I'm glad I'm here, too." She drew in the scent in his car. It was a fragrance of leather cleaner mixed with his spicy cologne, and it was more than appealing.

"So what did you do today?" she asked.

"I reinterviewed Megan's parents to see if there was anything else they could tell us about her and her life, then I went back into the station, where our little task force went over everything we have so far concerning the killer."

"What a hard day it must have been for you," she replied sympathetically.

"They've all been pretty hard since the first victim was found," he confessed.

"Well, tonight over dinner, anything to do with the Scarecrow Killer as conversation is strictly off-limits," she said firmly. "Besides, I thought Sunday was your day off."

"Normally they are, but I decided to go in for a while this morning."

By that time, they had arrived at the café. He found a parking space down the street and together they got out of the car.

"Beautiful night," he said as they walked toward the front door.

"Yes, it is." The sun was still bright overhead, but there was a slight chill in the air that whispered of autumn's fast approach.

When they reached the café door, he opened it and ushered her inside. On Sunday evenings, the place wasn't too busy, as most people were at home preparing for the new week ahead.

He led her to a booth and they sat. Almost immediately, Lauren Kane, one of the waitresses, appeared to take their orders.

"I'd like the cheeseburger with fries and a cola to drink," Bailey said.

"And I'll take the big bacon burger with fries," Benjamin said. "And a cola, too."

Minutes later, their orders were in front of them and their conversation was light and easy. "Autumn is my favorite time of year," she said as she squeezed a pool of ketchup on the side of her plate for dipping her fries.

"It's my favorite, too," he replied. "I enjoy the cool nights, when there is a bit of woodsmoke in the air and you can sleep with your windows open."

"Exactly, and you can cuddle up on the sofa with warm fuzzy blankets and drink apple cider or hot chocolate." She would so love to cuddle up with him. His big strong arms would surround her and his scent would infuse her head. Oh, it would be wonderful.

Their talk moved on to shows they had seen on television, and what sign they each were—she was a Libra and he was a Cancer. He talked a little about his work as a police officer. She found everything about his work interesting.

She then began to share stories about the antics of some of the women who came into her shop. She didn't mention any of them by name, but she did do some pretty fair impressions of them that had him laughing.

She loved the sound of his deep laughter and she had a feeling that he hadn't had much to laugh about lately. With his job so heavy and stressful right now with the Scarecrow Killer, she wanted to be his light and soft place to fall.

"Oh, Bailey, this has been so good for me," he said once she'd finished one of her tales and they had finished eating. "How about some dessert?"

"Not for me," she replied. "But you go ahead, I'm just too full to want anything else. As you can see, I ate almost all of my fries—they were my dessert."

"Yeah, I don't need any dessert, either. Shall we get out of here, then?"

Even though she hated to have the evening with him come to an end, she also knew his time right now was limited and he was probably exhausted from all the extra hours he was having to put in. She would just gladly take whatever time he had for her.

He paid the tab and then they left the café. Evening had fallen and the sky overhead was filled with bright, sparkling stars. "This is one of the things I love about being in small-town Millsville. There are no bright city lights to interfere with us being able to see the complete beauty of the stars," she said.

"I love it here. I've never wanted to live anyplace else," he replied.

"Me, neither," she agreed. "But I wouldn't mind doing a little traveling sometime in the future."

"I agree—there are several places I'd love to see."

They reached his car and got inside. As he drove her home, they made small talk about the little town they both loved. From the unique shops on Main to the new gazebo in the town square, Millsville had never tried to be anything bigger than a nice quaint town that wanted the best for its residents.

Before she knew it, he was pulling into her driveway. They both got out of the car. She saw it before they even reached her front porch. A rather large white teddy bear holding some sort of a sign was sitting right in front of her door.

You Belong to Me, the sign said.

"Ah, it looks like I have a little competition," Benjamin said with a touch of amusement.

She didn't pick up the bear. She didn't even want to touch it. It creeped her out, just like the rose at the fair had. Chills rushed up her spine as the back of her throat threatened to close up. First it had been a dead woman in her salon, then the rose and now this. What was going on? Who on earth was leaving these things for her?

"I don't know who it's from," she finally said. "I can't imagine who left this for me, but could you please take it away for me? I don't want it. I don't want anything to do with it."

"Sure, I'll be glad to if that's what you want," he replied.

"That's definitely what I want," she replied as tears pressed hot in her eye.

She turned to unlock her door and when she turned back around to face him, he stood just mere inches away from her. "Hey, are you okay?" he asked softly. It must have been obvious to him that she wasn't. "Come here," he said and pulled her into his arms.

"This is why I asked you if the Scarecrow Killer left gifts for his victims before he killed them," she said against his broad chest.

"Bailey, look at me."

She raised her head to meet his gaze with hers. "We have absolutely no evidence to show that the killer leaves items for his victims. Have you received anything else?"

"On the first night of the carnival when we were closing up, I found a rose on the tent floor with a note that said 'I love you,'" she replied.

"These things have the earmark of a secret admirer, not the killer."

His words lessened the fear inside her. She still found it creepy. But being in his strong arms definitely comforted her.

His eyes shone as bright as the stars overhead and before she could guess his intent, his lips claimed hers.

The kiss started out as a light one, but then he deepened it by dipping his tongue in to swirl with hers. Immediately, she was lost in the sweet, hot sensations that rushed through her.

However, all too quickly he released her and smiled. "That's just to let you know that I intend to be an active participant in this competition." He leaned down and picked up the teddy bear. "Are you sure you want me to take this with me?"

"Positive, and, Benjamin, trust me. There is no competition. There are no other men in my life," she replied.

"That's a good thing to know," he replied. "On that note,

what would you think about coming over to my place on Thursday night for a steak dinner?"

"I think it sounds absolutely wonderful," she answered, once again a warmth swirling inside her at the thought of another date with him.

"Then why don't I pick you up about five thirty on Thursday evening and I'll cook you dinner," he said.

"I'll be ready and thank you so much for tonight. I had a wonderful time," she said.

"Yeah, so did I." A small frown appeared across his forehead. "Bailey, with the fact that somebody you don't know is leaving you these uh…gifts, it's all the more important that you watch when you're out and around. Make sure you don't let anybody get too close to you. You know the drill."

"I do," she replied somberly.

"Good, so I'll see you on Thursday evening." He waited on the porch until she was safely in her house.

She stepped in, then closed and locked the door. Her lips were still warm with the imprint of Benjamin's. The kiss, although far too brief, had absolutely lit her up inside.

He was exactly the kind of man she'd always imagined him to be. So far, she'd found him kind and intelligent, and he had a great sense of humor. And that kiss they'd shared had been absolutely toe-tingling amazing.

The vision of the teddy bear suddenly intruded into her happy thoughts, making her frown. *You Belong to Me.* Who was behind these "gifts"? First the rose and now the teddy bear. She moved over to her front window and peered outside.

Was somebody out there right now? Watching her? Why? What did they want from her? Seeing nothing out of place and nobody lurking about, she let the curtain fall back in front of the window and fought against the shiver of apprehension that threatened to creep up her spine.

Benjamin followed Dallas's patrol car down Main Street. They were headed to the motel, where apparently another fight between two men who lived there was in progress.

It was just after ten and it was another beautiful day— far too beautiful for two men to be fighting and definitely not the way to start a new week.

This wasn't the first time they'd been called to the motel to settle a fight between Burt Ramsey, an alcoholic who worked as a handyman around town, and Rocky Landow, a vet who was in a wheelchair after losing a leg.

Even though Rocky was in a wheelchair, the man was strong with upper body muscles, and if Burt got too close to him, Rocky could pull himself up and out of the chair to do a lot of damage to the weaker and much thinner Burt.

The Millsville Motel was mostly populated by drug addicts and people who'd fallen on hard times. It was a low gray building that breathed of failure and hopelessness. A couple of the units sported broken windows covered over with thick cardboard. Several people lived there permanently, as was the case with the two men who were going at each other this morning.

Benjamin couldn't remember anyone passing through town choosing to stay there. Millsville definitely wasn't a destination location.

They now whirled into the motel parking lot and immediately saw Burt standing in front of Rocky, who had a gun in his hand. Benjamin's chest immediately tightened.

This was the first time a gun had been present in one of the many squabbles the men had and that instantly raised the stakes.

Dallas got out of his car, as did Benjamin. They both drew their own weapons, but they didn't move any closer.

"Rocky, put the damned gun down," Dallas demanded.

"No, I won't. I'm going to shoot this lying bastard through his black heart," Rocky replied, his voice deep with anger.

"He's crazy," Burt whined. It was obvious the man was already sloshed. "All I said to him was 'good morning' and he went off like a rocket."

"That's not what you said to me, you damned liar," Rocky yelled and lifted the gun higher. "You called me a dirty cripple and said I needed to die and save the taxpayers having to pay for my disability checks. Damn you, I lost a leg defending the likes of you."

"And thank you for your service, Rocky, but you need to put the gun down now," Dallas said.

"All I did was come outside for a little breath of fresh air and you started flapping your mouth at me," Rocky said to Burt.

"Rocky, you're a good man. You know you don't want to shoot Burt. For God's sakes, man, don't destroy your life because of him," Benjamin said.

"He needs to not talk to me. He's a damn drunk who talks way too much," Rocky said. Benjamin saw Rocky's hand on the gun start to relax.

"Hey, I can't help it that I drink a little bit," Burt said, his voice slightly slurred. "You know I love you, man," he said to Rocky. "I'm sorry if I ran my mouth at you."

Rocky stared at Burt for several long moments and then

he finally set the gun down in his lap. "Apology accepted," he replied gruffly.

Dallas holstered his gun, then approached Rocky and grabbed the gun away from him. Meanwhile, Benjamin walked over to Burt and grabbed the man by his arm. He reeked like a brewery and was unsteady on his feet. He'd obviously had a lot to drink despite the early hour of the day.

"Listen, you two are close neighbors here and you both need to be good neighbors for each other," Dallas said. "The next time I'm called out here for a fight between you two, somebody is definitely going to go to jail. I'm not even kidding, I'm dead serious about that. I've had it with you two and your petty fights that take up my time and resources."

He turned and looked at Burt. "Go get into your place and don't speak to Rocky again for the rest of the day." He then looked at Rocky. "And the same for you. Do you have a permit for this thing?" He held up Rocky's gun. Then he broke it open to check if it was loaded.

"Yeah, I've got it inside. Do you want me to go get it for you?" Rocky asked.

"No, I trust you, but if I see you brandishing it again, we'll be having another kind of conversation and it won't be so pleasant," Dallas said and handed the gun back to him.

Minutes later, the two lawmen were on their way back to the station. As Benjamin drove, his thoughts turned to Bailey and his date with her the night before.

He had found her absolutely delightful. From her intelligence to her quick wit, he couldn't remember ever enjoying being with a woman as much as her. She'd made him laugh and it had felt wonderful after his long days of dealing with law-enforcement issues and a vicious murderer.

She'd looked beautiful in the jeans that hugged her slender waist and legs and the red blouse that complemented her blond hair and bright blue eyes.

Kissing her had been beyond wonderful. Her lips had been so soft and so inviting. He could have kissed her forever. He couldn't wait until Thursday night to see her again.

However, apparently another man wanted her attention, too, even though Bailey had professed that she didn't know who he was. Who had left her a teddy bear?

Benjamin had never understood the whole secret-admirer deal. If someone really wanted to tell a woman they admired or cared about her, why not just tell her to her face? Why play games?

Certainly, he and Bailey weren't anywhere near exclusive with each other, but he was surprised to feel just a little bit of jealousy when he thought about her going out with another man.

This was what he'd been afraid of, that he would love spending time with her and that he would not want it to end. But eventually it would have to end. He just hoped nobody got hurt when that happened.

He reached the station and went inside, where he found Dallas seated in the break room with a bag of peanuts and a soda before him. Benjamin fed the vending machine enough money for a soda and then he sat next to his boss.

"I'm so sick of those two taking up our time," Dallas said, his irritation rife in his voice.

"It would help if Burt wasn't drinking so much or so often," Benjamin replied and cracked open his soda can. "The man definitely needs treatment for his alcoholism."

"Yeah, and it would also help if Rocky wasn't so damned sensitive," Dallas added. "I swear, I was really tempted to throw them both in jail today."

"I get it, as if we don't have more important things to focus on right now. Too bad all the criminals and fools in Millsville couldn't take a break for a month or so and let us focus strictly on the Scarecrow Killer crimes."

"Ha, yeah, that would be nice." Dallas finished off his peanuts and chased them with a drink. "And speaking of the Scarecrow Killer, I want us to start from the very beginning with the first murder and go through everything we have again."

They'd already done this half a dozen times, but there was always a chance that they'd somehow missed something. Benjamin finished the last of his soda and then the two men left the break room together.

They headed down the hallway to a room where the murder books were spread out on a table. On a whiteboard there were pictures of the victims in life and in death, with their names written next to the photos. There were also enlarged photos of the button that had been found at the last scene.

Benjamin took a seat at the table and Dallas sat across from him. "You start with the Cindy Perry file and I'll start on Sandy Blackstone."

"Got it." Benjamin grabbed the file and opened it in front of him. There had to be something...some clue they were somehow missing. Surely no killer was this organized...this utterly clean.

As the two men began to read, Benjamin was aware that there was already a clock ticking. It beat in his head, reminding him that if they couldn't solve these murders quickly, then there would be another victim.

They had to catch this man before he struck again, before he made up his mind that the pretty blond-haired, blue-eyed Bailey was perfect as his next victim.

Chapter 5

"And then Robin threw down her plate. I mean, she literally threw the whole plate down to the floor. Pieces of china and food flew everywhere," Liza Settle said. "Thank goodness my dining room floor isn't carpeted or it would have been a real nightmare to clean up."

"I always knew she had a temper, but I never dreamed it could explode like that," Sharon Burke replied. "Knowing this, I certainly don't intend to invite her into my home anytime soon."

"I will never have her back in my house," Liza replied. "And I told her that after her fit."

Bailey tried to ignore the gossip as she worked on Liza's nails. Poor Robin, whoever she was—she didn't know she was being gossiped about in the public nail salon by these two women.

That was part of Bailey's job, to do nails and ignore the gossip she heard…and she heard a lot. She knew who was mad at whom, who was having financial issues and who was sleeping with whom. However, she had never heard any gossip, good or bad, about Benjamin.

It was just after noon on Wednesday when Celeste Winthrop swept into the salon. Celeste was a striking blonde with big, doe-like brown eyes and a fashion sense to rival

Bailey's. Today she was clad in brown slacks and a tiger-striped blouse. A gold belt and earrings finished the attractive ensemble.

"I don't have an appointment today, but I was hoping you could work me in," she said.

"Naomi can take you in about five minutes," Bailey replied.

"Bailey, I would really much prefer you take care of me today," Celeste replied with a thin smile.

"Then it will be fifteen to twenty minutes," Bailey said. She still needed to finish up with Sharon's fingernails and she wasn't going to rush it just because Celeste was waiting.

"That's fine, I'll wait." Celeste sat in one of the chairs in front of the window that were for the waiting clients. She picked up one of the magazines Bailey kept on an end table and began flipping through the pages.

A small ball of dread formed in the pit of Bailey's stomach. If Celeste just wanted to have her nails done, she would have allowed Naomi to serve her. Celeste liked her nails dipped and Naomi had often dipped Celeste's nails in the past.

Celeste must have an ulterior motive for wanting Bailey, and Bailey had a feeling it had something to do with Benjamin. He'd obviously broken up with her before he'd started seeing Bailey. The dread increased inside her. She knew the conversation with Celeste probably wasn't going to be a pleasant one.

Fifteen minutes later, Celeste sat in a chair at one of the nail stations and Bailey began to give her a manicure. Celeste had already chosen her dipping color—a bright red with sparkles.

"So I hear through the grapevine that lately you and

Benjamin have been seeing each other," Celeste said, wasting no time in getting to what she wanted to discuss.

"We've been hanging out a bit together," Bailey replied as she began taking the old polish off Celeste's long, pointy nails.

"I just want to give you a little friendly advice because you seem like a very nice woman. I know Benjamin is quite a catch, but you better hang on to your heart where he is concerned. He'll only hang out with you for a little while and then he'll be back together with me."

Bailey looked up to meet the woman's narrowed gaze. "I guess only time will tell," Bailey replied, keeping her tone even and calm.

"Trust me on this. He'll give you the three- or four-date treatment and then he'll break it off with you. I know he'll come back to me. Benjamin and I shared a very special relationship. We had a little spat, but once he gets over being upset with me, he'll come back to me." There was a brazen confidence in Celeste's voice.

Bailey looked back down at Celeste's nails. "If that happens, then it happens. I don't intend to lose any sleep worrying about it."

"I just figured, you know, woman to woman, I needed to give you a heads-up so you don't get hurt in the process," Celeste said.

"I appreciate that. Who knows, maybe I'll be the one to stop seeing him," Bailey said, knowing that was probably what was going to happen, anyway.

"Oh, are you already tired of his company?" Celeste asked with a raised, perfectly plucked eyebrow.

"No, I just mean nobody can say what might happen in the future," Bailey replied.

Celeste spent the rest of her time in the chair in a sullen silence. Forty-five minutes later, she left the salon with her new fancy red nails and snide smiles.

"I'm surprised you didn't pull all her nails clean out," Naomi said with disgust. The two of them were momentarily alone in the place. "She is one nasty piece of work. It's no wonder she's been single for as long as she's been."

"I'm not sure why she thought it was necessary to have that conversation with me," Bailey said.

"She was just trying to stir up doubts in your head about Benjamin. Celeste has always been a brazen witch. Honestly, Bailey, I've never seen you as happy as you've been lately. I know how long you crushed on Benjamin from afar and I think it's wonderful that the two of you are now together," Naomi said.

"We're not exactly together. We've only gone out on one official date," Bailey replied. "Well, two if I count the drink after the carnival. Although he did ask me to his place on Thursday night. He's going to cook steaks for us."

"Oh, you are so definitely together," Naomi exclaimed. "When a man takes you to his house and cooks for you, it's definitely serious."

Hours later, as Bailey drove home, she thought about what Naomi had said. It wasn't serious with Benjamin... It couldn't be, because the moment things got too serious between them, then she'd have to bounce.

You're not right.

You're not a normal woman. You're selfish.

Those hateful words shot through her head with a stabbing pain—pain, because she knew Adam had been right about her. She wasn't normal and she would never seek out a long-term relationship again.

It had been a late night at the salon and the shadows of darkness were creeping in by the time she parked in her driveway. Before winter hit, she had to arrange everything in her double garage so that she could use half of it to park inside.

She got out of her car and before she even took one step, she felt it. The hairs on the nape of her neck rose up and she had the distinct creepy-crawly feeling of somebody watching her.

She looked all around. There were no strange cars parked on the street. Nothing appeared out of the ordinary and yet the feeling was strong enough to make her feel more than a little afraid.

She hurried to her front door, unlocked it and went inside. She locked the door after her and then went directly to the window and moved the curtains aside just enough so she could see outside.

Her heart beat a quickened rhythm as she peered out. There was nobody lurking around on her property. Maybe it had just been some sort of a false signal from her over-worked brain.

She was about to release the edge of the curtain when she saw him. Across the street in her neighbor's yard, a man looked out from behind a large tree.

The curtain dropped from her hand as she slammed her back against her door. Her heart pounded so loud in her head that for a moment she could hear nothing else.

There was no question that the man had been looking directly at her and her house. The shadows had been too deep and the distance too far for her to see exactly who it was.

With her heart still beating a million beats a minute,

she peeked out the window once again. She stared at the big tree across the street.

Seconds ticked by, then minutes passed and she saw no more movement. He was gone. Or maybe he hadn't really been there after all. It could have been a trick of the light or her overactive imagination.

She walked across the room and sank down on her sofa, waiting for her breathing to return to normal and her thoughts to become clear from the panic that had momentarily gripped her.

She was sure somebody had been there. Who had been out there? Who had been watching her and why? Who had left the rose and the teddy bear for her?

Somebody was stalking her and she needed to find out why. She wanted to know who it was. Should she call the police? If the man was already gone, then what could law enforcement do about it?

Her biggest fear was that it might be the Scarecrow Killer. Benjamin had told her there was no evidence to indicate that the man had left gifts for his victims before he'd killed them, but how did anyone know that for sure? Was he the one watching her? Was he trying to decide if she would be his next victim?

It took her a very long time to fall asleep that night. The next morning, she got ready for work and as she opened the door to leave her house, she nearly stumbled over a vase filled with bright, colorful flowers. She grabbed the note that was in an envelope and opened it.

You are mine.

She read the words and looked around, wondering if the bearer of the gifts was watching her now. In case he was, she kicked over the plastic vase and then tore the card into little pieces.

Was that what the man behind the tree had done? Waited until she was at home and in bed to leave the flowers? She'd had enough of this secret-admirer stuff. The day before she'd found a box of chocolates waiting for her at the salon door. She'd immediately thrown the box in the trash. There was only one person she could think of that might possibly be behind it all.

She stewed about it all the way to work and once she got to the salon, she sat in one of the chairs and pulled her phone out of her purse.

She hadn't heard from him for about two weeks and so she thought things had been ironed out between them. She found him in her contacts and hit the button to call him. Enough was enough and nothing was going to change her mind about him. If he was behind all the gifts, then she needed to tell him to stop it all now. He answered on the third ring.

"Bailey, it's so good to hear from you," Howard Kendall said warmly.

"Howard, this isn't exactly a social call," she said tersely. "I just need to know, are you leaving things for me? Like a teddy bear and flowers and candy?"

"No, but if I do, will you go out with me again?"

"Howard, we weren't right for each other and, no, I wouldn't go out with you again no matter how many gifts you left for me. Howard, this is really important to me, so please don't lie to me. So have you been leaving gifts for me?" she asked again.

"No, it's not me. I've pretty much moved on, Bailey. You've made it very clear to me that there's no way forward for the two of us. Besides, from the sound of things, you now have another man besotted with you," he replied.

She believed him. She didn't believe he would lie to her. He wasn't her secret admirer. Then who was it? Who was skulking around her house and leaving love notes and items for her?

She couldn't imagine who it was. She spent so much of her time in the salon with women. Was it possible it was Ethan Dourty? She didn't believe so. He hadn't even called her since they'd had coffee together at the café. So who? Who was possibly "besotted" with her?

Was she in danger from this person? She just didn't know what to think, but the whole thing definitely had her on edge. The good thing was that Thursday night she had a date with a cop. She was definitely going to bring it up with him and get his thoughts on the whole thing. Maybe he could tell her how often stalkers turned dangerous.

Thursday morning, the Scarecrow Killer task force was officially together again in the small room they worked out of. The task force consisted of Dallas, Benjamin and Officers Trent Lawrence and Ross Davenport.

If they had a bigger police force there would be far more people on the task force, but this was Millsville, Kansas, and manpower and resources were very tight.

So there were only four men completely dedicated to this case while the rest of the officers dealt with most of the petty crimes in town. Although with the investigation at a standstill when they weren't working on the case, they were all back to patrolling and dealing with various petty crimes that occurred.

"I got a tip this morning over the tip line," Dallas said. "And I think it's something we need to check out."

"What was the tip?" Trent asked. He was a middle-aged man who had been with the department for about ten years. He was sharp and dedicated, and Benjamin had always liked and trusted him.

"Somebody called in and said that George Albertson keeps a lot of straw hats in his barn," Dallas replied.

"He's got a pretty big barn on his property," Benjamin said thoughtfully.

"And he's isolated on all that farmland, too," Trent added. "Isolated enough that nobody would hear a woman if she screamed."

"He's always been kind of an odd duck. He keeps to himself and doesn't seem to have any friends or family," Benjamin said.

"I think this definitely warrants a visit from law enforcement," Dallas said. "What do you all say?"

"I say we don't have anything to lose in checking it out." Benjamin rose from the table where the four of them had been sitting.

"Benjamin, you can ride with me. Trent, take Ross and follow us in your car," Dallas said and also stood.

Minutes later, they were on their way to the large spread on the western outskirts of town where Alberton lived. "It would be nice if this tip panned out," Dallas said.

"Yeah, it would be good for the town if we could finally get this madman off the streets and into jail," Benjamin replied.

"If we could get him behind bars, maybe I'd start sleeping again. On another, more pleasant note, are you ready for your big date with Bailey tonight?" Dallas asked.

"As ready as I can be. The apartment is clean and the food is all ready to be cooked."

Dallas shot him a quick, amused glance. "Tell me the most important thing of all… Did you put clean sheets on the bed?"

Benjamin laughed. "A gentleman never tells." He sobered. "Seriously, man, we're not at that place in our relationship. In fact, I'm just trying to be a friend to her because I think she needs one right now."

"I'm sure she's probably still having a rough time with everything that's happened. It had to be horrible for her to walk into her salon and see our victim seated in one of her chairs," Dallas said.

"Yeah, it was horrible for her and she doesn't really have much of a support system." Benjamin hadn't seen Bailey all week and he was really looking forward to seeing her that night.

No matter what he'd told Dallas about the relationship with Bailey, it was beginning to feel like he didn't just want to see her to support her, but he wanted to get together with her because he really wanted to spend time with her.

He'd run into Celeste in the grocery store the night before. She'd been quite flirtatious with him, as if she'd never had words with him. But he had no interest in picking things back up with her again, especially not with Bailey now in his life.

Celeste had been so desperate to get married and have babies, and that's all she'd talked about when they'd been together. Her desperation had been exhausting to him. With Bailey, things were so much lighter and easier, and right now he was completely enjoying his time with her.

All thoughts of his dating life fell from his head as they

approached the Alberton place. The home was a relatively small one. It had once been white, but had weathered to a dirty gray.

The barn was set to the right of the house and was a huge structure that was also weathered and gray. The doors to the barn were closed as they pulled up in front of the house and parked behind George's beat-up black pickup.

The four officers left their vehicles and approached the front door of the house. Hopefully, George wasn't somewhere in his fields working. If he was, the odds of him hearing them were minimal.

Dallas knocked on the door. There was no reply. He knocked again, this time harder and louder. George had to be around somewhere since his truck was here. Hopefully, he was close enough for him to hear them.

"George," Dallas yelled. "George, are you here?" he yelled again.

They all turned in unison at the sound of a door screeching open in the barn. George Albertson was in his late fifties or so. He was a tall man with the shoulders and thighs of a linebacker. He was certainly in good enough physical shape to manipulate and move a dead woman's body.

"Chief Calloway…what's up?" George said as he approached them. He was wearing overalls and a straw hat rode the top of his head. He swept off his hat, exposing his thinning salt-and-pepper hair, as he reached where they were.

"I'll be honest with you, George. We need to see inside your barn," Dallas replied.

George's eyes narrowed as he frowned. "And why would that be?"

"We got a tip this morning and we need to check it out," Dallas replied.

"A tip, huh. I'm sure it was that bastard Sturgis Devons." George's gaze shot across his property and he glared at his neighbor's house in the distance. He looked back at Dallas. "That man's been trying to break me down for years. He wants my land, but as long as I'm alive he'll never get it."

"I really don't know who called in the tip," Dallas said. "We just need to check out a few things in your barn."

"You got a search warrant?" George asked, his blunt features radiating his intense displeasure at this whole thing.

"No, but if necessary, I can go get one. I just figured we could do this the easy, friendly way," Dallas replied.

George released a deep sigh. "All right. I got nothing to hide, so let's go to the barn."

Dallas walked alongside George while Trent, Ross and Benjamin brought up the rear. Would they find something in the barn to point to George as their killer?

Benjamin desperately hoped so, but the fact that George was now fully cooperating with them gave him little hope that they would find a den of evil inside the big, weather-beaten structure.

What they did find inside were neat stacks of hay, a clean floor and four straw hats hanging off nails in one wall. There was absolutely nothing to indicate that any women had been killed and dressed up like scarecrows in the barn.

Benjamin walked over to get a closer look at the hanging straw hats. They were in various conditions—one was neat and clean while the others were sweat- and dirt-stained around the headbands. The ones found on the victims had been brand-new and completely clean.

He turned to look at George. "Why four hats?"

"One is my go-to town hat and the rest of them are field

hats. The sun gets really hot if you're bare-headed out there all day. Why? Is it against the law to have more than one hat?" George asked rather sarcastically.

"Of course not. I was just curious," Benjamin replied evenly.

"Okay, I think we're finished here," Dallas said.

A few minutes later they were in their cars and headed back to the station. "I'm so disappointed that this didn't pan out," Dallas said, his frustration rife in his voice.

"Yeah, me, too," Benjamin agreed.

"At least you have something to look forward to," Dallas replied. "You have your date with Bailey tonight to take your mind off all this."

"But I also worry about her," Benjamin replied. "You know she fits the profile to become a victim of this guy. As long as he's out on the streets I believe she's in potential danger."

"After this latest murder, I think I need to have another town hall meeting to remind all the women in town to stay in pairs or a group when they're out and about. In fact, I think I'll set something up in the next week or so."

"Sounds like a plan to me," Benjamin agreed. "It never hurts to remind the women that they could potentially be in danger every time they leave their houses."

Dallas turned the car into the lot and parked behind the station in his official parking space.

The afternoon flew by and at four o'clock Dallas told Benjamin to take off for the day. Benjamin didn't argue about getting off early, then headed for the exit and quickly left.

He made one quick stop on the way home, and once there, he took a quick shower and shaved, then changed into a pair of jeans and a royal blue polo. He then went into his kitchen and turned on the oven to bake the potatoes.

He didn't particularly enjoy cooking, but it was ridiculous how much he was looking forward to cooking for Bailey. There was something about her that stirred something deep inside him. It was something he'd never felt before and it both excited and frightened him a little bit.

He enjoyed looking into her bright blue eyes and seeing her wide smile. He loved the sound of her full-bodied laughter. He even enjoyed the big colorful earrings she wore that seemed to be her trademark.

For the first time in his life, he really wished things could be different. But they weren't and they never would be, and so the odds were good he'd spend the rest of his life all alone.

He knew he couldn't get in too deep with her, but surely, they could continue seeing each other for a little while longer as long as things remained light and easy between them.

Chapter 6

Bailey stood at her front door and awaited Benjamin's arrival to pick her up for the evening at his place. She was excited. Her heart beat a little faster than normal and a delicious sweet energy swirled around in the pit of her stomach.

She hadn't seen him all week long and was eager to spend more time with him and to get to know him on an even deeper level. She was especially excited to see the place he called home. Surely, it would be a peek into what was important to him and what he surrounded himself with.

Once again, she'd dressed casually in a pair of jeans and a pink blouse. Her makeup was light, her hair in its usual spiked-up style, and large pink-and-denim-colored earrings hung from her ears.

Since she had gotten the flowers in the vase, there had been no more "gifts" left for her. She hoped whoever was responsible for them would either stop or simply reveal themselves to her. She still intended to talk to Benjamin about it.

For the past week, each day after work she'd gone into her garage and moved the boxes and bags of salon supplies to one side of the double garage. Thankfully, she was now able to pull her car into the garage and park there each night. She'd realized just how vulnerable she'd been walking from the car to her front door each evening and now that problem had been solved. She could go into her garage and enter into her kitchen without having to walk outside.

Her heart lifted up as his car pulled into her driveway. Before he could get out, she pulled her door shut behind her and practically danced out to his car.

She slid into the passenger seat and shot him a wide smile. "Hi," she said.

"Hi, yourself," he replied in what had become a pattern of greeting every time they saw each other. He offered her a wide smile of his own. "You look absolutely beautiful this evening, as usual."

"Well, thank you, kind sir. You cut quite a dashing figure yourself," she replied.

"Pink is definitely a good color on you," he said.

"Thank you, it's my favorite color. And I would guess that your favorite color is blue."

"You'd be right. Are you hungry?" he asked as he backed out of the driveway.

"Starving and I can't wait to taste your expert culinary skills."

"Ha, don't expect too much," he said with a laugh.

"It's another beautiful night," she said. The sky was clear and the temperature was a bit cooler than it had been. Outside, it smelled like autumn, but inside the car all she could smell was the delicious scent of Benjamin. It was a combination of shaving cream, his slightly spicy cologne and wonderful male that enticed her.

"It is a beautiful night," he agreed. "In fact, it's so pleasant out I decided it might be nice if we'd eat outside on my patio, if that's okay with you."

"That sounds lovely," she replied. "I didn't even think about you having a patio at the apartments."

"My place is on the ground floor so I have a very nice patio. Have you ever been to the apartments before?"

"No, I haven't," she replied. The Downhome Apartment Complex was the only one of its kind in Millsville. It was a two-story structure that she guessed had about fifteen units. It was only a couple of years old and she'd heard it was very nice.

"Living there works for me right now. With all the hours I work, I'm rarely at home, anyway. Maybe eventually I'll buy a house, but up to now I've never really felt the need," he explained.

"Home ownership isn't for everyone, especially in this day and age," she replied. "But it was important to me. I dreamed of having my own house since I was little." Still, she wouldn't have cared if Benjamin lived in a dark, dank cave. She was interested in the man, not his dwelling.

They reached the apartment complex, which was painted an attractive tan with darker brown trim. He turned in and parked in one of the covered spaces provided to the tenants. They got out of the car and he gestured toward one of the doors. "I'm in apartment 106," he said.

She followed him to the door, which he unlocked and then opened. "Welcome to my humble abode," he said as he gestured her inside before him.

She walked in and looked around the place with interest. The furniture indicated it was a typical bachelor pad. A glass-topped coffee table set before a black sofa. There was also a recliner chair and a huge flat-screen television hung on the wall.

What really drew her attention was an array of photos

hanging on another wall. She stepped closer to gaze at them. It was obvious they were photos of Benjamin's family. There was one of the family all together and then there were photos of Benjamin with his sister and her family. There was also one of the two siblings together and several of him alone with his niece and nephew.

"These are so nice," she said.

He came up to stand behind her. His body heat engulfed her at the same time his scent dizzied her senses. She turned and he took a step back from her, but not before she thought she saw a fevered blaze of desire in his eyes. It was there only a moment and then gone, but it was enough to light a small fire in the pit of her stomach.

"I only have one regret about photos," she said in an attempt to fill the sudden awkwardness between them.

"And what's that?" he asked.

"I never managed to get a good photo of my sister," she replied.

He laughed. "You should have used an imaginary camera," he returned, making her laugh. "Are you ready to head into the kitchen?"

"Just lead the way," she said.

She followed him through the living room and into a kitchen that had a small table and a long island with three stools in front of it. Bailey sat on one of the stools as Benjamin went to the refrigerator.

"The potatoes are already cooking in the oven and should be ready in about fifteen minutes or so," he said as he pulled out two beautiful steaks marinating in something that smelled wonderful. He opened a drawer and withdrew a torch lighter. "I'm just going to step out and start the grill. I'll be right back."

He disappeared out the sliding glass door that obviously led to his deck. She took the moments while he was gone to tamp down the wild physical desire that had gripped her the minute she had slid into his car.

She wasn't anywhere close to wanting to make love to Benjamin...was she? Only rarely did she sleep with the men she was dating. She always broke things off with them before that point came. She tossed the very thought of making love with Benjamin out of her head. Tonight, she was just looking forward to some good companionship and a delicious meal.

Benjamin came back inside. "We'll let that warm up for a couple of minutes and then we'll move outside so I can cook the steaks."

"Sounds like a plan to me," she replied. "So how was your week?"

He leaned with his back against the refrigerator. "Frustrating," he admitted. "We thought we had a good lead on the Scarecrow Killer from the tip line, but it didn't pan out."

"I'm sure the tip line is going to fill up with a bunch of foolish nonsense. Mad at your neighbor...call the tip line. Ticked off at a relative...call the tip line."

"I'm afraid you're right," Benjamin replied. "Dallas is doing his best to vet the calls that come in, but that's time-consuming in and of itself. He's also planning on having another town-hall meeting. It's going to be this Wednesday night."

"That's probably a good idea," Bailey replied.

"I hope every woman in town attends and that's including you."

"I'll plan to go," she replied.

"Ah, I've been remiss… What can I get you to drink?" he asked.

"What are you offering?" she asked.

"I've got soda, ice tea and beer. I'm going to have a beer."

"Make that two, bartender," she replied.

He grinned at her and then pulled two bottles out of the refrigerator. "Now, shall we move outside?" He grabbed the platter of steaks and his beer while she picked up her beer and followed him out the door.

The patio was a pleasant area. There was an umbrella table and the yellow-and-white-striped umbrella looked beautiful against the deep blue of the sky. He had set it with black plates and yellow napkins. He looked incredibly hot with the sunshine sparking in his blond hair as he grabbed a large pair of tongs off the grill.

"This is really nice," she said as she sank down in one of the yellow cushioned chairs at the table.

The grill was on one side of the patio, far enough away from where she sat that she couldn't really feel the heat from it. However, it was obviously hot, since the steaks immediately began to sizzle when he put them on to cook.

"Do you spend a lot of time out here?" she asked curiously.

"Not as much as I'd like to. To be honest, it's not much fun sitting out here all alone."

"I'm sure if you called Celeste, she would be more than happy to come over and spend some time with you here," Bailey replied.

He frowned. "Why would I call her? I don't want to spend any time with her."

"Not according to her. According to her you two will be

back together very soon." She told him about Celeste coming into the nail shop and having a conversation with her.

"That woman has a lot of damned nerve trying to interfere with my life," Benjamin said when she was finished. "I'm so sorry you had to deal with that… With her."

"Don't worry, she didn't bother me at all," Bailey assured him. "I found her to be more than a little bit desperate."

"She's definitely desperate to find a new husband," he replied. "But it's certainly not going to be me."

He turned the steaks, which had filled the air with their mouth-watering scent. "How do you like your steak?"

"Medium," she replied. "How do you like yours?"

"Medium." He smiled at her, that smile that melted her insides and made her want to fall into his arms.

It didn't take long for the steaks to cook and then they sat down to eat. The salad he'd made was crispy and fresh, the baked potatoes were perfectly cooked and the steak was seasoned and grilled to perfection.

As they ate, they talked about the week that had passed. He shared what they had done in an effort to find the elusive killer and she told him about what had happened in the nail salon.

In a perfect world, they were perfect together. He shared the darkness of his work with her while she tempered that darkness with the lightness of silly gossip and the latest in nail news.

But it wasn't perfect because she wasn't perfect. She wasn't normal and if she could help it, she would never be put in a position again for another man to tell her that.

"How about some dessert," he said once they had finished eating. "I stopped by the Sweet Tooth Bakery on my way home from work today and picked up a few things."

"Did you know the way to a woman's heart is anything from the Sweet Tooth Bakery?"

He laughed. "I didn't know that, but it's good information to know. Sit tight and I'll bring them out." He picked up their two dinner plates, then went into the house and returned a moment later with a pink-and-white-striped box from the bakery and two small plates.

He gave her one of the plates and then opened the bakery box. Inside was an array of sweets. There were cinnamon and cream-cheese bars, little chocolate fudge squares and bite-size raspberry fritters.

"Hmm," she said as she helped herself to one of each. "Now this is what I call a real dessert."

"I wasn't sure what you would like, but I figured cinnamon, chocolate and fruit was a good combination," he said as he took a couple of the cinnamon bites for himself.

"Definitely a good combination," she agreed. "I've never had anything bad from the bakery. I'm so glad the place is up and running again after the fire."

Harper Brennan owned the bakery, and several months ago one of her customers had tried to kill her by trapping her inside and starting the place on fire.

Thankfully, Sam Bravano, the man who Harper had been dating, had managed to save her. Sam and his brothers, all carpenters, had worked hard to rebuild the place after the fire. The man who had set the fire had been a regular customer and had developed an obsession with Harper. Thinking about all this made her remember that she wanted to talk to Benjamin about her "secret admirer."

She waited until after dinner, when they'd cleaned up

the dishes and were seated in his living room and having coffee. "Benjamin, I want to talk with you about something serious," she said.

"Okay." He moved a little closer to her on the sofa. "What is it?" He looked at her with concern.

"I might be overreacting, but you were there when the teddy bear was left for me and since then there's been a couple more things left for me."

"Things like what?"

"A box of candy and a vase full of flowers, and each one has a note attached that says something like 'you belong to me' or 'you're mine forever.' I think this person might be stalking me."

"And you don't have any idea who it might be?" he asked.

She frowned. "I thought it might be Howard Kendall. We went out a few times and then I broke it off with him and he tried for weeks after that to get me back. But I called and asked him point-blank if it was him. He denied it all and I've never known Howard to be a liar, so I believe him."

"Is there anyone else you might have dated in your past or anyone who has indicated an interest in you recently?" he asked.

"I had coffee with Ethan Dourty not too long ago, but it was just a friendly cup of coffee at the café and nothing more. And before I dated Howard, I also went out a few times with RJ from the tattoo shop, but this isn't RJ's style. RJ would be all up in my face. My main question for you is should I be afraid? How often do stalkers get dangerous?" She searched his beautiful blue eyes.

"To be honest, I don't know. But my first instinct is to tell you not to worry too much. I really believe this man is going to reveal himself to you very soon. He's just hoping to win you over before that happens." He looked at her intently. "Is it working?"

"God, no. I'm finding it all very creepy and irritating. So you don't think I need to be afraid?"

"I think you need to be very cautious," he replied. "It's the same thing about the Scarecrow Killer. You need to watch your surroundings and be aware of who is around you." He reached out and slowly slid a finger down her cheek. "Bailey, if you are ever afraid, call me and I'll be at your place immediately."

He dropped his hand, but his eyes suddenly burned with a light that made her breath catch in her throat. "Bailey, I really want to kiss you right now."

Her heart fluttered as she held his gaze. "Oh, Benjamin. I would really like for you to kiss me right now."

He leaned forward, gathered her into his arms and then his lips took hers in a kiss that shot fire through her veins and made her realize just how difficult it was going to be to stop seeing him.

Chapter 7

Kissing Bailey was like taking a powerful drug. Benjamin's head dizzied and his heartbeat accelerated the moment his lips met hers. She tasted of a hint of cinnamon and warm coffee and sweet hot desire.

He deepened the kiss by dipping his tongue in to dance with hers. She tightened her arms around his neck and pressed herself closer to him, making him half-mad with his own heightened desire for her.

He reminded himself that he didn't want to get in too deep with her, but it was hard to remember that when she filled his arms and her mouth was so hot and so hungry against his own.

What he wanted to do right now was to take her into his bedroom. He wanted to strip her naked and then make slow, sweet love to her. However, he still had his wits together enough to know he couldn't let that happen. That definitely wouldn't be fair to her.

He cared about her enough not to sleep with her and then dump her. With that thought in mind, he finally pulled away from her. She dropped her arms from around his neck and sat back with a sigh.

"I could kiss you all night long, Bailey," he said.

"And I would let you kiss me all night long," she replied softly.

"Unfortunately, I have an early morning at work tomorrow, so I think it's time for me to take you home."

"Of course. I would never want you to be too tired at work because of me. That could be very dangerous for you."

He smiled at her. "Thank you for being so understanding."

"I've really enjoyed tonight," she said minutes later when they were in his car and headed back to her house.

"I have, too," he agreed. "But I always enjoy spending time with you. You're very easy to talk to, Bailey."

"And I find you very easy to talk to," she replied. "I don't know what I would have done without you after... you know... Megan and everything."

"You've impressed me with your strength. Bailey, you're far stronger than you think you are."

She laughed. "You keep telling me that, but maybe I just have you fooled."

"Sorry, I'm a police officer and that means you can't fool me," he replied.

She laughed once again. "So you're telling me you're like a human lie detector?"

"That's me," he answered lightly. "Don't you know that officially I'm a detective and so I can detect lies?"

He pulled up in her driveway and parked. "Maybe Saturday night you could come over here and we could get pizza?" she said.

"Better yet, why don't I pick you up and we go to the pizza place to eat?" he suggested. With the physical-attraction level so wild between them, he thought it was better if they spent their time together in public places.

If he had his way, he'd package her in bubble wrap to keep her safe from harm, but he couldn't exactly do that. He also didn't want to parade her out in public too much, but the pizza parlor was a small place off the beaten path and so he thought it would be safe to take her out there.

"Okay, we can do that, but only on one condition," she said.

He looked at her curiously. With darkness having fallen outside, the only illumination came from his dash lights and they painted her face in a lovely way. "And what's that?"

"I pay for the pizza."

"That's not necessary," he immediately protested.

"Yes, it is," she replied firmly. "And really, I insist, so don't argue with me now and don't argue with me at the pizza place."

"Well, okay then. I don't want to argue with you. How about I pick you up around six."

"Sounds good to me," she concurred. She looked so beautiful in the faint lighting that stroked her features in a soft aura and it made him want to kiss her all over again.

Instead, he unbuckled his seat belt, and she did the same, and together they got out of the car. When they reached her porch, her gaze shot all around, including across the street. Initially, he could feel her tension, but it faded away quickly and she smiled up at him.

"You okay?" he asked.

"Fine. I'm just happy there's no new gifts left for me and there doesn't appear to be anyone hiding behind the tree across the street."

"Whoa, you didn't tell me anything about a man across the street," he replied with surprise.

"It was on the night before I found the vase of flowers on my doorstep. I was sure I saw a man lurking behind that big tree over there, but honestly, now I'm not sure if I really saw somebody or if it was just a figment of my over-active imagination. If he was real, all he did was leave me the flowers on my porch."

"If you think you see something like that again, you call me and I'll come check it out immediately," he insisted. He would hope that if she really saw somebody lurking around her house or across the street, she would call him and he could get out here fast enough to catch the creep.

"I'm so glad I have a personal lie-detector detective bodyguard to keep me safe."

He laughed. "That's a pretty heavy title for me to wear."

"But you do it with such grace and style," she murmured, her beautiful eyes sparking in the moonlight.

"On that note, I think it's time I make my exit." He kissed her on the cheek and then took a step back. "I'll see you Saturday night."

"Thanks again for the great food and conversation to-night," she said and then moved to unlock her door. When that was done, she turned back to face him. "Good night, Benjamin."

"Good night, Bailey." He waited until she was safely inside her house and then he walked back to his car. God, he'd wanted to kiss her again and not just on her cheek. He'd wanted to take her in his arms and kiss her properly. Still, it was a good thing he hadn't.

For a few minutes, he merely sat in his car and gazed all around the area. It bothered him that she'd thought she'd seen a man across the street watching her. When she'd asked him about stalkers turning dangerous, he'd tried to downplay the threat.

However, the whole gifts thing coupled with the possibility of somebody watching her, stalking her, did trouble him. There was no way to know if the person was a threat to her or not. He was certainly hoping whoever was leaving the things for her wasn't dangerous.

At this point there wasn't much he could do about the situation except be there for Bailey. He could definitely ask Dallas for more nightly patrols down her street.

He finally pulled out of her driveway and headed back home. His mind shifted to when he'd held her so close and had kissed her so deeply.

In those moments, he had wanted her badly. But making love to Bailey wouldn't be fair to her. He had no intention of having a long-term relationship with her. She was a beautiful, bright young woman and deserved a man who wanted to be married and have a family. And that wasn't him, and it would never—could never—be him.

He should stop seeing her now, but with a potential stalker in her life, it wasn't the right time for him to just walk away from her.

"Is it a possibility to get a couple of extra night patrols down Bailey's street?" he asked Dallas the next morning. Dallas was in his office and Benjamin stood just inside the door.

"I'm sure I could arrange for that," Dallas replied. He gestured to the chair in front of his desk. "Want to sit and tell me exactly what's going on?"

"It seems that Bailey might have picked up a stalker," Benjamin revealed as he sat in front of his boss. "She's been getting anonymous gifts and love notes from somebody and she thought she saw a person hiding behind her neighbor's tree a couple of nights ago."

"And she has no idea who is behind it?" Dallas asked with a frown.

"None," Benjamin replied. "I'd just feel better if some officers had eyes on her place throughout the night."

"Got it, and I'll arrange for extra patrols down her street." Dallas leaned back in his chair and his frown deepened. "I think we can write off this being the Scarecrow Killer. None of the family members or friends of our victims mentioned anything about them receiving anonymous gifts or notes before their deaths. I just hope this doesn't blow up into anything serious. That's the last thing we would need right now."

"I completely agree," Benjamin offered.

"Do you have any of the notes she's received?" Dallas asked.

"No."

"That's too bad," Dallas mused with a shake of his head. "At least if we had one of the notes, we could fingerprint it and possibly get an identity off it."

"I'll tell her the next time she gets one to give it to me," Benjamin replied, irritated with himself that he hadn't thought about it before now.

"In the meantime, I've got you on street patrol today since we're stalled out on the Scarecrow Killer investigation," Dallas said.

"Fine with me." Benjamin stood. "You know I never mind patrol. I just came in to talk to you about the extra patrols for Bailey, so now I'll head on out and hit the streets."

"I'll see you sometime before the end of the day," Dallas said.

Minutes later Benjamin was in his patrol car and headed down Main Street. He parked and got out to walk. He always enjoyed being on foot and talking to not only pedestrians who were out shopping, but also the people who owned the shops. It was especially important now that law enforcement was seen out and about. With the Scarecrow Killer on most everyone's mind, it was imperative that the people of Millsville saw the presence of law enforcement.

One of the first things he saw just up ahead of him was Fred Stanley following closely behind Annie Cook. Annie was an attractive mother of two young children and Fred was known as the town's lech.

Benjamin sighed and hurried toward the two. "Hey, Annie," he called out.

She stopped and turned to face him and he saw the relief that quickly flashed across her pretty features. He reached the two and stopped Fred, as well. "Annie, is Fred bothering you?" he asked and turned a stern look at the old man.

"Yes… I mean, no, it's fine," she replied, her cheeks flushed with color. "Fred was just, uh, giving me some suggestions of things we could do if I came to visit him at his house."

"Like what kinds of things?" Benjamin asked, easily able to imagine what sorts of things the old widower had suggested.

"Oh, that's not important now," Fred interjected hurriedly. "Annie looked kind of sad so I was just trying to be friendly and cheer her up." Fred offered Benjamin his most innocent smile.

"Annie, I'm sure you have more important things to do than listen to Fred's suggestions. So why don't you go on about your day and I'm going to stay here and have a little chat with Fred."

"Thank you." She looked at him gratefully and then turned and hurried on down the sidewalk. Benjamin turned to look at the old man who smelled of an ancient cologne and a menthol muscle cream. "Fred, you have got to stop accosting women on the street," Benjamin said sternly.

"I wasn't accosting nobody. I was just trying to be a little friendly," he protested. "The poor woman looked a bit lonely and sad and I was just trying to cheer her up some."

"You definitely need to be a little less friendly with the women. If you aren't careful, you're going to end up in jail," Benjamin replied. "I know Dallas has warned you over and over again about this."

"I hear you," Fred responded grumpily. "Now can I go?"

"Where are you headed now?"

"I suppose I'm going home."

"That sounds like a very good idea," Benjamin replied. He watched as the old man ambled away. Fred had been warned a million times about speaking inappropriately to the women in town. He was a problem, but at least he was a fairly harmless problem.

Benjamin spent the morning walking the streets and visiting with the people he came across. The day was fairly cool and everyone he encountered was pleasant. Much of the conversations were about how much fun people had had at the fall-festival celebration and the upcoming town meeting. As he passed the salon, he shot a quick gaze inside and saw Bailey seated at one of the workstations painting a woman's nails.

At noon he got back into his car to continue patrolling the streets. By midafternoon, a thick layer of clouds had diminished the sunlight overhead, turning the day a miserable gray.

He stopped two people going too fast and gave out a warning to one and a ticket to the other, who was a teenage chronic speeder. The rest of his day passed uneventfully.

It was about six thirty when he decided to knock off for the night. He called and checked in with Dallas then did a final drive-by of the nail salon. It was closed up and Bailey's car was gone.

It was ridiculous how much he'd wanted to pop in to see her today… Just to see her beautiful face…just to enjoy her beautiful smile for a minute or two.

Before heading home for the night, he decided to do a quick pass by her house. In the preternatural darkness of the evening, the streets were fairly deserted.

He turned down Bailey's street. Her car must have been parked in her garage, since it wasn't in her driveway, but lights flooded out of her front window, letting him know she was probably home. His gaze shot across the street and all his muscles tensed as he saw a figure attempting to hide behind the big tree there.

He stomped on the brakes, shut off his car and locked it as he bolted from it. The figure took off running and Benjamin raced after him. The person looked relatively thin and appeared to have a ski mask on to hide his identity. He was clad all in black—black pants and a black sweatshirt.

He left the yard and ran down the side of the street. Dogs barked in alarm as the man passed each of their territories. Who in the hell was he and what did he want from Bailey? Why in the hell was he watching her home?

Benjamin followed as fast as possible, desperately wanting to catch the person. His breaths became deep pants as he tried to shorten the distance between him and the man he now believed for sure was stalking Bailey.

However, the masked person ran across the street and disappeared into a dark backyard. Benjamin chased after him, but when he reached the yard, he saw no sign of the man and he had no idea which direction he might have run.

He searched the area as he fought to catch his breath. Damn, he'd lost him. He stood for several long moments, but he saw and heard no movements anywhere. Whoever it was, he was definitely gone or hiding so well that Benjamin couldn't find him. And the odds that he would be behind that same tree on another night were slim to none.

"Dammit," Benjamin said aloud as he finally headed back to his car. This had probably been his best opportunity to find out who Bailey's stalker was and he'd totally blown it.

He clicked on his flashlight and headed for the tree across the street from her place. Maybe the person had dropped something there that could identify him. The only thing he found there was a box of candy. He went across the street to his car and opened his trunk. He was thankful that even in his personal car he carried things for an emergency.

He grabbed a pair of latex gloves and a brown evidence envelope big enough to hold the box of candy. Once he'd taken care of that, he did a check around her house before getting back into his car and heading toward home. What bothered him was the possibility her stalker could be the Scarecrow Killer.

Despite what Dallas had said on the matter of gifts, they really didn't know what might have happened to the women before they'd been murdered.

They didn't know anything about what the murderer did before ultimately leaving his victims to be found. Was it possible he left them little gifts and notes? Absolutely, although none had been found when they checked the victims' homes. That didn't mean the killer hadn't gathered them up at some point before the victims had been found.

The fact that Bailey had a stalker worried him, but the possibility that it could be the Scarecrow Killer scared him half to death for her.

There was no question Bailey was a little bit disappointed that her date with Benjamin was going to be at the pizza parlor and not at her house. That meant there would be no hot kisses or hugs or physical interaction between them at all.

Still, she was looking forward to spending more time with him. In fact, she couldn't remember enjoying a man like she enjoyed him. He was warm and witty and so very easy to talk to. She felt safe when she was with him and loved the way he seemed to really listen to her.

This was about the time in most dating situations when she walked away from whomever she was seeing, but she wasn't quite ready to do that with him. She didn't want to stop seeing him yet. He stimulated her intellectually. Their shared laughter moved her and his mere presence comforted her. Surely, she could see him a few more times without any harm.

It was now just a few minutes before six and she stood at her front door waiting for him to arrive. As always, her heart beat a little faster at the thought of being with him again.

When he pulled up in her driveway, she flew out of her

door. She reached his car and slid into the passenger seat, then offered him a big smile.

"If you aren't careful with your running out to my car like this, you'll make me think you actually like me," he said teasingly.

"Oh, no, I'm just really looking forward to the pizza," she replied.

He laughed. "Then I better get you to the pizza place as quickly as possible." He backed out of her driveway and headed toward Main Street, where the pizzeria was on the other side of town from the café. "How was your day?" he asked.

"Fairly boring as nail days go," she replied. "It was a slow day and I'd much rather be busy than slow. What about you? What was your day like?"

"Fairly boring as police days go, but in my line of work you definitely want slow days," he replied. "However, I did have a rather eventful evening last night."

"Really? How so?" She looked at him curiously. He had such a nice profile. As usual, this evening he looked hot as hell. He wore blue jeans and a navy blue polo shirt. His short, neatly trimmed blond hair looked clean and shiny, and he smelled of his delicious scent. She would never, ever get tired of looking at him.

"I decided to drive by your place on my way home from work last night and guess what I saw behind the tree across the street from you?"

She straightened up in the seat and looked at him intently. "You saw somebody?"

"I not only saw him, but I got out of my car and chased after him. Unfortunately, I lost him in a backyard down the street from you." His regret was heavy in his voice.

"At least I know now that I'm not crazy and imagining things. I'm assuming you didn't get a good look at him."

"He definitely doesn't want to be identified. He was wearing all dark clothes and a ski mask." He pulled into the pizzeria parking lot. He parked, unfastened his seat belt and then turned to look at her. "We really need to work on trying to figure out who this guy is. We can talk about it more while we eat."

Gino's Pizza was a quaint little place just off Main Street, with red-and-white checkered cloths on the booths and tabletops, and an overweight Gino wearing a sauce-splashed white apron that made him appear as if he'd just walked away from a crime scene.

He greeted them at the door and gestured them to seat themselves. There were two couples already there, one settled in at a booth and the other at a table.

She was glad Benjamin guided her to a booth. She always found a booth more intimate and conducive to more cozy conversations. And from the sounds of things, she and Benjamin had a lot to talk about.

They had just seated themselves and agreed on a pizza when Gino approached their table. "Officer Cooper, it's nice to see you here…and Bailey, it's always good to see you."

"Thanks, Gino," Benjamin replied as Bailey smiled at the older man.

"Have you two decided on what you want?" Gino asked.

"We have," Benjamin answered. He ordered a large pizza, one side filled with meats for himself and the other side with mostly vegetables for her. He also ordered sodas for them both.

The drinks were quickly delivered and then they were

left alone to wait for the pizza. "Shall we talk about the elephant in the room now?" she asked.

He frowned. "How about we eat first and then talk about it after."

"That's fine with me. I hate talking about negative things while I'm eating."

"Me, too. I'm assuming since Gino knew you that you've eaten here before."

"Yes. Occasionally, I'll order over the phone and pick up a small pizza for dinner on the way home from work," she replied. "I think there's going to be plenty of leftovers with you ordering a large pie."

He grinned at her. "Ah, but you've never seen me eat pizza before."

She laughed. "No, I haven't, but I'm looking forward to it. Do you fold it or eat it as is?"

"As is. I've never really understood the whole fold thing. Why smoosh all that goodness together?"

"You have a point." She took a sip of her soda.

"By the way, you look quite lovely tonight." His gaze on her was warm across the table.

"Thank you." Her body heated from head to toe. Drat him. Why did he have to affect her on such a visceral level? Why did he have to affect her on every single level she had?

She wanted to hear his every word, whether he was talking about silly things or heavy, important topics. She loved the way he looked at her, as if she was beautiful and every single thing she said to him was equally as important as whatever he said to her. She wanted to kiss him and feel his touch all over her body.

Thankfully, before those kinds of things began to play

too much in her mind, their pizza arrived. As they ate, they talked about the different kinds of pizza they would eat.

"I would never eat it if it had any kind of fish on it," she said and made a face. "That sounds absolutely disgusting to me."

"For me it's fruit," he added. "I prefer my pineapple separate from my pizza."

Their talk continued to stay light and fun as they ate. It was so easy with him. There were never any awkward silences or stuttering around for something to say.

A few more couples came in, along with a family of five, raising the noise level in the small restaurant. Still, they had no problem hearing each other as the children in the group were well-behaved.

"Your sister has a couple of kids, right?" she asked.

"Yeah, she has two. She has a three-year-old little boy and a five-year-old girl," he said.

"And are you a good uncle to them?"

"Apparently so because they seem to love their Uncle Benjy."

"That's what they call you? Uncle Benjy? Oh, that's so cute," she said.

He laughed. "I don't know about that, but I find them really cute and very entertaining." He leaned back against the booth and looked at the leftover pizza. He had a piece left of his and she had three pieces remaining of hers. "Do you eat leftover pizza?"

She nodded. "As far as I'm concerned there's nothing better in the morning than a warm cup of coffee and a cold piece of pizza."

"Then I'll make sure you get home with your leftovers. Would you like some dessert?"

"Heavens no, I'm absolutely stuffed," she replied. "I should have stopped eating a piece ago."

"Then shall we go?" He dug in his back pocket for his wallet.

"Put that away," she said sternly. "Don't even go there with me, mister. Have you forgotten our deal for tonight? I'm paying and that's the end of it." She reached into her purse and pulled out her credit card.

"I don't like this," he replied with a frown.

"Well, deal with it, macho man," she said jokingly. When Gino came to their table, Benjamin instructed him to box up her leftovers and she handed the man her card.

A few minutes after that they were back in his car and headed to her house. "Thank you for dinner," he said.

"You're more than welcome. Why don't you come in for a nightcap and we can talk about the elephant in the room," she suggested.

"Yeah, we definitely need to have a talk about it," he concurred.

The evening had been so pleasant and she dreaded ruining it by talking about stressful things like her stalker. But she couldn't exactly hide from what was going on in her own life.

When they reached her house, she was grateful to see nothing had been left on her porch, although she was aware of Benjamin's gaze shooting all around the area.

"What's your poison?" she asked once they were inside. "I think I'm going to have a small whiskey and cola."

"That sounds good to me," he replied.

"Sit tight and I'll be right back." She went into the kitchen and fixed their drinks, then carried them back into the living room, where she placed both of them on the coffee table and then sank down on the sofa next to him.

She picked up her glass. "Cheers," she said.

He lifted his glass and clinked it with hers. "Cheers."

They both took a drink and she could only hope the warmth of the alcohol as it filled her could keep away the chills she knew their conversation might produce.

"Okay." He set his glass back on the coaster on the coffee table and gazed at her soberly. "There's no question that you have a stalker. So far, he's been harmless and I'd say that's a good sign and he might stay that way or he might eventually turn his attention to somebody else. Are you sure none of the three men you mentioned to me before is the person?"

"I'm as positive as I can be," she replied. "Maybe you chasing after him scared him away permanently," she added hopefully.

"Maybe, but in the meantime, I've asked Dallas to make sure we do extra patrols by your house each night and he agreed to do so. I wish we could put somebody on you full-time, but that's just not feasible with our manpower issues."

"I understand that," she replied. "I like the part where you said he might eventually turn his attention to somebody else, although I wouldn't wish this on any other woman. It's so creepy to know somebody is watching you and leaving you things you don't want. At least I've got good locks on my doors." She picked up her drink and took another long sip. "If and when this creep reveals himself to me, I swear I'm going to punch him right in the face."

He laughed. "I would hate to have to arrest you, Bailey."

"Hmm, I might like you putting me in handcuffs," she replied teasingly.

His eyes darkened and lit with a fire that shot a flame into the very pit of her stomach. She leaned forward, her heart suddenly racing with a sweet and fiery anticipation. "Kiss me, Benjamin," she said softly. "Please, kiss me."

Chapter 8

She didn't have to ask him again. He scooted closer to her, drew her into his arms and then took her mouth with his. Oh, the man could kiss. His lips were wonderfully soft, yet masterful, and being in his arms felt like being home.

She was the one who deepened the kiss, dipping her tongue in to dance with his as the flames inside her burned hotter. She leaned into him closer and his arms tightened around her.

This is what she'd thought about all evening while they'd been eating. She had fantasized about kissing him again and being held in his big, strong arms. Now that it was happening, her heart sang with joy.

The kiss continued to build in intensity as his hands moved up and down her back in slow, sweet caresses. She wanted more. The need for more of him grew deep inside her.

His lips left hers and slowly slid down her throat in nipping, teasing kisses. She was more than half-breathless as electric currents flooded through her veins.

"Bailey, you drive me absolutely crazy," he whispered, his voice slightly deeper than usual.

"You drive me absolutely crazy, too," she replied.

He took her mouth with his once again in a fiery kiss

that sent her half out of her mind. She had never wanted a man as much as she wanted him. She wanted him naked in her bed and against her body. She wanted to feel his warm skin against hers. She wanted to be as intimate with him as a woman could be with a man. No matter what happened in the future, she wanted to make love with Benjamin right now.

She finally leaned back from him. "Come to my room with me, Benjamin. Please, come and make love to me."

She saw the start of a protest in his beautiful eyes before he spoke. "Bailey, I don't think…" he began.

"Don't you want me?" she asked.

"Of course, I do, more than you know, but…"

"Shh." She placed her index finger against his mouth. "Don't think, Benjamin. Don't think and just be in this wonderful moment with me." She got to her feet and held a hand out to him. He hesitated only a moment and then he stood and took hold of her hand.

They were both silent as she led him up the stairs and into her bedroom, where the lamp on her bedside table created a soft glow. Once there, he gathered her back into his arms and kissed her once again.

The flames between them were still there, hotter than ever. As their kissing continued, she began to unbutton her blouse. Once it was fully undone, she shrugged it off her shoulders and it fell to the floor behind her.

In turn, he pulled off his polo, exposing his beautiful, broad chest to her view. She took off her earrings and put them on the nightstand, then turned out the lamp. Then the fire between them quickly exploded and they both finished undressing in a frenzy, finally sliding into her pale pink sheets.

He took her back into his arms and she loved the feel of his warm, naked skin against her own. Their kisses became frantic, filled with a hungry need and passion.

His mouth left hers and he kissed the sensitive skin just behind her ears, making her grateful she'd taken off her earrings. She wanted to melt into his warm, smooth skin and never be found. She had never felt this incredible kind of need before.

His hands cupped her breasts for only a few moments before his mouth moved down to lick first one erect nipple and then the other. Electric currents raced through her, from her breasts and into the very center of her. He teased and tormented her breasts until she thought she'd go absolutely mad.

At the same time one of his hands slid slowly down her stomach, caressing down to the place where all her nerve endings met. She gasped and moaned his name as his fingers began to move against her.

"You're so beautiful, Bailey," he whispered.

"So are you," she replied mindlessly as the tension inside her rose higher and higher. He quickened his finger dance against her and suddenly she was there…soaring and unraveling as her climax crashed within her. She clung to him and cried out his name.

Once the exhilarating wave had passed, and despite her still gasping for air, she reached down to encircle his hardness with her hand. He was fully aroused and just feeling him pulse with life in her grasp awakened a new hunger inside her.

He allowed her to caress him for only a few moments before he rose up and positioned himself between her hips.

He slowly eased into her and she gripped the side of his hips to urge him in deeper.

He completely filled her up inside and the feeling was beyond wonderful. His gaze held hers intently, visible from the hall light that spilled into the room. He then groaned her name and began to move against her. Slowly at first, he stroked in and out of her.

The sensations inside her were overwhelming as his lips sought hers once again. When the kiss ended, he pumped into her harder and faster. She welcomed him, raising her legs behind his back and clinging to him as the tension inside her rose higher.

The waves of pleasure came faster and faster, and suddenly she was there once again, spiraling out of control as another powerful orgasm gripped her.

As she began to crash back down to earth, he climaxed, as well. When it was done, he collapsed to the side of her, and for several minutes they remained that way as they each tried to catch their breath. It was at that moment she realized she was madly and desperately in love with him.

Benjamin stood in the guest bathroom down the hallway from Bailey's bedroom and stared at his reflection in the mirror. "Dammit, man," he said aloud with self-disgust. This wasn't supposed to have happened. This was the very last thing he'd wanted to happen between them.

With the scent of her still clinging to his skin, all kinds of regrets swept through him. Oh, making love with her had been beyond wonderful. He'd half imagined it in his head, but nothing had prepared him for the heart-stopping act of actually making love with her.

She'd been so passionate and giving and had stirred a

passion deep inside him he'd never, ever felt before in his life. Damn the fact that he hadn't stopped things, that he hadn't just kissed her good-night and left it at that. Damn the fact that he hadn't been stronger than his own desire for her.

One of the reasons he'd insisted they go the pizza place and eat in public in the first place was to prevent any kind of intimate physical contact between them. He should have known coming inside with her for a nightcap was a bad idea. He'd set himself up for failure by coming into her house. And he'd failed miserably.

He sluiced cold water over his face and then got dressed in his clothes, which he'd plucked up off the floor on his way out of her bedroom.

Okay. What was done was done and he couldn't go back and change it. However, he could never, ever repeat this mistake with her again. What he needed to do now was see her a few more times and then begin to distance himself from her. It was what was best for both of them.

He'd made love to her, but he certainly hadn't proposed to her. He'd made no promises about any future with her and before he left to go home tonight, he needed her to understand that.

He left the bathroom and realized she was no longer in her bedroom. "Bailey?" he called out.

"I'm down here." Her voice came from the lower level. He went downstairs and found her seated in the corner of the sofa. She had pulled on a pink robe over what appeared to be a pink nightgown. Her short hair was slightly tousled, her lips appeared pink and slightly swollen and she looked absolutely beyond gorgeous.

"Benjamin," she said with a soft smile and patted the

sofa next to her. "That was positively wonderful. I can't tell you how much I loved being in your arms."

He sank down and looked at her somberly. "It was wonderful," he replied. "But, Bailey, it shouldn't have happened."

She frowned. "But it was what we both wanted, wasn't it?"

"In that moment, yes. But I should have had better control over things...over myself. We didn't even have protected sex."

"If you're worried about me, I haven't been with anyone for a very long time and I'm on the pill," she replied.

He frowned. "Okay, but I just need you to understand that I'm not in a position to make you promises about any kind of a future," he said.

She shifted positions on the sofa and moved her arms across her chest. "Benjamin, I swear, you think way too much. We are just two consenting adults who slept together. I certainly don't expect anything from you, except maybe to repeat this again soon," she said with a naughty smile.

Her words set him somewhat at ease. Maybe he had overthought everything. Still, he was determined that this wouldn't happen again in the future. There was no reason for it to happen again.

"I wanted to ask you to spend the night with me, but I know tomorrow is your day off and you probably have a lot of things you need to do before going to your parents' house for your family dinner. I knew if I asked you, you'd probably say no," she added.

"You're right, I would have said no." The last thing he'd want to do was fall asleep with her in his arms because he would like it too much and it would just make things even more complicated between them than they already were.

Thirty minutes later, when he was in his car and driving home, he knew it was time to stop seeing her. He was getting in too deep with her. Initially, he'd worried about hurting her, but the truth was his heart was the one that would hurt when she was no longer in his life.

Still, you didn't stop seeing a woman after making love with her. That certainly wasn't the right thing to do and he would never do something like that to Bailey.

So he would see her a few more times and then stop seeing her. A wave of depression swept through him at the very thought of not having her to talk to and to laugh with anymore. She had been the welcome lightness in his life that he'd desperately needed.

He called her the next day and asked her to dinner at the café on Monday evening. She readily agreed and he hated how much he was looking forward to it. Dammit, he'd never felt so out of control when it came to a woman before.

Sunday afternoon he drove out to his family's farmhouse for an early dinner with his parents, his sister and her husband and their kids. The Sunday gathering was a long-standing tradition and Benjamin always had Sundays off unless something popped up that needed his attention at work. Or in the case of last weekend, when he'd taken Bailey out to dinner on Sunday.

The farmhouse where he'd grown up was a rambling three-bedroom ranch style. Benjamin's father, Johnny, had worked hard all his life as a farmer on the land. Benjamin's mother, Marie, had spent her life as a loving support to her husband and her children.

Benjamin had a lot of wonderful memories from growing up on the farm. He'd loved sitting on the back porch and watching lightning bugs dance in the yard while they all ate homemade ice cream or a piece of freshly baked pie.

There had been snowy days when the four of them had built snowmen, had snow fights and made snow angels. They'd gone apple picking together and shared picnics, among so many other things.

His parents had worked hard to instill a strong sense of family. Although there had been times growing up when the last thing he'd wanted to do was spend time with his parents, he could now appreciate those family times.

He pulled up and parked next to Lori and her husband's car. The minute he entered the house, he was attacked by his sister's children.

"Uncle Benjy," five-year-old Amelia squealed and hit him midcenter for a hug. He pretended to be knocked off his feet and fell backward on the floor.

That set Amelia into a giggling fit. Three-year-old Aaron crawled on top of him and pulled on his nose. Benjamin pretended to sneeze and then made other noises with his mouth that had the two little ones giggling with delight. He absolutely adored Lori's children.

"Ah, I should have known my brother had arrived by the noise coming out of this room," his sister said as she stood in the threshold between the living room and the kitchen.

Lori was a pretty woman with light brown hair and blue eyes. Her husband, Charlie Statler, was a good guy who was also a farmer working on their own land.

"Kids, leave Uncle Benjy alone, and Benjamin, get up off the floor and stop tormenting my children," she said teasingly.

"Ha, they're tormenting me instead of the other way

around," he protested with a laugh. "Okay, kids." Benjamin got to his feet. "Uncle Benjy needs to go talk to the grown-ups now."

"And you two come with me, it's almost time to eat," Lori said to her children. She picked up Aaron and put him on one hip and then grabbed Amelia's hand and led them into the kitchen.

Benjamin followed behind and entered the large airy kitchen where the table was set for five and a toddler and high chair were present. "Hi, Ma," Benjamin said and walked over to the stove where his mother was pulling a large tray of chicken breasts out of the oven. He leaned in and gave her a quick kiss on the cheek. "Need some help with that?" he asked.

"No, I've got it. Go sit down with the other men," she replied. "You know how I am about men in my kitchen."

"Right," Benjamin responded. She'd never wanted help in the kitchen. She only allowed Lori to help out occasionally.

Benjamin's dad sat at the head of the table with Charlie seated on one side of him. Benjamin sat across the table and down one from his brother-in-law, leaving the other chair next to his father waiting for his mother.

The kids were wrangled into their chairs, and ten minutes later the food was on the table and they'd all begun to eat. Besides the baked chicken, there was a bowl of noodles, seasoned green beans that were from their garden and homemade yeasty rolls. There was also a red gelatin mold with applesauce in it.

Meals when they were all together usually involved a form of controlled chaos as Lori fed the two children while trying to feed herself. Benjamin tried to help her out, encouraging the kids to eat their green beans as they slurped up the noodles.

As they ate, and in between the children's needs, they all talked about the week that had just passed. Johnny and Charlie spoke about farming issues and the preparations already being made for the winter and then the conversation turned to the latest murder.

"Is Buddy riding Dallas's back about a solve?" Johnny asked, referring to Buddy Lyons, the town mayor.

"No. Actually, he's been surprisingly very supportive so far. He knows we're all doing everything possible that we can to catch the killer."

"Poor Bailey, I can't imagine walking into my place of business and finding a dead body sitting there," Lori said and visibly shuddered.

"Yeah, it was pretty rough on her," Benjamin replied.

"The word on the streets is that you and Bailey have gotten pretty close." Lori gave him a knowing grin. "In fact, that same rumor mill said you skipped out on us last Sunday to have dinner with her at the café."

"Is that true?" his mother asked. "Are you seeing her... dating her? From what I've heard, Bailey is a lovely young woman."

"Yeah, we've been hanging out together a bit, but it's nothing serious," he replied.

"It's never anything serious with you, Benjamin. You aren't getting any younger, son," Johnny said. "Surely you don't want to be all alone for the rest of your life. You need to find a good woman and get married."

"Of course, I don't want to spend the rest of my life all alone, but I can't help it that I haven't met the perfect woman for me yet," Benjamin protested. Except that he had and yet he knew it would never work out with her.

They finished the meal and after the cleanup Lori and her family left while Benjamin hung around for a little while longer, especially since he'd missed last Sunday's family meal.

"Benjamin, why don't you come out to the front porch and sit with me for a while," his mother suggested after his father left the table and turned on the television in the next room.

"Sure," he agreed.

Minutes later the two were seated in the wicker chairs on the front porch. "How are you really doing, son?" Marie's blue eyes searched his face. She was still a beautiful woman with salt-and-pepper hair and delicate features.

"I'm doing okay," he replied.

"I worry about you, Benjamin. I know how much weight these murders have put on your shoulders and how much you take your work to heart."

"Dallas is the one who is really taking the brunt of it."

"But I know you and how deeply you care about what you do," she continued.

"Really, Mom. I'm okay." He smiled at her in an effort to reassure her.

"I do wish you had somebody special in your life," she said.

"I know…maybe someday I will," he said. "What I need most right now is for you to stop worrying about me because I'm doing just fine."

She laughed. "Don't you know? That's my job as a mother—to worry about my children until the day I die."

"I love you, Mom."

"I love you, too, son."

He got up from the chair. "And on that note, it's time for me to get out of here." His mother also stood and he gave her a quick hug. "Tell Dad I said goodbye and I'll check in with him later in the week."

"You take care of yourself, Benjamin. And take care of that beautiful heart of yours," she advised.

He walked out to his car, got in and then headed home. As he drove, his mother's words played and replayed in his mind. *Take care of that beautiful heart of yours.* That's what he was trying to do and that was ultimately the reason he needed to stop seeing Bailey.

Chapter 9

After making love with Benjamin, Bailey was torn about what she needed to do where he was concerned. She was more than crazy about him. She had fallen in love with him and she hadn't felt this way in years. In fact, she'd never felt this depth of love for a man before.

She'd always been able to easily walk away from the men she dated, especially knowing what she did about herself. *You're not normal. You're selfish and not right.* All the things that Adam had said to her when he'd broken up with her years ago flew around and around in her head as she drove to her mother's house on Sunday afternoon.

She'd called earlier and told her mother she was bringing over some things from the bakery as a treat. What she really wanted was some advice from her mother. She also needed to confess the reason she had relationship issues. It was past time she had that conversation with her mother. Maybe Angela would be able to give her some concrete advice.

As she pulled into the driveway and parked, intense nerves tightened her stomach. Her throat threatened to close up with dreadful anxiety. Surely, she shouldn't be so nervous about talking candidly with her own mother.

She grabbed the pink-and-white-striped box from the

bakery that was on her passenger seat and then left the car and headed for the front door. "Hello?" she called as she stepped into the house.

"In the kitchen," her mom replied. "Ah, you're just in time," she said as Bailey walked in. "The coffee just finished making. Have a seat and I'll pour us each a cup."

Bailey sank down at the table. "Have you had a good day so far?" she asked. As usual, Angela looked impeccable today. She was clad in a blue-flowered blouse that pulled out the blue of her eyes, and navy slacks. Her ash-colored hair was perfectly coiffed and dainty blue earrings completed her look. Her mother waited to answer until she had the two cups of fresh brew on the table, along with two small plates. "I've had a lovely day so far. I slept in a little bit and then watched videos on jewelry-making. I figured I'd do a little research before I actually started the process for myself."

"That sounds like a smart thing to do," Bailey replied.

"And how has your day been so far?" Angela asked.

"Not too bad," Bailey responded.

"Now, tell me, what is the special occasion that has you bringing me goodies from the bakery?"

"Can't I just do something nice for you without it being a special occasion?" Bailey asked.

"Of course, and I'm eager to see what you brought me from the bakery."

Bailey untied the white ribbon across the top and opened the box to display the strawberry bars that she knew her mother loved. "Oh, what a lovely treat," Angela exclaimed. She immediately took two of the bars and placed them on the little plate in front of her. Bailey took one for herself as nerves once again tightened her chest and made her feel slightly sick.

Angela took a bite and then sipped her coffee, her gaze direct on Bailey over the rim of the cup. She lowered the cup, but kept her gaze focused on her daughter. "So tell me why you're really here? What do you need? A loan? You know I'm not made of money, especially since I retired. Or do you want to borrow something? A dress or maybe a blouse of mine?"

"Of course not. You should know by now I'm financially solid. The salon is doing very well and I've never had to borrow money from you," Bailey replied. "And let's be honest, we don't exactly share the same fashion sense." She drew in a deep breath. "Actually, I need some advice from you."

"Advice about what?" Her mother eyed her curiously.

"I'm sure you've probably heard through the grapevine that I've been seeing a lot of Benjamin Cooper lately."

"Yes, I have heard that through the grapevine. I've also heard he's a good, solid man, although I'm sure his job has been quite difficult lately."

"It's been very difficult for everyone in law enforcement right now," Bailey agreed. "Are you going to the town meeting this Wednesday evening?"

"Yes, I'm planning on attending, but you didn't come by here to get my advice on whether I should attend the meeting or not. So what advice do you need from me?" Angela eyed her curiously.

Bailey drew in a deep breath and then released it. "Mom, it's finally happened. I'm in love. I have fallen madly in love with Benjamin." It was the first time she'd said those words aloud and they sang in her heart, but also caused a shaft of pain to rush through her as she thought of ending things with him.

"Well, that's wonderful. Do you know if he feels the same way about you?" Angela asked.

"I'm not sure. He hasn't said the words to me, but I know he cares about me a lot." She was sure she'd seen love shining from his eyes when he gazed at her. She was positive she'd tasted love in his lips when he kissed her. Yes, she believed in the depth of her heart that he was in love with her, too.

"So then what's the problem?" Her mother took another bite of her strawberry bar.

Bailey once again drew in a deep breath and released it before answering. This was the moment of truth. It was past time she told her mother her secret. "Mom, I don't want to have children," she blurted out.

Her mother's eyes widened. "Whatever do you mean? Bailey, you're being silly. Of course, you want children," Angela scoffed. "Every woman wants children."

"Not me. Mom, I've given it a lot of thought, but I just don't have that maternal feeling. I've never had it. Most of my friends have had babies and seeing them hasn't moved me or given me the feeling that I couldn't wait to have one of my own. I just don't want any of my own."

"Bailey, you're being absolutely ridiculous." Angela frowned at her. "Maybe you need to see a therapist about this. It's just not normal to not want children."

Those words stabbed a sharp sword through Bailey's heart. *You aren't normal.* "I love my life just the way it is. Isn't it better not to have children than to have them and then somehow resent them?" Bailey asked. "Mom, I'm fulfilled by my career and by my life the way I'm living it right now. My life is full enough already."

"You know what your problem is, Bailey? You're very

selfish. Only a selfish woman wouldn't want to have children." Her mother leaned back in her chair and crossed her arms. "You know, I could have decided not to have you after your father left me, but I wanted a baby."

Bailey shook her head. "And I just don't want any babies."

Angela's nose thinned as she blew out an exasperated sigh. "I know I certainly did nothing in your upbringing to warrant you feeling this way. Well, this certainly explains why you haven't married yet," she continued. "Most men want children. It's important to them to have a family. No man would want you knowing this about you. So what possible advice could you want from me?"

Bailey wasn't sure why she'd thought it would be a good idea to come here and bare her heart to her mother. So far Angela had told her she wasn't normal and she was selfish, repeating the same things Adam had said to her so long ago. She supposed unconditional love from a mother wasn't a given when it came to somebody like Angela.

"I guess I was just wondering if you thought it was wrong of me to keep seeing Benjamin without telling him where I stand on the children issue," Bailey said.

"Well, of course, it's wrong. Bailey, he has an absolute right to know this about you. I can't believe you haven't told him already. You shouldn't tie up his heart any longer. He deserves to move on from you and find a woman who isn't so self-absorbed and will give him the family he probably wants."

"But we haven't had any talks about the future yet. It's not like we're planning on getting married next week. Everything has been kept pretty casual so far." There was no way she intended to tell her mother that they'd already made love.

"I still think you should have the conversation with him immediately, although I suppose there's always a possibility that you'll change your mind about having children."

"Mother, I'm thirty-four years old. I know myself pretty well by now. Trust me, I'm not going to change my mind about it," Bailey said.

"Then you'll wind up a bitter old woman and will be all alone for the rest of your life," her mother replied.

Bailey left soon after that. She drove around for about an hour, tears chasing down her cheeks as she played and replayed the conversation in her head.

You aren't normal. You're selfish. Maybe you need to see a therapist. The words went around and around in her head as sobs escaped her.

Had Adam been right about her after all? Was her mother right about her? Was it selfishness that made her not want children? Was it some sort of a weird abnormality? Was it really so wrong for a woman to know instinctively…intellectually that she didn't want to have any kids?

She finally found herself pulling up in front of Joe and Lizzy's place. She swiped the tears from her face and drew in several deep breaths to get her broken emotions under control.

She'd never told Lizzy her feelings about children, although Lizzy had talked often about her desire to have children. Bailey's mother's words had hurt her horribly and she just wanted—just needed—to talk to her best friend right now.

She got out of her car, walked to the door and then knocked. Lizzy answered. "Hey, Bailey," she said with a smile.

To Bailey's surprise, she burst into tears. "Oh, honey,

what's going on?" Lizzy instantly put an arm around her shoulder and pulled her into the living room and to the sofa. Bailey collapsed there with Lizzy by her side. "Bailey, what's going on? Why are you crying? Did Benjamin break up with you?"

Bailey shook her head and tried to pull herself together as quickly as possible. "Where are Joe and Emily?" she asked, not wanting them to walk into the room and find her such a blubbery mess.

"They went into town. It's just us two here. Now, talk to me," Lizzy insisted. "What's going on?"

Bailey drew in a deep breath and expelled it slowly. "I just left my mother's place and she really hurt my feelings."

"This isn't something new, Bailey," Lizzy said softly. "Your mother has hurt your feelings many times in the past."

"I know, but she was way worse today. I went over to talk to her because I was hoping to get some advice from her and then I told her something that really set her off. It's something about me that really nobody knows, not even you."

Bailey's chest tightened. If she told Lizzy her secret, would her best friend also tell her she wasn't normal? That she was selfish? Would she not want to be friends with Bailey anymore?

"What is it, Bailey? Do you want to tell me?"

"Oh, Lizzy, it's been a secret of mine forever and I'm so afraid you'll hate me once I tell you."

Lizzy pulled Bailey's hand into hers and squeezed. "There is absolutely nothing you can tell me that would make me hate you, Bailey."

Bailey drew in a deep breath and it slowly shuddered

out of her. "Lizzy… I don't want to have children," she finally blurted out.

"And?" Lizzy looked at her with confusion.

"And nothing. That's it—that's my big secret. According to my mother that makes me not normal and selfish." Tears once again blurred Bailey's eyes. "She told me I need a therapist."

"Well, that's all utterly ridiculous. Motherhood isn't for everyone," Lizzy replied.

Bailey straightened up and stared at her friend. "So you don't think I'm abnormal or selfish?"

"I think you're very smart to know that about yourself before you bring any children into the world. Bailey, if you were selfish, I wouldn't be friends with you. I'm sorry your mother said those hateful things to you because they simply aren't true. They're nothing but small-minded nonsense."

"But Adam said those same kinds of things to me when I told him I didn't want children," Bailey admitted. "He told me that when he broke up with me."

"Adam was a total jerk who wanted to own you. He wanted nothing more than to keep you pregnant and barefoot in the kitchen. You were really lucky to be rid of him." Lizzy looked at her curiously. "So what advice did you want from your mother?"

"I wanted to know how to handle this situation with Benjamin. Do I owe it to him to tell him this about myself now or can I wait?"

"Really, Bailey, only you can answer that question," Lizzy said. "The two of you haven't talked about children yet?"

Bailey shook her head. "It's just never come up in our conversations. We really haven't talked about any kind of a future together at all. But I'm in love with him, Lizzy, and I'm afraid he won't want to see me anymore if he knows I don't want children."

"Maybe he doesn't want children, either," Lizzy replied.

Bailey frowned thoughtfully. "I don't know. I do know he absolutely adores his little niece and nephew, which makes me think he'd want some children of his own."

Emotion pressed tight against her chest once again. "Oh, Lizzy, I've never allowed myself to fall in love before because I knew this part of me was probably a game-changer for the men I dated. But somehow, Benjamin got beneath all my defenses. So the way I see it is I either sacrifice my own wishes for a man or I wind up alone. And I just can't sacrifice who I am and what I want in my life."

"Then talk to him, Bailey. If you think your relationship is at the place where you need clarity about this, then just have the conversation with him. That's the only advice I can give you," Lizzy said.

"And you don't think any less of me because I don't want kids?" Bailey asked with uncertainty.

"Of course not. I admire you for knowing what is right for you. Besides, from what I hear, more and more women are choosing not to have children. Part of it is the economy right now, but women are also being fulfilled by their careers, or travel, or hobbies, or whatever. You are certainly not alone."

"But I feel so all alone," Bailey replied mournfully.

Lizzy leaned over and gave her a big hug. "You aren't alone, girlfriend. You've always got me," she said as she released her.

"Thanks, Lizzy. I appreciate your friendship more than you'll ever know." Bailey got up from the sofa, utterly drained by the emotional afternoon. "And now, I think I'll just go home, get into bed and pull the covers up over my head."

Lizzy laughed and also stood. "You'll be okay, Bailey. No matter what happens with Benjamin, or what your mother says to you, you're going to be just fine."

Bailey headed for the front door with Lizzy at her heels. "Call me, Bailey, or just come by. You know I'm always here for you."

Bailey smiled. "I know, and I really appreciate it."

Bailey left the house, then got back in her car and headed home. There was no question that talking to Lizzy had made her feel better, but it also hadn't solved anything. She still didn't know what she was going to do about Benjamin.

She saw it when she pulled into her driveway. The brown teddy bear on her porch was twice the size of the last one. She pulled into her garage and parked, then watched to make sure the door shut behind her.

Once inside the house she went directly to the front door, opened it and grabbed the bear. She looked around the area and thankfully saw nobody lurking about. But what bothered her was the fact that somebody had to have been watching her to know she'd left the house and it was safe to leave the bear without risking his identity.

Her first thought was to call Benjamin, but what could he do now, after-the-fact? At least nobody had broken into her house or done anything scary like that. It was the same old thing…a gift she didn't want from somebody she didn't want to know.

There was an envelope stapled to the bear's paw. She ripped it off and opened it. *You are going to be mine for-*

ever very, very soon. She tossed the note on her coffee table and then threw the bear across the room. Finally, she sank down on her sofa and began to cry once again, this time with a combination of fear and heartache.

This note definitely sounded more threatening than the others. Did this mean he was escalating? Was he getting ready to make a move on her? What kind of a move?

Who was it that was stalking her? It was terrifying to know that somebody was watching her. It was even more terrifying to think that the person had some sort of a deadly obsession with her.

She thought about calling the police to make a report of it, but she knew there wasn't much of anything they could do about it. Even if they caught him red-handed on her property, he probably wouldn't be charged with much. He'd probably be charged with trespassing and given a warning to stop leaving her things. She had no idea what it took to have somebody actually charged with stalking. Would the legal system see the notes as threats?

The sobs ripped from the very depths of her. She had a stalker and she was afraid. And she had a man she loved desperately and she had a definite feeling she was going to lose him.

On Monday evening, Benjamin dressed casually for his dinner at the café with Bailey. Along with his jeans, he pulled on a silver polo-style shirt and called it good.

They'd made plans for him to pick her up at six. It was still a bit early for him to leave. He sank down on the sofa and as always, when his mind was empty for just a moment, it filled with thoughts of Bailey.

He'd always been so careful, so cautious, when it came

to his relationships with women. But somehow, Bailey had barged into his heart with her warm, big smiles and her obvious zest for life. She'd sneaked under his defenses with her full-bodied laughter, sharp wit and intelligence.

Then there was the way she kissed him and the way she felt in his arms. Making love to her had stirred him to the very depths of his soul. There was nothing he'd like more than to make love with her again and again, but, of course, he couldn't allow that to happen.

When it was time for him to go pick her up, he couldn't help the little edge of excitement that filled him. There was no question that he enjoyed her company immensely. She was a welcomed respite from the frustrations that plagued him at work.

But in his heart, he knew she was much more than that to him. He would enjoy her company just as much when his job became easy again.

The Scarecrow Killer remained elusive and he was picking off young women one by one without making any mistakes. The button was their only clue and if he realized he'd lost it, he'd probably throw away the shirt it came from. Then the button would be worthless in their investigation.

They'd spent the day running on a damn hamster wheel, checking and rechecking all the murders, throwing out suppositions that had no real merit.

They combed the internet for sites that sold straw hats and frayed jeans, but had no real way to check sales. There were hundreds of sites that sold straw hats and none that sold frayed jeans, but who knew what might have been available for sale when. It had been an exhausting day, but now that he was on his way to pick up Bailey, a burst of new energy filled him.

He pulled into her driveway and, as usual, she immediately ran out toward his car. And, as usual, she looked positively lovely.

She was clad in a royal blue dress with a silver belt that showcased her slender waist and her shapely breasts. The short length of the dress displayed her shapely legs. Big, silver earrings danced on her ears, and the smile she wore cast a deep warmth inside him.

She slid into his passenger seat, bringing with her the wonderful scent of hers that half-dizzied his senses. "Hi."

He grinned at her. "Hi yourself," he replied. He backed out of the driveway. "Are you hungry?"

"Starving. I spent the whole day trying to get the supplies in my garage in order and so I skipped lunch," she explained.

"Then I hope the café has enough food for you," he said teasingly.

"Ha ha, you're a funny man," she replied. "You know I eat like a little bird."

"Ha ha, you're a funny woman."

They both laughed at their own silliness. It took only minutes to get to the café. He parked, and together, they got out of his car. It was another beautiful evening. The sky was clear and it was a bit cooler than it had been. September was gone and Halloween was just around the corner.

"Winter is going to be here before we know it," she said as they walked toward the café's front door.

"Ugh, don't remind me. I'm definitely not a big fan of winter," he replied.

"That makes two of us. I hate the cold and the snow makes business slow down, as getting nails done isn't a necessity when the streets are slick. Although I do love a white Christmas, but I just want it for that one day."

He laughed. "It rarely happens that way."

"I know, but I can wish," she replied.

There weren't many people in the café on Monday nights so they easily found a booth. She opened a menu and began to look at the offerings. He already knew he was going to have the bacon cheeseburger with fries on the side.

"Seeing anything exciting?" he asked.

"Several things. For a change I'm really not in the mood for the usual burger and fries, but I am thinking of having the special."

"And what is the special on Monday nights?" he asked.

"Spaghetti with meat sauce, garlic toast and a house salad."

"Sounds good, but I'm going to stick with my burger," he replied.

At that moment, their waitress arrived and took their orders. "So how were your days off?" he asked once they were alone again.

She frowned. "Kind of a mixed bag. Like I told you before, I worked in my garage all day today and yesterday I had a difficult visit with my mother and then stopped by Lizzy and Joe's place." A flash of pain swept quickly across her features.

"You want to talk about your visit with your mom?" he asked, hating to see the sadness in the depths of her beautiful eyes. If she needed to talk about it, he certainly wanted her to know he was available to listen.

She smiled. "No thanks. It was just kind of the usual bash-on-Bailey party. I've gotten used to it by now."

But she wasn't used to it. Benjamin knew from the pain

he'd momentarily seen in her eyes that she definitely had been hurt by her mother. Personally, he couldn't imagine such a thing. Mothers were supposed to be a child's biggest champion, weren't they?

"Anything else new in your world since last time I talked to you?" he asked.

Once again, a dark shadow filled her eyes. "Yes, but I don't want to talk about it right now. What about you? Anything new in your life?"

"Not really. I had dinner with my parents and my sister's family yesterday." He couldn't help but smile. "My niece and nephew decided to start calling me Uncle Benjy poo-poo head, much to my sister's dismay."

She laughed. "And what did you do to earn such an esteemed title?"

"I might have made some noises with my mouth while I was wrestling with them," he admitted.

"Bad Uncle Benjy," she replied. She looked down at the table and then gazed up at him once again.

"What?" he asked. She looked like she wanted to say something else.

She shook her head and smiled at him. At that moment, the waitress arrived not only with their drinks, but also with their orders.

"I know you were off work yesterday, but tell me about your day today," she said as they began to eat.

"There's not much to tell. The Scarecrow Killer case is still stalled. We spent the day going over and over things, and then this afternoon we spun our wheels to check out a tip that came in. Unfortunately, the tip was wrong and so it was just another total waste of our time."

"I'm sure you all are beyond frustration," she replied.

"Definitely." He watched with interest as she twirled a bite of spaghetti on her fork and then neatly popped it into her mouth. "You look like an expert eating that pasta. If I was eating it, I'd have it all over my chin and probably down the front of my shirt, as well."

She laughed once again. "The spaghetti twirl was taught to me by my mother when I was about eight years old. She wanted me to know the proper way to eat it so I wouldn't embarrass her if I ordered it when we ate out in public."

"I've never ordered the spaghetti here. Is it good?"

"Delicious," she replied. "You want me to twirl you a forkful?"

"Sure, if you don't mind sharing," he said. "I wouldn't mind a taste of it."

She smiled at him. "I never mind sharing with you." She neatly got the spaghetti on the fork and then they both leaned forward so he could eat it from her. It was just a simple, quick bite, but as she looked into his eyes, it became something far more intimate.

"What do you think?" she asked.

I think I want to kiss you, right here and right now in the middle of the café, his brain whispered, but, of course, he said none of that aloud. "It's good," he responded. "But I'll stick to my burgers."

They continued their small talk as they ate. As always, it was easy with her. He felt so very comfortable with her except for one issue.

He wanted her again. She was definitely deep in his blood now and as he sat across from her the memories of their lovemaking filled him with a wild hunger to repeat it.

"You've gotten very quiet," she said when they were halfway through the meal.

"I guess I'm just focusing on eating this burger," he replied. He couldn't tell her he was focused on her lush lips or the way the top of her breasts peeked out of the scoop-necked dress. He couldn't exactly tell her his head was filled with images of her naked in his arms.

She grinned. "I swear, we need to widen your horizon when it comes to food, otherwise you're going to become a burger."

He laughed. "Hey, leave my burgers and me alone. Besides, you love burgers, too."

"That, I do," she agreed. "Have you had a Big Jolly's burger?"

"Oh, yeah, that's my favorite go-to for lunch when I'm on duty," he replied.

The rest of the meal passed with more banter between them. He loved teasing her and hearing her witty comebacks. She would be the perfect woman for him if he was open to a serious relationship.

They talked about where they'd like to travel to. "I'd love to visit New York City," she said.

"I wouldn't mind that, but I'd also like to see the Grand Canyon and some of the desert area. I'd also like to see Niagara Falls."

"Both of those places are supposed to be pretty spectacular," she replied. "Most of the places I'd like to visit are right here in the United States. I really don't care about traveling abroad."

"I agree. There's enough in the US to visit without going to other countries," he said.

They finished their meals and then left the restaurant. "Benjamin, can you please come into my place when we get there? There's something I want to show you," she said when they were almost to her house. "It's important," she added.

He was reluctant to go into her house, especially since he'd been on sexual sizzle the whole night with her. But there was a serious tone in her voice that made him realize he probably needed to go inside.

"I can do that," he agreed as he pulled into her driveway.

They got out of the car and as always, when they walked to the front door, his gaze swept the area. Seeing nothing amiss, he waited for her to unlock her door and then he followed her inside.

He saw it immediately—a big, brown teddy bear sitting in the chair in the living room. "I assume that's a new gift and you didn't buy it for yourself."

"Yes and no," she replied. "It was on my porch yesterday afternoon when I got home from Lizzy's place." She sank down on the sofa. "Here's the note that came with it." She pointed to a small envelope on the coffee table.

He sat next to her and reached for the envelope. He carefully took the note out and read it aloud. "'You are going to be mine forever very, very soon.'" He looked back up at Bailey. Her blue eyes simmered with uncertainty and what appeared to be more than a touch of fear.

"The 'very, very soon' is what bothers me the most," she said. "I mean, what does that mean? Is this guy going to abduct me off the street tomorrow? When is very soon? Is it tomorrow…? The next day or a week from now…when?"

Benjamin took her hands in his. Hers were cold and trembled slightly in his. "Honey, don't get yourself too worked up. I think if this person really wanted to harm you, he would have done it already and he wouldn't give you a note warning you that it was coming. Maybe this just means he's about to reveal his identity to you. Maybe he believes he's won you over with his gifts and notes."

Although he was somewhat concerned about this note, he would say anything he could to take the fear out of her beautiful eyes. The bottom line was he didn't know just how seriously he should take all of this, and even if he did take it seriously, then what could he do about it?

Thankfully, her hands had warmed in his. "I hadn't thought about that," she said slowly. "It would be wonderful if he did finally reveal himself to me." She leaned forward and kissed him on the lips. It was a short, sweet kiss. "Thank you, Benjamin, for always being there for me."

Her eyes lit with a flame that had nothing to do with uncertainty or fear and he felt the sear clean down in his very soul. She leaned forward again and he couldn't help his desire…his need to kiss her long and deep. And just that quickly he was completely lost in her.

"Stay the night with me, Benjamin," she whispered once the kiss ended. "I've been so on edge lately and I always feel so safe with you. Please stay with me for this one night." Her eyes pleaded with him and he couldn't deny her. Dammit, he couldn't deny himself.

He knew he was making yet another big mistake with her. He knew they were going to make love again, but he swore this would be the very last time. Then he would have to find the perfect time to stop seeing her.

Chapter 10

Bailey awakened and slowly opened her eyes. It must be early, as dawn's light wasn't yet peeking into her bedroom window. The first thing that came into her consciousness was the fact that Benjamin was spooned closely around her back. He made a perfect big spoon to her little spoon.

His breath warmed the back of her neck and his scent surrounded her. Oh, she felt so safe, so wonderful in the shelter of his body. She closed her eyes once again and savored the feel of his naked skin against her own.

They had made love again last night and it had been just as amazing as the first time. It also left her more confused than ever on where they were with their relationship. Were they just good friends with benefits? Or were they working toward something more serious? But it couldn't be serious.

She was just so confused. She knew how she felt about him, but she didn't know exactly how he felt about her. He wasn't talking about a future with her. In all the time they'd spent together, he hadn't mentioned anything except the next time they'd see each other. Yet here he was in her bed after the two of them had made love for the second time.

If they could just remain friends with benefits then maybe she'd never have to tell him about her little secret. It would be the perfect world for her. She'd have his wonderful companionship and his beautiful lovemaking in her life without having to worry about any real future with him.

Even as she told herself that would make her very happy, she knew deep down in her soul it wouldn't. She wanted a wedding. She had always wanted to be a bride and she needed the full commitment that something like a marriage would bring to her. That was what she'd always dreamed of.

As far as she could see it, this was a lose-lose situation all the way around and eventually she was going to get her heart broken. She couldn't help the deep sigh that escaped her and at that moment he stirred against her.

He slowly pulled his arm from around her waist and slid back from her. It was obvious he was trying to get up without awakening her. "Good morning," she said to let him know she was already awake.

"Good morning to you," he replied. He rose up and kissed her naked shoulder. "Do you know what time it is?"

She looked at the clock on her nightstand. "It's a little after six, early enough that I can make us some breakfast before we start our days."

"Bailey, that isn't necessary," he protested.

She turned to look at him, barely able to make out his features in the semidarkness of the room. "It's not necessary, but it's something I'd like to do. Are you afraid to eat my cooking?"

"Bring it on, woman," he replied with a laugh and they both got out of bed.

Ten minutes later she was in her nightgown and a robe and in the kitchen frying up some bacon. The fresh coffee was dripping into the carafe and Benjamin was in her shower. He was taking one here so that all he'd have to do when he left here was go home, change into his uniform and then go in for his eight-o'clock shift.

Since she had no appointments until eleven today, she'd called Naomi and asked her to open up shop at the usual time and take care of things until Bailey showed up. So she had more time to get ready for work than he did.

She was just taking the crispy bacon strips out of the skillet when he walked into the kitchen. He brought with him the scents of fresh soap and shampoo and clean-smelling male. He was dressed in the same clothes he'd had on the night before, and he looked wonderfully handsome.

"Have a seat and I'll pour you a cup of coffee," she said.

"Wow, a full-service restaurant," he responded humorously as he sat in one of the chairs at the table.

She laughed and set the cup of fresh brew in front of him. "How do you like your eggs?"

"How ever you want to make them," he replied.

"Then I'm making it easy. You're getting them scrambled with cheese." She got the eggs out of the refrigerator, along with the milk and a bag of shredded cheese.

"That sounds good to me." He took a sip of his coffee. "How did you sleep last night?"

She smiled at him. "Very well. What about you?"

"I definitely slept well. You make a nice, warm little spoon."

She laughed, pleasantly surprised by how their minds worked alike. "And you make a wonderful big spoon." She scrambled the egg mixture and then poured it into the awaiting skillet. Once it was cooking, she pressed the bread down to toast.

By the time she had the meal on the table, the sun had risen over the horizon and filled her kitchen with a golden light. They made small talk as they ate, chatting about the forecast for some stormy weather over the next couple of days and she shared with him how much she hated thunderstorms.

"I remember when I was five or six there was a terrible thunderstorm one night and I got so scared. I ran into my mother's bedroom, hoping she would let me crawl into bed with her, but that didn't happen. Instead, she told me to stop being so ridiculous about something that couldn't hurt me. She called me a big baby and then she sent me back to my room." Bailey released a deep sigh and then smiled. "To this day I'm still afraid of something that can't hurt me. I absolutely hate thunder."

"I'm so sorry you are afraid of it. To be honest, it's never bothered me. Maybe it's because when I was young, my mother told me that thunder was actually the angels up in heaven taking a break from their heavenly duties and enjoying a game of bowling."

"Oh, that's a nice vision to have. I'll try to keep that in mind the next time it storms," she replied.

It wasn't long before they were finished eating. He insisted on helping her with the cleanup and then it was time for him to go.

They walked into the living room, where the teddy bear still sat in the chair and the note was in its envelope on the coffee table. Just that quickly, a wave of apprehension swept through her.

"Do you have a plastic bag?" he asked. "I just need one big enough to hold this envelope. I want to take it in and see if we can pull some fingerprints off it."

She went back into the kitchen and grabbed a quart-size baggie from the box in a drawer, then hurried back into the living room. "Can you hold it open for me?" he asked. She held the bag open while he picked up the envelope by its very top and then dropped it into the bag.

"You know my fingerprints are on it," she said.

"And mine, but we'll check it to see if there are any others on it."

"It would be wonderful if you could get his prints off it and we could finally identify him," she said.

He smiled at her. "Yes, it would be wonderful." He reached out and ran his finger down the side of her face. She turned her face into his caress. She so loved his touch.

"I'd love to see you without the edge of apprehension in your eyes." He dropped his hand back to his side. "And I assume you want me to take away the teddy bear."

"Yes, please—destroy it like I assume you did the last one," she replied.

"Actually, I didn't destroy it. I have it in the trunk of my patrol car so if I ever have a traumatized child on my hands, I can give it to them. Every officer tries to keep some stuffed animals on hand for that very purpose."

"Oh, that's so nice," she said. "Then I'd love it if you use the bears for that purpose."

"Okay, then it's time for me to get out of here and go home to get ready for my shift." He grabbed the bear from the chair and she walked with him to the front door. Once there, he leaned in to kiss her. It was a sweet, quick kiss that warmed her from head to toe. "I'll call you later," he said.

"Have a good day and catch a lot of bad guys," she said.

He laughed. "That's always the plan. And you paint pretty nails today and try not to worry too much about things."

She watched as his car pulled out of her driveway and

disappeared up the street. She closed the door and locked it, and then headed upstairs for a shower.

This morning it seemed as if they were a married couple, eating breakfast together before they parted ways to go to work for the day. It had felt so right and she desperately wished it would be like this every morning.

The truth was, she wished she was married to Benjamin and they could build new dreams together. They could travel together to all the places they had talked about, or maybe get a puppy to raise together. She wanted to fix him breakfast every morning and sleep in his arms every night.

You're not normal. You're selfish You need therapy.

The words crashed over and over again in her head as she got beneath the warm shower spray. Why should she expect Benjamin to love her when she believed her own mother didn't really love her?

It was almost time. He had worked so hard for the past few months preparing things for her. The isolated house was all ready for her. He'd worked diligently to make it a place where she would feel comfortable and be at home.

She would never have to work in the nail salon again. Being his spiritual bride would be enough to fulfill her. Once she got comfortable with their arrangement it would all fall into place.

He'd left all the gifts and notes to make her see the absolute depth of his love for her. He'd wanted her to know that he was thinking about her all the time.

Without a doubt, he knew she was the perfect woman for him and eventually she would see that he was the perfect man for her. It would probably take some time for her to adjust to everything, but he had all the time in the world for her. And once he made his final move, she would have all the time in the world for him.

Just sitting in his living room right now and thinking about what was to come with her stirred a wealth of sweet anticipation and happiness inside him.

It was just a matter of timing now. He needed to find the perfect time and place to take her away and get her into the home where they could live together without outside voices and opinions intruding.

He frowned as he thought of the cop whom she'd been spending a lot of time with. Maybe Benjamin Cooper thought he was the perfect man for her, but Benjamin couldn't be more wrong.

She obviously didn't know what was best for her right now, but he did. The time he'd had with her had been all too brief, but that was going to be rectified very soon.

Oh, he couldn't wait to have her all to himself. He couldn't wait to make her realize they belonged together forever.

Benjamin called Bailey on Monday evening and made arrangements to bring Chinese takeout to her house for dinner on Friday night. There was a new Chinese place in town and several of the men at the station had raved about it, so he'd decided to give it a try.

Bailey had told him she liked sweet-and-sour chicken, but he'd make his mind up on what to order for himself when he went into the place and looked at their complete menu.

Normally, he wouldn't want to be alone with her in her house, but this was not going to be a normal date. He'd have dinner with her and then he intended to break things off with her.

It was past time for it to happen, even though the thought of it broke his heart. He was deeply in love with her and he knew with certainty she was in love with him. It didn't matter that the specific words hadn't been spoken between them, since the sentiment, the emotion, was there between them every time they were together.

But he had to let her go. She needed to find a real man who would fulfill all her dreams. And he just wasn't that man. He'd never be that man. He'd been selfish in seeing her for as long as he had.

Even now, as he sat on patrol, his heart ached at the very thought of not having her in his life anymore. She'd brought such happiness to him. She'd brought laughter and passion, and there would be an aching void in him for a very long time to come when she was gone.

The worst part of it was he knew he was going to hurt her and that was the last thing he'd ever wanted to do. But it couldn't be avoided any longer.

He'd fingerprinted the envelope and note that had been left for her and unfortunately there had been nothing. He had also fingerprinted the box of candy that had been behind the tree on the night he'd chased the culprit. There had been no prints on it, either. Apparently, whoever had left it for her was smart enough to wear gloves.

He wished like hell he could discover who was behind it all and take away the fear he knew she felt before he broke things off with her, but that probably wasn't going to happen.

As he watched the traffic from where he was parked, just off Main Street, Celeste drove by. Celeste. He hadn't thought anything about the woman since Bailey had told him the divorcée had come into Bailey's salon to try to put her off him and then later when he'd run into her at the grocery store.

Celeste. Her name now thundered in his head. Was it possible she could be behind the gifts and notes to Bailey? Was it possible she was hoping Bailey would be excited about a new man in her life and that Bailey would break things off with Benjamin?

He thought about the night he'd chased the person lurking behind the tree. He'd just assumed it was a man, but could it have been a woman? Was it possible it could have been Celeste? Physically, he supposed it could be possible. But surely, it was a crazy idea.

He stewed about it until lunchtime, when he grabbed a burger and fries at Big Jolly's for himself and the same for Dallas. When he got back to the station, he and his boss went to the break room to eat their lunch and it was then that he brought up the Celeste question.

"So what do you think? Is it too far-fetched of an idea to think that Celeste might be behind the gifts and the notes to Bailey?" Benjamin asked his friend and then popped a fry into his mouth.

Dallas frowned thoughtfully. "I wouldn't have even thought about her if you hadn't brought her up. But to be honest, I wouldn't put anything past Celeste. I've always thought she had more than a little crazy inside her. Have you checked with the florists to see if anyone has ordered the flowers Bailey has received?"

"I checked and it's a negative. I also checked with the drugstore that sells the kind of candy she got. Again, the answer was no. I'm thinking whoever it is must be ordering the bears and the other stuff off the internet."

"Celeste would certainly know how to order things off the internet. Those fancy clothes she wears certainly don't come from the dress shop in Millsville," Dallas replied.

"I'm sure you're right about that," Benjamin agreed.

"I suppose you could question her, but I'm also sure Celeste has the art of lying down to a fine science," Dallas said.

"I imagine you're right about that, too," Benjamin said.

For the next few minutes, the two men ate in silence. "If Celeste is behind all this, then what would be her endgame?" Benjamin asked.

"I imagine she's hoping either you'll break up with Bailey or Bailey will break up with you and then you'll find yourself back in Celeste's arms." Dallas grinned at him. "This is what you get for being such a hot stud of a bachelor in town. You are the endgame for Celeste."

Benjamin released a dry laugh. "Under no circumstances would I ever go back to dating Celeste." He hesitated just a moment and then added, "Although this Friday night I'm breaking things off with Bailey."

Dallas looked at him in surprise. "Why? I thought things were really going good with you and her. I've got to be honest, buddy, I've never seen you as happy as you've been since you've been seeing her."

"Things have been going great with her, but you know my feelings about marriage. And it's not fair for me to keep seeing Bailey and deepening our relationship knowing it's never going to go to the next logical step."

Dallas shook his head. "I swear, I've never understood

your aversion to marriage. Don't you want to have some-body special in your life forever?"

"Nah, that's really never been for me. I'm good with dat-ing casually, but I know in the end I'm meant to be alone. Bailey and I have gotten in too deep with each other and I need to break it off with her before she gets hurt."

"I imagine she's going to be hurt, anyway," Dallas re-plied soberly.

"Yeah, I know and I hate that. But better I do it now than after we've spent even more time together." The mere thought of hurting Bailey caused a crashing pain inside him.

Why had he let their relationship go on for so long? After the second or third date, why hadn't he stopped see-ing her then? Before they'd made love…before things had gotten so—so complicated.

The answer was he'd been utterly enchanted by her. He'd enjoyed each and every moment in her company. The answer was he'd fallen deeply in love with her and he kept wanting to see her one more time…and one more time again. And Friday night he would walk away from her and from that love for good.

He now released a deep sigh and wadded up his fast-food wrappers. "Guess I'll hit the streets again, unless anything else comes up."

"And let's hope like hell nothing else comes up," Dallas replied. "Unless it's a valid tip on the Scarecrow Killer." The two men rose from the table and disposed of their trash in the nearby trash can. "In case you need me, I'll be in my office for the rest of the afternoon."

"Copy," Benjamin replied.

Minutes later, Benjamin was back in his car, driving up

and down the streets to check for any trouble. He knew in which homes law enforcement had been before due to domestic violence and where an underage chronic shoplifter lived with his wealthy parents.

Benjamin pretty much knew everyone who lived in town and most of the farmers who lived on the outskirts of town. But he didn't know where the Scarecrow Killer lived. And he couldn't imagine one of the neighbors he knew who probably smiled at him and passed the time with him harboring such a deep, evil darkness inside him.

Where was this murderer? Where did he live? He knew with certainty the killer would strike again and all he could hope for was that the man got sloppy and left behind a fingerprint or something else that would finally get him behind bars.

If that didn't happen and the man continued to kill, then eventually there would be no more blond-haired blue-eyed women left in town, and that included Bailey.

His heart clenched tight. It was bad enough that he was going to hurt Bailey on Friday night, but the thought of her being one of the Scarecrow Killer's victims drove him absolutely crazy.

The hours slowly crept by and all that was in his heart was the dread of Friday night. He fought the desire to call her, just to hear her voice and to see how her day had been.

Each time he drove down Main Street and passed her salon, he wanted to stop his car and go inside, just to see her pretty face and her beautiful smile.

On Wednesday night when he got off duty and after the town meeting was over, he parked his car down the street from her house. It was a dark night with storm clouds gathering overhead. The forecast was for thunderstorms tonight and then again on Thursday night.

As he gazed toward her house, he looked for any movement in or around her property. It just made him feel better to sit here for a couple of hours and watch over her place. Unfortunately, he couldn't stay here all night as he was on duty in the morning. Once again, he wished they had a bigger department, so that somebody could sit on Bailey's place all through the hours of the night.

As a rumble of thunder sounded in the distance, he remembered her telling him how afraid she was of the sound. God, he wished he could go inside her house and get in bed with her. He wanted to hold her while it stormed overhead.

He wished he could comfort her like nobody else ever had. But he couldn't go in. He couldn't give her any more false hope that he would continue in a relationship with her.

While he dreaded what he had to do on Friday night, he also couldn't wait to get it over with. The anxiety of what was to come was eating him up inside. He was finding it difficult to concentrate on anything else. Finally, at midnight, when a torrential rain began to fall, he headed home.

Thursday night found him parked in the same place, watching her house as again storm clouds darkened the sky overhead. He really wasn't sure why he was here other than these nights were his long goodbye to her.

Every minute he sat in his patrol car down the block from her house, he spent the time going over each and every moment he'd spent with her. Every minute he sat there, he grieved deeply for the loss of her.

Tomorrow night it would be over, but memories of their time together would haunt him for many years to come.

When raindrops began to fall, it felt as if the sky was weeping the tears that pressed tight and hot against his eyes.

Tomorrow night it would be all over and he knew he would never be the same again.

Chapter 11

Bailey couldn't wait to see Benjamin on Friday night. The hours of each day dragged by as she gave manicures and pedicures and listened to the gossip of her clients, all while anticipating spending more time with him. She would never be able to get enough time with him. She would always want more.

The days were gray and dreary and Wednesday night she'd suffered through the thunderstorms, alone as usual and by hiding her head under her bed pillow.

Thursday morning, she awakened a little cranky from not getting enough sleep the night before due to the thunderstorms. She wasn't thrilled that the same weather was forecast for later that night, too.

She spent most of the day battling with herself about having the serious talk with Benjamin, the one she knew she needed to have with him. It was time—past time—that he knew who she really was. It was past time that she let him decide if she could be enough for him without the addition of a family.

It was about four thirty in the afternoon when Letta Lee and her good friend Mabel Treadway came in for their appointments. The two older women were the last appointments of the day. Bailey got them both in the chairs and their feet soaking in the scented water and then she helped them pick out new nail color.

Naomi began working on Mabel's feet while Bailey started on Letta Lee's. Right now, they were the only clients in the salon. Hopefully, there wouldn't be any walk-ins at this time of the day.

"The local gossip is that you seem to be seeing quite a lot of Benjamin Cooper lately," Letta said. "Do I hear wedding bells finally ringing for you in the near future?"

"Oh, no, we haven't really talked about the future. We're just enjoying each other's company for now," Bailey replied.

"Maybe it's a case of why buy the cow when you can get the milk for free," Mabel said with a side-eye at Bailey.

"Mabel!" Letta said and then tittered.

"I'm just saying," Mabel replied in mock innocence.

"As I said, we're just enjoying each other's company for now," Bailey said, slightly irritated by the whole conversation. She tried to tamp down her crankiness.

"In my day and age, things were certainly different between men and women," Mabel continued. "Marriage and family were the most important things."

"Bailey, whether you think so or not, you're getting fairly old and I can't believe you haven't married and started a family of your own by now," Letta said.

"I'm not that old," Bailey protested with a small laugh that she hoped masked her annoyance.

"All I know is some of the ladies in the gardening club are making bets on when your engagement to Benjamin is going to happen," Letta said. "Half of them are betting before Halloween and the other half are saying it will happen after Halloween."

"Well, it's nice to know I'm the subject of gossip for all you ladies in the gardening club," Bailey replied. "But I wouldn't hold your breath waiting for any engagement between us to ever happen."

Even though she said it lightly, the fact that she knew it would never go further with Benjamin than what they had now, or even less than that, sent a shaft of pain through her.

She had finally decided that tomorrow night she should definitely have the discussion with him. If he was going to break up with her over the children issue then it needed to happen sooner rather than later.

She'd let things go far too long between them and now it was going to hurt badly when he walked away from her. She had allowed him to get far too deep inside her heart, deeper than anyone she'd ever let in before, and he was the one she would never, ever forget when he went away.

The absolute worst thing about it was that he wouldn't go away completely. They would still be residents of the same small town. They would still run into each other from time to time and she knew each time she'd see him, her heart would break all over again.

"The town meeting was just another grim reminder of the awful killer that's living among us," Letta said, pulling Bailey from her thoughts.

"Bailey, aren't you scared going out and about on your own?" Mabel asked.

The town meeting the night before had consisted of Dallas updating the people about the latest murder and him reminding all the women in town to travel together.

She had only seen Benjamin briefly when she'd first gone into town hall as he was on duty and stood with other officers near the podium where Dallas had spoken. When the town meeting was over, the officers had been gone.

"I'm not overly scared, but I'm being as cautious as I can be," Bailey replied to Mabel.

"I'm glad I'm too old to make into a good scarecrow," Letta said.

"That makes two of us," Mabel agreed.

The last thing Bailey wanted to think about was the Scarecrow Killer when she had to go home alone on a dark and stormy night.

At least the conversation changed to the more pleasant matters of the gardening club as the women finished up getting their toenails and then their fingernails done.

"We're putting together a nice fall display for the lobby in town hall. We're hoping to get it up by the first of November," Letta continued.

"I think it's going to be beautiful," Mabel said. "We have so many beautiful fall colors to work with."

"And we hope everyone in town will stop by to see it," Letta added.

"I can't believe that Halloween is just around the corner," Mabel said.

"I hate Halloween," Letta replied. "It's my least favorite holiday of the year. I always keep my shades tightly closed and my porch light off so no little goblins will come to my door."

"I don't know about you, but I find the two of them utterly exhausting," Naomi said when Letta and Mabel finally left the salon.

Bailey laughed. "They can be a lot. Thankfully, we're done for the day." She walked over to the front door and flipped the Open sign to Closed. "I've been half-sleepy and kind of cranky all day."

"Well, you're a true professional because you didn't show your cranky to any of the clients," Naomi said. "And if anything, the last two women should have pushed you over the edge considering they were gossiping about your relationship right in front of you."

Bailey laughed. "All I know is I'm ready to get home and hopefully tonight the thunder will stay quiet tonight so I can get a good night sleep."

"Unfortunately, the forecast isn't in your favor on that. We're supposed to get storms after midnight."

"Maybe they'll pass us by," Bailey said hopefully.

"That would be just fine with me," Naomi replied.

A few minutes later Bailey stepped out of the salon. The air outside was hot and soupy with humidity, a perfect combination to brew up bad weather. It was a little bit odd to be having this kind of weather in October, as usually the stormy season was in the spring. But in the Midwest all bets were off when it came to the weather.

When she got home, she changed into her nightgown and robe, then fixed herself a microwave meal of seasoned chicken and broccoli. After eating, she went into the living room and turned on the television.

She had a few hours before bedtime and so she turned on a movie she'd recorded earlier in the week. Still, even the antics of the romantic comedy couldn't keep her from thinking about the next night.

Benjamin would be here with take-out Chinese and she had to decide if she was going to have "the talk" with him. If history meant anything then they would probably eat and then wind up in her bed.

Should she talk to him before that happened? Or did she want one more night in his arms and she'd talk to him after they made love and before he went home? She knew what she really wanted. She wanted Benjamin in her life forever and always, but that probably wasn't going to happen.

She'd seen the way his eyes lit up when he'd talked about his niece and nephew. He obviously loved children and she refused to compromise on the fact that she didn't want to have babies.

She couldn't give in on what she believed was best for herself. The salon was her baby and it not only required a lot of her time, but it also fulfilled her. She'd like to do a little traveling or explore a hobby. Did that mean she was selfish? Was it wrong to know what was best for herself?

She hadn't heard from her mother since she'd gone to the farmhouse to share her secret and ask for advice. She knew the silence from Angela was a punishment for Bailey's choice in life. There was no question that she was hurt by her mother's lack of support. But there was nothing she could do about it. The only real time she'd felt her mother's full support was when Bailey had decided to move out of the farmhouse and make her own way.

When the movie was halfway over, she stopped it. She'd watch it another night when she wasn't so distracted by her own thoughts. Instead, she turned on a half-hour comedy show and once that was over, even though it was relatively early, she decided to call it a night.

She got up off the sofa and walked over to the front window. She moved the curtains aside and peered outside. She was relieved that there was nothing on the front porch and there didn't appear to be anyone in the area. She let the curtain fall back into place, double-checked to make sure her front door was locked and then headed upstairs.

Once there, she went into the bathroom and washed her face and then brushed her teeth. She hung her robe on the hook on the back of the door and then headed for her bed. She was absolutely exhausted.

As her mattress enveloped her, her thoughts once again went to the man she loved. Wouldn't it be wonderful if she told him she didn't want children and he admitted he didn't want them, either? Then there would be nothing standing between them as their relationship deepened.

Then there would be the real possibility of an engagement happening between them. Then she would have a wonderful life loving and being loved by Benjamin.

She drifted off to sleep and into sweet dreams of Benjamin. She was back in his arms and they were laughing together, and then they were making slow, sweet love. But then the dreams changed. Benjamin disappeared and suddenly it was raining little teddy bears. She was outside and running for some sort of cover as the bears hit her in the head and glanced off her shoulders.

There was a loud boom and she shot straight up. Wildly, she looked around the room. It took a moment for her to orient herself as to what was happening. She was in her bed and there were no teddy bears. It had only been a dream… a very unsettling dream.

She settled back against her pillow at the same time a flash of lightning rent the darkness of the room. It was followed quickly by a loud boom of thunder. She realized that was probably what had awakened her.

She squeezed her eyes tightly closed and then opened them once again. At least if she saw the lightning, she would know to expect the thunder. The storm appeared to be right on top of her, as the lightning came over and over again, along with the deep roars of the thunder.

It can't hurt me, she told herself. *It's loud, but it can't hurt me.* She tried to think about it the way Benjamin had told her. It was just a band of angels taking the night off and enjoying bowling.

It couldn't last all night. Surely, the storm would move away fairly quickly. Another flash of lightning illuminated the room and then she saw him. A man wearing a ski mask and dark clothing stood in the threshold of her room.

She screamed as sheer terror exploded in her veins. Any sleepiness she felt disappeared beneath her wild fear. With a deep sob, she grabbed the lamp off her nightstand and threw it toward him. She didn't know if it hit him or not. She quickly rolled to the opposite side of her bed and dropped down to the floor.

She crouched there as her brain frantically struggled to work. Oh, God, this had to be her stalker. Who was he? The answer to that question didn't really matter now. He was here, in her bedroom, in the middle of the storm, and he wanted to make her his forever. Her heart thundered inside her as sheer terror shot through her veins.

The room was in utter darkness between the lightning flashes and so for a moment she didn't know where the man was, but she sensed he was close to her...far too close. If she could just make it to the bathroom, she could close the door and lock herself inside.

What did he want? Why was he in her house? Of course, she knew the answers to those questions. He wanted her. How had he gotten inside? What did he intend to do to her?

Wild questions flew through her head as she tried to crawl as silently as possible toward the bathroom.

She couldn't believe this was actually happening. She swallowed against the deep sobs of fear that threatened to burst out of her. Rain pelted at the window, making it impossible for her to hear him. She had to get away. Dear God, she somehow had to get away from him.

She was almost to the bathroom door when he grabbed one of her legs by the ankle. She flipped over on her back and kicked at him, screaming once again as she tried to fight him off.

"Who are you?" she screeched as she kicked at him with all her might. Lightning flashed and the thunder boomed overhead, further adding to her terror.

She managed to kick him hard in the groin. His hand slipped off her leg and he groaned. She scrabbled forward and was halfway through the bathroom door when she felt the tiny pinprick in her thigh.

Oh, God, what had he done to her? She continued to kick at him, but before long she began to feel woozy. Her head swam and she knew she was in deep trouble.

Sleepy…she was so sleepy. "What do you want?" Her words were slurred.

"You."

The single word was punctuated by a loud crash of thunder and Bailey knew no more as a deep, darkness descended.

Friday morning, Benjamin woke up with a huge ball of dread sitting tight and heavy in his chest. As he dressed for work, he thought about the night to come. It would be one of the most heartbreaking nights of his life. Saying goodbye to Bailey would be the most difficult thing he'd ever do in his life. But it had to be done.

Once again, he was on regular patrol today since nothing was happening with the Scarecrow Killer case. The mood in the police station was grim. They knew the killer would strike again soon and right now there was absolutely nothing they could do to stop him.

Dallas and the others on the task force continued to go over the murders that had occurred, looking for something, anything, that might prove useful. But other than the button, which they suspected had come off a man's shirt, there was nothing. The killer was extremely organized and wasn't making mistakes.

Benjamin checked in at the station and then went out to patrol. As he sat in a spot just off Main Street to watch for speeders, his mind once again went to Bailey and the night to come.

He'd stayed awake half the night thinking about her as it had thundered overhead. He wished he could have been the one to comfort her through the stormy night. The thought of her all alone and afraid had chewed into his very soul.

But he wasn't going to be her hero. He wasn't going to be the one who comforted her when she was afraid. He wasn't going to be the man to enjoy laughing with her or making love to her. He definitely wasn't going to be the man to grow old with her and that was what broke his heart most of all.

After tonight, it would be over. At least he'd gotten a taste of what it felt like to love and be loved. He would always be grateful to her for that. It would be memories of her that warmed him on many a cold, lonely, wintry night.

He'd decided he would never date again. Even the abstract idea of going out with another woman was intensely unappealing. There would be no more dating after Bailey.

He didn't want to play this game anymore of seeing a woman a couple of times and then breaking it off with her. He'd find another way to deal with his loneliness, but it wouldn't be by randomly dating.

It was around eleven when his phone rang. He looked at the caller identification, but didn't recognize the number. "Officer Cooper," he answered.

"Uh, Benjamin… Officer Cooper. It's Naomi—Naomi from the nail salon," she said. "I was just wondering if you'd talked to or seen Bailey this morning?"

"No, neither, although I have plans to see her later for dinner. Why? Is there a problem?" His stomach clenched.

"I don't know…maybe not. She's just usually in the salon by now, but she didn't have any appointments scheduled for this morning."

"Did you try to call her?" he asked.

"I did, but it went directly to voice mail," Naomi replied.

"Maybe it's possible she was kept up by the storms overnight and knowing she had no appointments, she just decided to sleep in," he said.

"I guess that's possible," Naomie agreed. "She just usually calls if she's going to be late. I just got a little worried about her and wanted you to know."

"How about if she doesn't come in by some time this afternoon, you give me a call back," Benjamin replied.

"That sounds good," Naomi said in obvious relief. "Thanks so much."

He tried not to overly worry about the phone call, but given the evidence that she was targeted by somebody, it bothered him enough that he decided to do a quick drive-by of Bailey's house. A few minutes later he pulled up in her driveway, got out of his patrol car and then walked to the front door. He didn't see anything amiss, nothing that would warrant his immediate concern.

He left the porch and headed for the garage. He peered inside the small window in the door and saw her car parked there. He then returned to his car and got back inside.

Bailey was a grown woman, and if she decided to turn off her phone and sleep until noon, then that was her prerogative. The fact that she didn't have any appointments that morning made him believe this was the case. She'd probably been up all night with the storms and was now catching up on her sleep.

He pulled out of her driveway and decided to head to the local convenience store to grab a soda and maybe one of the hot dogs they grilled.

He was pulling into the convenience-store parking lot as a teenager burst out of the door with two eighteen-packs of beer in his arms. He took off running around the side of the building as Benjamin parked and jumped out of his car.

Raymond Smythe, the owner of the store, came flying out of the establishment, cursing and yelling at Benjamin to catch the thief. The kid dropped the beer as he came to a fence. He scrabbled over the top of the fence and dropped down to the other side.

Benjamin didn't bother to follow after him. Instead, he picked up the beer and carried it back around to the front of the store. "Did you catch the little bastard?" Raymond asked angrily.

"Nah, he jumped over the fence. I don't need to chase him down now. We both know who he is," Benjamin replied in disgust. Raymond held open the door for him, and Benjamin carried the beer inside and set it on the counter.

"It's not like he hasn't done this before," Raymond said, anger still lacing his voice. "How many chances does he get before the prosecuting attorney does his job and keeps the kid behind bars for a while? When in the hell will his parents step up to discipline that boy?"

"I wish I had some answers for you, Raymond, but I don't. All I can do is arrest him for shoplifting again and then it's out of my hands," Benjamin replied.

"I know... I know, I don't mean to yell at you. I'm just frustrated as hell," Raymond said. "Times are hard enough without seeing your merchandise walk out the door. I'm for sure pressing charges against him."

"Don't worry, Raymond. I'll go hunt him down now," Benjamin said.

"Thanks, Officer Cooper," Raymond responded.

Minutes later Benjamin was back in his car and headed toward the Kane residence, where sixteen-year-old Bradley Kane would probably be hiding out.

Ida and Emmett Kane lived in one of the biggest houses in Millsville and word was they were one of the wealthiest families in town. Their son, Bradley, was their only child and this wasn't the first time Benjamin had been to their house to arrest the young man.

The kid probably had had enough money in his pocket for the two packs of beer and a dozen other things. But he was underage and so he thought it was okay to just steal the beer he wanted.

He pulled into the driveway of their oversize, two-story home and got out of the car. The house was only about a block away from the convenience store so Bradley should have had time to get here before Benjamin.

He got out of his car, went to the front door and then knocked. Ida Kane answered the door. She was a tall woman with dark hair and green eyes. Those vivid green eyes narrowed as she greeted him. "Officer Cooper," she said stiffly.

"Afternoon, Ida. I'm here for Bradley. I just caught him red-handed stealing beer from the convenience store," Benjamin explained.

Emmett came and stood behind his wife. "Officer Cooper, why do I get the feeling you have a vendetta against my son?"

"I have a vendetta against people who break the law and about fifteen minutes ago Bradley broke the law," Benjamin replied.

"You said this was at the convenience store?" Emmett asked.

"That's right."

"I'll give Raymond a call and make things right with him. I'm sure we can work it out man-to-man. There's no need to arrest my boy again," Emmett insisted.

"I'm sorry, but it doesn't work that way, Emmett. Now, you want to go get Bradley for me?" Benjamin asked.

"He's not here," Ida said, her gaze averted from Benjamin's, which let him know she was lying.

"You're just wasting time because as soon as I see him, he's going to be arrested. It can either happen here in relative privacy or out in the street somewhere," Benjamin said.

The couple hesitated a moment and then Emmett released a deep sigh and turned around. "Come here, son," he shouted. The three of them waited a long minute.

"Bradley, come on out here," Ida shouted angrily.

Bradley was a tall, thin young man. He showed up at the door, not with contrition on his features, but rather a whine waiting to happen. He tied his long, dark hair back with a strip of rawhide and then looked at Benjamim.

"Man, I just wanted a little beer for a party that's happening tonight," Bradley grumbled.

"First of all, you know you're underage and secondly you can't just steal what you want," Benjamin said. "Now, turn around."

"Bradley, don't say another word," Emmett said. "We'll get the lawyer and get you out as soon as we can."

Fifteen minutes later Benjamin was headed to the station with Bradley in his back seat. The kid was sullen and quiet on the ride, but Benjamin didn't feel sorry for the spoiled thief.

If Ida and Emmett didn't draw some boundaries and have Bradley face some serious consequences now, then they were going to have a real problem on their hands once Bradley hit legal age.

It took over an hour to book him in and then he checked in with Dallas before heading out for more patrol work. As he drove through Big Jolley's to get a burger for a late lunch, he wondered if Bailey had finally made her way into the salon.

He hadn't gotten any more calls from Naomi, but it suddenly felt important that he check in and make sure everything was okay and Bailey was in the salon, where she belonged.

Instead of calling, he decided to drive to the salon and check on Bailey. He wouldn't mind confirming with her that they were still on for that night.

He pulled up to the salon and was surprised that her car wasn't there in its usual parking space. An edge of concern shot through him. It was just after two o'clock. Where was Bailey?

Had she decided to take the entire day off work? Certainly, as the owner of the business, she had that right.

He got out of his car and went into the salon, where there were no clients and Naomi was seated in one of the chairs flipping through a magazine.

"Hey, Naomi, have you heard anything from Bailey yet today?"

"No, nothing," she replied as a crease danced across her forehead. "In fact, I was going to give you a call soon to see if you'd heard anything from her."

"No, I haven't. Has she ever done something like this before? Just not shown up?"

"Never," Naomi replied. "And she would never do something like this without calling me."

The edge of anxiety that had brought him into the salon now exploded into full-blown apprehension. "I stopped by her house earlier and saw that her car was in the garage, so I just assumed she might be sleeping in later than usual. But I'm going to head over there to check on her again right now."

Naomi got up from the chair and followed him to the door. "Could you call me and let me know what's going on with her?"

"I'll call you as soon as I know something," he agreed and then he left the salon.

As he headed toward her house, he tried to come up with all the reasons why she wouldn't be in the salon and why she wouldn't have called Naomi to check in. He couldn't come up with a single reason, considering the lateness of the day, and that definitely had him concerned about her.

The first thing he did when he arrived at her house was to peek into the garage. Her car was still there. He then went to her front door and knocked.

When there was no reply, he knocked even harder. "Bailey," he yelled. "Bailey, are you in there?"

Still, there was no response. Dammit, what was going on here? With her car in the garage, where else could she be? He stood on the porch for several long minutes and then decided to look around the house.

God forbid she had gone outside for some reason and had fallen and couldn't get back up. Or for some ungodly reason she'd gone out in the storm last night and been hit by a falling tree branch. God forbid she was lying in the yard, helpless and unable to call for help.

He headed around the corner of the house, where nothing appeared amiss. Thankfully, the gate on her backyard fence wasn't locked so he could head around to the back of the house.

Again, he saw nothing there to give him pause. He looked all around the yard and then exited and went to the last side of the house.

He saw it immediately. A screaming alarm shot through him at the sight of the broken window. The glass was completely gone, leaving a gaping hole big enough for somebody to get through. Oh, God, somebody had gone into her house. With trembling fingers, he called Dallas.

"Dallas… I think she's gone. Somebody broke into her house and I don't know if she's dead inside or if somebody took her away."

"Where are you now?" Dallas asked quickly.

"I'm at her house… I'm at Bailey's."

"Just sit tight, I'll be right there," Dallas said.

"Dallas…hurry." Benjamin's heart crashed painfully in his chest. Something had happened to Bailey and he didn't know if she was dead or alive. Dear God, what had happened to her?

Chapter 12

A headache...pounding at her temples and making her feel half-nauseous. Bailey slowly climbed to consciousness, although she kept her eyes closed against the severe banging in her head.

Was it morning? Did she need to get up and get ready for work? That thought made her open her eyes. She stared around her in utter confusion.

For several minutes she simply looked around her and she couldn't make sense of anything. She was tied to a chair at a table in a kitchen she didn't recognize. It looked kind of like her kitchen, but it wasn't. Where in the hell was she?

Her brain struggled and worked to figure it out. Was this some kind of a strange dream? No, she was definitely awake. Suddenly the events of the night before exploded in her brain. The storm...the man... Oh, God, who was the man who had come into her house? And where was she now?

Her heart pounded with intense fear as she pulled on the ropes that bound her arms and feet to the chair. She had to get up... She needed to get away now—now!

Panic seared through her to her very soul as she tugged and yanked at the ropes, hoping to find some give to them, but there was none. She began to sob in fear as she twisted her wrists first one way and then the other. She only stopped when her wrists burned painfully and she was out of breath.

She gave in to her tears then, sobbing until she felt as if she had no more tears left to cry. She leaned back in the chair, exhausted and afraid.

She assumed she was in a house somewhere, but there didn't seem to be anyone inside with her right now. The place was completely quiet, other than her occasional hiccupping sniffles.

As she once again gazed around the kitchen, a new sense of horror filled her. The room was painted a bright yellow, just like her kitchen in her house. There were colorful roosters hanging on the walls, just like at her place.

Somebody had gone to a lot of trouble to try to re-create Bailey's kitchen here. Why? What did it all mean? The only real difference in this kitchen was that the refrigerator and stove appeared brand-new.

This was too weird for her to comprehend. Why had somebody done this? It scared her as much as anything and she began to pull and tug at the ropes with a renewed fervor.

What was going on here? Who had drugged her and carried her out of her house to this place? And when was that somebody going to return here? And what was he going to do to her?

You are going to be mine forever very, very soon.

As the words to the last note she'd received flew around and around in her head, she began to scream.

When Dallas and a couple of other offices arrived at Bailey's house, Benjamin quickly filled them in on the fact that nobody had seen or heard from Bailey all day and he took them directly to the broken window.

"This gives us cause to go inside the house," Dallas said tersely.

Together they all moved to her front door. To everyone's surprise the door was unlocked. Benjamin was the first one in. As Dallas went to the room that had the broken window, Benjamin began to search the house for Bailey.

His heart thundered in his chest as he went from room to room. She wasn't anyplace on the lower level, so he quickly headed upstairs and directly to her bedroom. It was there he found the signs of a struggle.

Fear shot through his veins as he stared around. The blankets appeared to have been dragged off one side of the bed and one of the bedside lamps appeared to have been thrown or knocked to the floor. What had happened in here? "Dallas," he yelled down the stairs urgently as his heart beat a frantic rhythm. "Up here."

Dallas and Officer Ross Davenport ran up the stairs and into Bailey's bedroom. Dallas looked around with a deep frown. "We need to process this as a crime scene," he said. "Here and the dining room downstairs, where apparently somebody entered the house through that window. I'll call in more men and they can get started. The most important thing we need to investigate is Bailey's disappearance."

"Somebody took her, Dallas," Benjamin said, his heart sick with fear for the woman he loved. "She's been kidnapped. Where can she be? Dammit, I should have taken the notes and gifts she'd received more seriously. Whoever sent her that stuff is behind all this…behind her disappearance. We have to find her. We just have to…"

"Benjamin, calm down," Dallas replied sympathetically.

"You need to hold it together for Bailey. The first thing we need to do is contact her mother and see if she knows anything about any of this." Dallas pulled his phone from his pocket. "I should have her number in my contacts from when she was working for the mayor."

Benjamin's heart pounded so hard in his chest that for a moment he couldn't hear anything else and he could scarcely take a breath. Why hadn't he taken the notes she'd received more seriously? Why hadn't he staked out her house throughout the nights to keep her safe from danger?

Exactly when had she been taken? If he'd stayed outside her house for another hour last night, could he have prevented this from happening? If he'd stayed just another fifteen minutes, would he have seen the person go into her house?

And how much danger was she in? Was she being held somewhere or had the worst already happened and had she been killed? No… No, he couldn't think of that right now. He had to maintain the hope that she was alive no matter where she was.

"Angela," Dallas said into his phone, which was on speaker. "It's Dallas."

"Yes, Dallas." Angela's voice came across the line.

"Have you heard from or seen Bailey today?" Dallas asked.

"No, I haven't. Why? Is she in trouble for something?"

"She hasn't done anything wrong, but we think she's in trouble." Dallas explained the fact that nobody had seen or spoken to Bailey that day and that they believed she had been taken against her will from the house.

"What do you mean she's missing?" Angela asked when

Dallas was finished. "More importantly, what are you doing to find her?"

"We're going to do everything in our power to find her, Angela," Dallas replied. "Did she ever mention to you about her getting love notes and little gifts from somebody?"

"No, she never said anything about that to me. Why?"

Once again Dallas explained what had been going on in Bailey's life.

Benjamin wanted to scream. Minutes were passing by...long minutes that they couldn't get back. Too much time was being wasted. He wanted action right now. They needed to be beating down doors to find her.

They had no idea exactly when she had been taken or how much time they'd already lost. All Benjamin knew for sure was he wanted her found right now. He needed to see her now, alive and well immediately. He couldn't live with any other outcome.

It killed him that while he'd been busy dealing with a petty shoplifter, he could have been out hunting for Bailey. While he'd sat and eaten a hamburger, who knew what she'd been going through?

Dammit, he should have checked things out the first time Naomi had called him. Sheer terror gripped him as he remembered the words from the last note she'd received.

You are going to be mine forever very, very soon.

Now she was gone, but he prayed it wouldn't be forever.

Bailey screamed until she was hoarse and her throat hurt. She fought against the ropes until her wrists were raw and she thought they may be bleeding. Finally, despite her intense fear, drained by all of her exertions, she drifted off to sleep.

She jerked awake some time later and began to cry once again. She'd hoped this all was some sort of a nightmare and everything would be all right when she woke up, but it wasn't. It was real and she didn't know what would happen next.

There was no way she could get out of the ropes. There was no way for her to escape and save herself. She looked over to the window. She couldn't see anything outside, but she assumed it was late afternoon by the cast of the sun.

Did anyone know she was missing? Surely, Naomi would have been concerned when she didn't show up in the salon this morning. Were the police out looking for her? Was Benjamin searching for her?

How could they find her when she didn't even know who had taken her? She knew it was whoever had left the gifts and the notes for her. But who was it?

Looking around the kitchen only freaked her out more. The fact that somebody had gone to so much trouble to try to re-create her kitchen was totally creepy. Damn, who had gone to all this trouble? The same questions kept swirling around and around in her head.

Her heart crashed inside her chest as she heard a door open and close in the direction of what she assumed was the living room of the house. Her nerves screamed in her veins and her heartbeat ramped up as footsteps sounded, coming closer and closer.

A familiar voice rang out... "Honey, I'm home."

She gasped as he came into the kitchen. "Howard," she said in stunned surprise.

Howard Kendall smiled at her. "Hi, darling. Surprised?"

"Howard, what are you doing? Let me go right now. You lied to me," she said. He'd lied to her about it all. He'd said he wasn't behind the gifts and the notes, and she had believed him. Yet it had been him all along. She'd been such a fool to believe him.

"It was a harmless little lie," he replied. He went to the refrigerator and pulled out a package of hamburger and then bent down and took a skillet out of one of the lower cabinets. "I hope you like tacos because that's what's on the menu tonight for dinner."

She stared at him for several long moments. Was he mentally ill? How could he think anything about this was right? "Howard, I don't want to eat dinner with you. I just want to go home. You need to let me go now."

He put the hamburger into the skillet and then turned to face her, another smile curving his mouth. "Bailey, I know this will be a little difficult for you at first, but we belong together and eventually you'll come to realize that. I'm the perfect man for you and I'm all you need."

"Howard, if you care about me at all, then you'll let me go. We can talk about everything once I'm home," she replied, trying to keep her voice calm and even.

"I'm sorry, Bailey, but that's just not going to happen. I know what's best for the both of us and you being here with me is what's for the best."

He turned and once again opened the refrigerator. He pulled out a head of lettuce, a tomato and bagged shredded cheese. She watched him work, her mind still reeling from what he'd just said…by everything he had done.

"Howard, you have to know this isn't right. Untie me and let me go," she said frantically. "Please, let me go," she insisted, her voice rising.

"Just stay calm, Bailey, everything is going to be wonderful," he replied. He took a spatula and stirred the hamburger.

"It will only be wonderful if I'm at home," she responded.

"Honey, this is your home now," he answered.

For several minutes, she simply sat and stared at him, still unable to believe this was all happening.

"I need to use the restroom," she said suddenly. Maybe if he untied her and took her to the bathroom, she might find a way to escape this place. She might find something in the bathroom that would help her get away.

"Of course." He moved the skillet off the burner and then approached where she sat. "I will warn you, Bailey. I need you to behave," he said as he untied the ropes that held her arms. "If you don't behave, there will be consequences that won't make you happy."

She thought about punching him. God, she wanted to hit him, disable him in some way so she could run. But she didn't. She knew she wasn't strong enough to really hurt him and she was afraid of what consequences she might face if she tried anything physical right now. He untied her legs, but kept a length of rope tied around her waist.

He helped her to her feet and she was surprised that she was weak and rather wobbly. Was it because of her fear or because she'd been tied up all day? Or was it the residue of whatever he'd used to drug her the night before?

He led her out of the kitchen, down the hallway and to a door that apparently led to a bathroom. "I'll just be right out here," he said as he dropped his end of the rope and then leaned with his back against the hall wall.

She opened the door and stepped into the bathroom, and instantly a deep wave of sick frustration hit her. The bathroom was completely empty. Instead of a mirror over the sick, a steel plate reflected her image back to her.

The small, high window above the bathtub was boarded up. Still, she ran over to it and tried to pry off the board. But the nails that held it in place must have been long because she couldn't make the board budge.

There was nothing in here to help her. Absolutely nothing. She couldn't get out the window and she couldn't break the mirror in order to get a weapon. The only thing in the room was a roll of toilet paper. New tears burned at her eyes. This was madness…utter madness.

Minutes later, she opened the door and Howard smiled at her once again. She was growing to hate his smile. He was acting as if everything was perfectly normal and it wasn't. There was nothing normal about any of this.

He took her back to the table and then retied her arms and legs to the chair. Once she was secured, he went back to frying the hamburger.

"Are you hungry?" he asked. "I know I am. It will be so nice for us to eat together for breakfasts and dinners. Unfortunately, I won't be here for lunch tomorrow as I'll be at work. But Sunday we can spend all our time together."

"Howard, people will be looking for me. The police will be out searching for me," she replied.

"They're never going to find you," he said with an easy conviction.

"Where is this place?" She knew Howard lived in an apartment in the same complex where Benjamin lived. This was definitely not his apartment.

He looked at her and frowned. "I guess it doesn't hurt for you to know. This place used to be my parents' home. Of course, they moved away years ago and abandoned this house. Nobody will think we're out here. On the outside, the place is a total wreck. The wood is weathered and decayed. The windows are all boarded up and it looks completely deserted. But inside I've worked really hard to make it your dream house."

He was definitely mentally ill. This was way beyond obsession. "Howard, you need some help," she said. "What you're doing isn't right."

"It will all be right in the long run," he insisted airily. "It will just take time and now we have all the time in the world together. You'll come to understand that we belong together."

He chopped up the lettuce and then began to dice up the tomatoes and she wanted to scream. "Unfortunately, I'll be leaving you tonight right after dinner. I have to maintain a certain presence at my apartment until the police clear me from suspicion."

"Why don't you just release me and we'll never talk about this again," she said. "I won't tell anyone about this or about you."

"I went to a lot of trouble to make things right here for you," he responded. "You should be damned grateful for everything I've done for you."

"Well, I'm not grateful," she said angrily. "I hate everything you've done and I hate you for what you're doing to me."

He walked over to her and slapped her hard across the face. She cried out at the blow, hurt by the impact and shocked by the physical abuse.

"You will respect me, Bailey. I love you with all my heart and soul, but I won't stand for any disrespect from you. Now, the tacos will be ready in just a few minutes and we can have a nice meal together."

She remained quiet. It was obvious he wasn't just going to just release her and now she didn't know what to expect from him. Her cheek burned and now she knew he was capable of physical violence.

He apparently had a sick fantasy in his head. All she could do right now was continue to look for a way to escape. All she could really do now was pray that somehow, someway, somebody found her here.

Chapter 13

Within thirty minutes, Dallas had commandeered Bailey's kitchen table as his temporary headquarters. A couple of officers were in the dining room processing the broken window, while others were on the stairs and in Bailey's bedroom to see what they could find there.

Much to Benjamin's surprise, Angela arrived shortly after, obviously very worried about her daughter. It was now dinnertime—the time that Benjamin should have been eating Chinese food with Bailey.

It didn't matter that he had intended to break things off with her. His love for her was thick and rich and his fear for her was like a clawing, savage animal inside him.

"Did Bailey mention anybody she thought might be behind the notes and gifts to her? Anyone from her past?" Dallas asked Benjamin.

Benjamin was seated across the table from Dallas. As much as he wanted every officer out searching for Bailey, he knew they had to be smart with their resources. It would be a waste of time for the men to just head out and scatter with no plan in place.

"She did mention a couple of men. I know she dated RJ for a while and right before we started seeing each other, she had coffee at the café with Ethan Dourty. She also told me she dated Howard Kendall for a while and he continued to want to see her after she broke things off with him. Those are the only three she mentioned to me."

He looked at Dallas with a sense of urgency. "It's got to be one of those three men, Dallas. It's just got to be."

Dallas looked over at Angela, who stood with her back against the refrigerator. "Angela, has Bailey mentioned to you anyone who might have been giving her trouble?"

Angela shook her head, her eyes filled with worry. "No, I didn't even know about the gifts and the notes she got. The only man she ever talked about with me was Benjamin. I wish…" She shook her head and stopped whatever she was about to say. "Just find her…please find her," she finally said desperately.

Dallas looked back at Benjamin. "I know Howard lives in one of the apartments in your complex. I also know RJ and Ethan both live in houses. RJ's place is isolated and on the edge of town. I say we start there."

Benjamin popped up out of his chair. "Okay, then let's go." Finally, some real action. If the tattooed man had taken Bailey…if he'd done anything to harm her, then Benjamin would make sure the man was sorry. He swore before Dallas would be able to get RJ into handcuffs, Benjamin would get in at least one good punch.

As if Dallas knew his frame of mind, he told Benjamin that he would be riding in Dallas's car. Two other officers followed in another patrol car. Four other officers were dispatched to Ethan's house just off Main Street. The rest of the men on duty would remain at Bailey's house, waiting for further instructions.

"I know emotions are running high with you right now,"

Dallas said as they sped toward RJ's house. "But, Benjamin, I need you to remain professional."

"If he's hurt Bailey, then I can't promise anything," Benjamin warned.

"If I can't trust you to keep yourself under control, then I'll assign you to stay back at Bailey's place and not be a part of the search team," Dallas said firmly.

Benjamin stared out the window, willing the car to go faster and faster. Once again, a sense of deep urgency flooded through him. Hopefully, this would be the beginning and the end of their search for her. And hopefully, they would find her alive and well.

Surely, the person who had left her those love notes and gifts wouldn't take her to harm her. From the sound of the notes, the person was in love with her and that was the only thing that kept hope for her alive inside him. Surely, if he loved Bailey, he wouldn't hurt her.

RJ's home was a small ranch set on three or four acres of land that was mostly wooded. There was a detached garage and a large shed. His black pickup truck was parked outside, letting them know the muscled, tattooed man was home.

Dallas and Benjamin got out of their car and the two officers in the other car joined them. "You let me handle this," Dallas said with a pointed look at Benjamin.

The four of them moved to the front door, where Dallas knocked. They waited for a response. When there was no answer, Dallas knocked again, this time harder.

"I'm coming, I'm coming. Give me a damn minute," RJ cried out. After another couple of minutes, RJ opened the door. He looked at Dallas in obvious surprise. "Chief

Calloway. Uh, what's going on?" He gazed at the other officers and then looked back at Dallas.

"When was the last time you saw or spoke to Bailey Troy?" Dallas asked.

RJ frowned. "Bailey? I guess it was at the fall festival. Her tent was next to mine. Why? What's going on?"

"She's missing," Dallas replied succinctly. "Mind if we come in and look around?"

"What do you mean she's missing?" RJ asked in what appeared to be obvious confusion.

"Somebody broke into her house last night and kidnapped her," Benjamin said, unable to contain himself. "So are you going to let us inside?"

RJ looked from Benjamin to Dallas. "And you think I had something to do with this? I would never harm a hair on Bailey's head. I adore that woman," he exclaimed.

Was the man stalling them? Why hadn't he already opened the door to let them inside? Benjamin itched to get in and find out if Bailey was there.

"Do I mind if you come in and invade my privacy? Hell yes," RJ said and then opened the door wider. "But come in and knock yourselves out. I'm offended that any of you would think that I'm capable of such a thing."

He stepped aside and the four officers entered into a small living room. "Check out the bedrooms," Dallas said to the two officers. While they headed down the hallway, Dallas and Benjamin checked the living room and kitchen.

They opened every door and each cabinet. Anywhere that an adult woman could be stashed away, they checked, but found nothing to indicate Bailey had ever been in the house.

They all converged back in the living room. "RJ, we need to check your garage and the shed," Dallas said.

The big man heaved a deep sigh. "Come on then." He grabbed a set of keys off a key holder just inside the front door and then led them out of the house and toward the two outbuildings.

He unlocked the garage door first. Inside were boxes of supplies for RJ's tattoo store. There was little else there and no place to stash a woman. They then moved to the shed, which held a lawn mower and everything necessary for lawn care.

She wasn't here. RJ's had been a bust, a total waste of time. When they were in the car and headed back to Bailey's place, one of the officers who had been dispatched to Ethan Dourty's place called in to report that they had found nothing there to indicate Bailey's presence.

"We'll head on over to Howard's place, although it would be very difficult for him to keep a woman against her will in the apartments," Dallas said.

"Unless he has her bound and gagged." This particular vision of Bailey ripped through Benjamin. He didn't want to think about her being tied up and with duct tape or something else in her mouth to keep her quiet.

And if she wasn't at Howard's place, then where could she be? If none of the three men he knew about had taken her, then who?

Howard had to have her, otherwise every single man in town would be a suspect. It would be a sea of suspects. A deep, breathless anxiety once again pressed tight in Benjamin's chest. He was grateful Dallas didn't talk on the ride to Howard's. Benjamin's fear and apprehension was so great inside him, he had no words.

He fought against tears that burned hot at his eyes. He didn't want to cry now. Tears would mean failure and he wasn't about to admit failure yet.

It seemed to take forever to get to the apartment complex. Darkness had now fallen and the idea of her being somewhere out there alone and afraid tore at his insides.

Benjamin rarely saw the banker as Benjamin lived on one end of the building and Howard lived at the other end. Before they got out of the car, Dallas made a quick call to the landlord to see exactly what apartment number Howard lived in. Once they had that information, they pulled down the complex and parked in front of his place.

Nerves jangled inside Benjamin as he got out of the car. She had to be here, she just had to be. It was the mantra that went around and around in his head as they approached the apartment. He followed behind Dallas and waited impatiently as Dallas knocked on the door.

Howard immediately opened the door and looked at them in surprise. "Chief… Officer Cooper… Uh, what can I do for you all?"

"Do you mind if we come in for a conversation?" Dallas asked.

"Of course not. Please come in." He ushered them into a neat and tidy living room. For a brief moment, Benjamin smelled her…the wonderful spicy scent that stirred him in so many ways. It was there only a moment and then gone. It had to be his imagination and him wanting to believe so badly that she was here someplace.

Dallas sat on the sofa and Benjamin sank down next to him while Howard sat on a chair facing them. "When was the last time you saw or spoke to Bailey?" Dallas asked.

"I haven't seen or spoken to her in weeks," Howard said

with a frown. "Oh, wait, she did call me a little over a week ago to ask me if I was leaving little gifts and notes for her. I told her I didn't know anything about it and that was the extent of us talking with each other. Why? What's going on?"

"We believe Bailey was kidnapped from her home last night," Dallas said.

Howard straightened up in the chair in what appeared to be in genuine shock. "What? Oh, my God, what can I do to help?" He leaned forward in the chair and appeared sincerely stunned at the information.

"Right now, what you can do is let us search this place," Dallas replied.

Howard looked surprised all over again. "You think I had something to do with this? I would never…" Howard's voice trailed off as he stood. "Please, feel free to look around all you want. I would never do anything to harm Bailey and I certainly have nothing to hide."

Dallas and Benjamin checked everywhere in the two-bedroom apartment, but there was nothing to see there. There was no sign that Bailey was there or had ever been there.

As they left the apartment, a soul sickness filled Benjamin. The three men who were the most viable potential suspects had been cleared, so now every man in town was a potential suspect.

Where did they go from here? Where did they even begin? How did they search an entire town for one missing woman? The tiny ray of hope he'd had now threatened to go out. He felt utterly empty inside.

"We'll find her," Dallas said fervently as he pulled back up in her driveway. "I swear we're going to find her, Benjamin."

Once again, Benjamin couldn't speak. Deep emotion ripped at him and the burn of tears pressed heavily against his eyes. Bailey...Bailey. Her name flew around and around in his head...in the very depths of his heart.

When they walked into Bailey's kitchen, Angela looked at all of them and then collapsed into one of the chairs and burst into tears. "Where is she? Oh, dear God, who has her?" She began to weep.

Lizzy Maxwell, who had shown up while Dallas and Benjamin were gone, immediately tried to console the weeping woman. She managed to get Angela up and out of the kitchen chair and led her into the living room, where her sobs were still audible.

Benjamin wanted to fall into a chair and weep as well, but he couldn't. He had to stay strong until Bailey was found. And he could only pray she would still be found alive.

Minutes ticked by, turning into hours. Bailey could tell by looking out the window that night had fallen. She tried once again to get free from the ropes, but she couldn't.

Her cheek still stung and she was still completely shocked that he'd slapped her. While she'd been dating him, she had never seen any red flags that would indicate the man was capable of any violence. But now she knew differently and this new Howard absolutely terrified her.

He'd untied one of her hands so she could eat the tacos with him. However, the last thing she'd wanted to do was eat. But as he talked about how much trouble he'd gone to in making the Mexican food, she knew the best thing for her to do was to take several bites and tell him how wonderful it was. And that was exactly what she had done.

After eating and cleaning up the kitchen, he'd left the house. But that had been hours ago.

When was he coming back here? And what would he expect from her when he got back? The idea of him taking her sexually against her will made her want to throw up. She didn't want him to touch her in any way.

The only man's hands she wanted on her were Benjamin's. She closed her eyes and instantly an image of the man she loved filled her mind. Would she ever see him again? Would she ever feel his big strong arms surrounding her? Would she ever gaze into his beautiful blue eyes or hear his deep laughter again?

His image swam as tears filled her eyes. She'd been missing for hours and hours now, and she feared she would never be found. She'd exist in this strange and sick scenario that Howard had created for the rest of her life…or until the time she ticked him off or he tired of her. And then what would happen? Her blood ran cold. She knew the answer. Then he would have to kill her. There was no way he could just let her go now or in the future.

Why couldn't this all just be a terrible nightmare? Why couldn't she wake up and find herself safe and sound in her own bed?

But this wasn't a nightmare. She wasn't going to just wake up from this. Howard wasn't an imaginary boogeyman. He was the real deal… The monster in the closet… The creature under her bed.

She stared in the direction where he'd come in before with dread coursing through her entire body. How long before he returned? What kind of mood would he be in?

She didn't know how long she'd waited or what time it

was when she finally heard the door open and close. She steeled herself as his footsteps came closer and closer.

"Hello, darling," he said as he came in. "I'm sorry you've had to wait so long for me to return." He threw his car keys on one of the counters and then sank down in the chair at the table across from her.

"It's been quite an exciting evening," he said. "The police showed up at my apartment. I have to say I wasn't surprised since we dated a few times. Anyway, they were out searching for you. Needless to say, they didn't find you in my apartment." He laughed. "I insisted that I would never do anything to harm you and I made sure they knew I'd do anything I could to help them in the search for you. So I'm now completely in the clear. I'm not a suspect."

"Howard, for God's sake, please let me go. If you truly love me at all you'll release me and let me go home. I promise I won't tell anyone about this. I won't mention a word about you. I swear I won't get you into any trouble."

Of course, this was all a big lie. If he did release her the first thing she would do was go to Dallas and tell him all about Howard. The man shouldn't be out on the streets. He was a danger to all the women in town.

He smiled, but the gesture didn't quite reach the cold depths of his dark eyes. "I'm not going to release you and I don't want you asking me again. You're going to learn to love, Bailey. You're going to learn to love me as much as I love you." He stood. "And now, I don't know about you, but I'm completely exhausted. It's time for bed."

Every muscle in her body tensed up and her nerves all screamed. He moved over to her and began to untie her and she had to fight with all her might not to kick him, not to scream and punch him.

But she knew it was a struggle she would lose and it would only make things worse for her. Although she couldn't imagine how things would get any worse. She couldn't fight him. She'd just have to continue to look for an opportunity to escape. Maybe while he slept, she'd be able to slip away and get out of here.

He untied her arms and legs, but she remained tied around the waist with Howard on the other end of the rope. He led her down the hallway and into a bedroom where a pink nightgown and panties were lying across the queen-size bed. The bed was covered with a navy blue spread and the headboard had thick wooden bars that would make it perfect for tying somebody up. An icy chill rushed through her.

Oh God, was that what he had planned for her? Did he intend to tie her to the headboard and then have his way with her? Her stomach twisted and turned as a nausea filled her. She didn't want his hands on her. It would be rape for anything he did would be against her will.

"Go ahead, take the nightwear and we'll go back down to the bathroom, where you can change into it," he said.

She couldn't help the tremble of her body as she grabbed the nightgown and panties off the bed. He led her back to the bathroom she'd been in before and only then did he untie the rope from around her waist.

Once she was alone inside the room, she fought against the need to dry-heave. She couldn't believe this was really happening to her. She couldn't believe that she was actually going to have to get into a bed with him.

She changed into the nightgown, grateful that at least it wasn't too skimpy. But as she thought about what might follow, she felt sick all over again.

She lingered as long as she could in the bathroom, but after several minutes he knocked impatiently on the door. She grabbed the clothing she had just removed and then stepped outside and back into the hallway.

"Ah, Bailey, I knew you'd look lovely in that nightie and I was absolutely right. You look beautiful." He paused a moment and then frowned. "That was a compliment, so what do you say, Bailey?"

"Thank you," she mumbled.

"Good, now let's get situated for the night." Once again, he wrapped the rope around her waist and then tugged her back down the hallway and into the bedroom. He pulled the covers down on one side of the bed and gestured for her to get in.

Once she did, he tied one of her wrists to the bed railing and then her other one, as well. She was forced to lie on her back with her arms up over her head. This position left her utterly vulnerable to him. Once again, nausea rose up inside her, but she swallowed hard against it. The last thing she wanted to do was choke on her own vomit and die that way.

Once she was secure, he stripped down to a pair of boxers. "I know it's been a bit of a stressful day for you, so tonight we'll just get a good night of sleep. But tomorrow night we both should be fully rested and we'll explore our love for each other in a more physical way."

He turned out the overhead light and crawled into the other side of the bed. She remained stiff and still as a statue. Could she really trust that he wasn't going to touch her through the rest of the night?

She hated the way he smelled and the warmth from his body that drifted over to her. She even hated the sound of his breathing. She was afraid to go to sleep and yet longed for the sweet oblivion she knew it might bring.

Please, let somebody find me before he physically wants to share his love with me. Please let somebody find me before tomorrow night comes. That was her mantra as she remained wide-awake and scared.

Chapter 14

Somebody had brought in a couple dozen doughnuts early in the morning. Even the yeasty sweet scent of them nauseated Benjamin after the long and fruitless night. They all had agreed that Bailey probably wasn't being held in the apartment complex. They also agreed that the man who had taken her had to be physically strong.

Dallas delegated the officers to begin a grid search, starting at the south side of town. Three officers would search one side of Main Street and three other men would search the other side. They would be knocking on doors and checking out empty buildings and storefronts.

Benjamin had decided to hang back with Dallas and help guide the search parties. RJ, Howard and Ethan all showed up, eager to help in the search, so Dallas sent an officer with each of them and gave them specific rows of houses to check.

Angela had slept on Bailey's sofa all night. Benjamin had never seen the tough woman as broken as she appeared to be by Bailey's disappearance. Lizzy, along with Naomi and Jaime, had also arrived at the house early that morning, offering to do anything they could to help.

Benjamin was momentarily in a fog of exhaustion, yet his mind kept trying to think of all the places Bailey could be. As the hours crawled by and the search teams checked in again and again with no news, he began to lose any hope that he'd had.

It would take forever for all the homes and businesses in town to be searched. She had been missing all night… possibly for two long nights. The police department was so small and the search area was so big. Benjamin's heart ached with an emptiness that frightened him. He couldn't give up hope yet, not while there was a possibility that she might still be alive. Dammit, they had to find her.

At noon, a knock fell on her door. "I'll get it," Benjamin said, grateful to do something…to do anything. Letta Lee and a half a dozen women from the gardening club stood on the front porch.

"We're here to help," Letta said. She sidestepped Benjamin and entered the living room. She looked over at where Angela and Lizzy were seated on the sofa. "Angela, I'm so sorry this has happened."

"Thank you, Letta," Angela replied and swiped a tissue over her eyes.

"You know we all think the world of Bailey," Letta said.

"I just can't believe this has happened," Angela replied and began to cry once again.

"You need to come on into the kitchen and talk to Dallas," Benjamin said to the older woman.

Letta immediately swept past him and went into the kitchen. "Dallas, we've heard what's happened to Bailey. I'm here with a lot of women from the gardening club and we want to help in the search."

"Letta, I appreciate it, but—" Dallas began.

"Dallas Calloway, don't you dare tell me we're all too old to help out," Letta said.

"I wasn't about to tell you that," Dallas replied. "It's just that we don't know how dangerous this situation might become and so I can't send you all off without an officer and right now all my officers are already out working the streets."

Benjamin didn't volunteer for the job. He'd seen that one of the women was on a walker and another one was on oxygen. As much as he appreciated their desire to help, the truth was they would probably be more of a hindrance.

"If you really want to help, then maybe you could make us all some sandwiches for lunch." Dallas pulled his wallet from his back pocket and got out three or four twenty-dollar bills. "I'm sure the officers would appreciate having something to eat besides doughnuts as they come to check in."

"We can definitely take care of that," Letta said as she picked up the money. "We'll make sandwiches and I'll have Mabel make her good coleslaw and Eileen can put together the pasta salad that everyone raves about whenever we have a potluck dinner."

Letta was still talking about her plans for food as she walked out the front door. "At least I know the men will be fed good this afternoon," Dallas said. Benjamin didn't want to be here that afternoon without Bailey. He had no interest in any food that might be offered. He just needed Bailey. Where could she be?

Dallas leaned back in his chair with a deep frown. "This is like the damned Scarecrow Killer case. I feel like there's something we're missing. I can't believe those notes came from just some random person."

"If not random, then who?" Benjamin asked in deep

frustration. "We already cleared the three men that she'd mentioned to me."

Dallas's frown deepened even more. "What we didn't check was if any of those three men own other property besides where they live." He turned to Officer Ross Davenport, who was in the process of pouring himself a cup of coffee.

"Ross, I need you to head over to city hall and get all the property records for Ethan Dourty, RJ Morgan and Howard Kendall." Dallas looked back at Benjamin. "Maybe it's time that we start at the beginning once again. I should have thought to have these records checked before now."

"Don't beat yourself up," Benjamin said to his friend as Ross left. "I didn't think about any one of them having other property here in town or anyplace else."

Benjamin waited impatiently for Ross to return. He poured himself a cup of coffee and then returned to his seat at the table with Dallas. A map of the town was spread out before Dallas and as officers checked in from various addresses, Dallas marked them through with a red pen.

It didn't take too long before Ross returned. Surprisingly, two of the men had other property. RJ had been left his family's place and Howard had also been left a property when his family had moved out of town.

"I know these two places," Dallas said as he stood. "As far as I know they've both been empty for a very long time. Let's head to RJ's property first. It's not in as bad a shape as Howard's parents' old house is."

Benjamin jumped up, a renewed energy racing through him. How had they overlooked this? They'd apparently had tunnel vision and had possibly believed in the innocence of a person who had lied to their faces.

Minutes later, Dallas and Benjamin were in his car and

two more officers followed behind them as they raced to the property that RJ owned on the southern edge of town.

"Why didn't either of these men mention that they had other property when we questioned them?" Benjamin asked.

"Why would they? It's probably because they didn't even think about it. Both of the homes appear badly weathered and deserted, Howard's worse than RJ's. It's obvious they aren't living in the homes."

"This has got to be it," Benjamin said fervently. "She's got to be in one of these places otherwise I'm afraid we'll never find her and, Dallas, we have to find her."

It didn't matter that Benjamin had intended to break up with Bailey. He needed to see her driving her little red sports car around town. He needed to watch her prance down the street in one of her stylish outfits with her oversize earrings dancing on her ears. He desperately needed to see her happy and vibrant and very much alive.

It took them only a few minutes to arrive at the house that RJ owned and, on the way, Dallas called the officer he'd sent with RJ to search earlier that day. Assured that the bald, muscular man was still out with the lawman, there was no reason to believe anyone would be in the house except Bailey.

The place looked completely deserted, with windows boarded up and spray paint in neon shades adding colorful images and words to the otherwise dark brown house paint.

Benjamin's heart began to pound against his ribs as an enormous rush of adrenaline flooded through his veins. The minute Dallas stopped the car, he jumped out of the passenger side and then impatiently waited for Dallas.

The two officers who had come with them also got out of their car, and together the four of them approached the front door. It didn't appear as if anyone had been inside the house for some time. Spiderwebs hung across the doorway and were destroyed as Dallas kicked open the front door. However, Benjamin knew spiders could spin an intricate web in a matter of hours.

There was no furniture inside and dust covered the floor. There were nests in the corners of the front room where animals had made their home. Benjamin knew she wasn't here. They all knew she wasn't, although they checked all the rooms, anyway.

"Okay, this was a bust," Dallas said once they were all back outside. "Let's head on over to Howard's parents' old place and see what we find there."

Dallas called Officer Andy Edwards to check to see if Howard was still with the search party. He wasn't. Edwards told Dallas that Howard had taken off just a few minutes before, indicating that he needed to go back to his job at the bank before the workday was over.

"We need to hurry," Benjamin said as they headed toward Howard's parents' abandoned home.

"I'm going as fast as I can," Dallas replied tersely as he stepped on the gas.

Had Howard really gone back to the bank to work or was he right now with Bailey? Benjamin leaned forward, straining against his seat belt as if that might make the car go even faster. Howard's old property was on the other side of town from RJ's and each minute they were in the car, they weren't there to check about Bailey.

Were they finally going to find her? Or would this just be another bitter disappointment? Would she be alive or was it already too late for her? Had Howard treated her all right or had his love obsession turned deadly? Was Howard even the guilty party?

The questions flew fast and furious around in his head. Dallas turned right on a side street that saw little traffic. The road was narrow with tree limbs encroaching over the asphalt. After several miles, he made a left on a road that was little more than a dirt path.

"The house is up here on the right," Dallas said as he slowed down.

He turned into a long gravel driveway. The house looked as deserted as RJ's had. The wood had weathered to a bleached gray and the windows were all boarded up. Squirrels played in the trees overhead, adding to the look of complete abandonment.

Benjamin's very last vestige of hope dwindled out of him. All four of them got out and approached the front door. Once again, Benjamin thought he smelled a trace of her in the air. His damn memory was apparently playing tricks on him again.

When they reached the front door, it was locked and the lock looked shiny and new against the old wood. Once again, a wave of adrenaline flooded through Benjamin. Why would anyone want to lock up a place like this? Unless they had something to hide inside.

Dallas threw himself at the door, his broad shoulders leading the way. Once… Twice… And on the third crash, the door frame splintered enough for him to kick the door down.

He stepped inside with Benjamin at his heels and the two men froze. They entered into a living room that looked like Bailey's. It had a black sofa with pink and yellow throw pillows. A bookcase was against one wall and held the same books and knickknacks as the one in Bailey's home.

"What in the hell?" Benjamin said in disbelief.

"Benjamin?" Her voice came from what he assumed was the kitchen. The sound of it shot an electric thrill through his entire body and nearly cast him to his knees. She was alive!

"Bailey?" he shouted as he ran toward the doorway that would take him to her. He was aware of the other officers following closely behind him.

She was tied to a kitchen chair. She had a black eye and blood had dried from an apparent nosebleed. She saw him and began to weep. "Thank God," she cried. "Oh, thank God, you found me."

"Just sit tight, we're going to get you out of here," Benjamin replied. "Somebody call for an ambulance," he yelled as he raced to the kitchen drawers, looking for a knife or anything sharp to cut the ropes that held her. He couldn't even begin to process the injuries to her face. Right now, all he wanted was to free her so he could pull her into his arms.

"He—he's insane," she continued through her sobs. "I—I... He told me he loves me, but I—I think eventually he was going to kill me. I was never going to l-love him...never, no matter how long he held me here."

"Don't cry, honey. You're safe now." Benjamin found a couple of sharp knifes in one of the drawers and he began to cut at the ropes that held her legs while Ross began to saw at the ropes around her arms.

Dallas got on his radio to call for more men. There was a sudden roar of rage as Howard burst into the room. "Stop it," he screamed. "She's mine. You all have no right to be in here. This is my private property. You have no right to take her from me."

Benjamin dropped his knife to the floor and rose to his feet. A simmering rage had been inside him since the moment he'd seen Bailey's face. That rage now exploded.

He rushed at Howard and before the man knew what to expect, Benjamin punched him as hard as he could in his face. Howard reeled backward and howled as his nose began to bleed.

"Benjamin," Dallas yelled. "Leave it now. Bailey needs you."

Benjamin wanted to hit the man again…and again for everything he'd done to Bailey. But reason warred with his rage and as Bailey called out to him, he rushed back to continue to use the knife to free her. Howard was lucky Benjamin didn't use the knife to stab him in his black heart.

"I'm going to sue you all for trespassing and entering my private property without a search warrant," Howard said as Dallas handcuffed him. Blood dripped from his nose. "Then I'm going to sue for police brutality. You saw him, Dallas. You saw your officer hit me."

"I didn't see anything," Dallas replied.

"You can take Bailey now, but she'll come back to me. She'll always come back to me," Howard said confidently.

"Never," Bailey screamed at him. "You'll never have me again. I hate you. Do you hear me, Howard? I hate you."

Howard laughed, the sound of evil with a sense of humor. "Trust me, I'll have her again. Bailey is my soul mate and we belong together."

"Why don't you shut up?" Benjamin said tersely. At that moment, the ropes around Bailey's legs fell to the floor.

"I'll get Howard into the back of my car," Dallas said.

It took only minutes after Dallas took Howard out of the house that Bailey was finally free of all the ropes that had held her.

Benjamin immediately drew her up and into his arms and held her tight as she cried against his chest. Her entire body trembled like a leaf in a windstorm. He stroked her back and whispered into her ear. "You're okay now. You're safe and nobody is ever going to hurt you again."

"H-he thought if he could keep me here long enough, I'd fall in love with him and never want to leave him. But his temper was so scary," she said.

The sound of a siren blared in the air. It suddenly stopped, indicating the ambulance had arrived. He was still holding her when two paramedics came in with a gurney.

"This isn't necessary," she protested as Benjamin gestured for her to lie down.

"You need to go to the hospital and get checked out. Bailey, aside from the physical wounds on your beautiful face, you've been through a terrible trauma. Please, go and let a doctor take a look at you."

She hesitated only a moment and then complied. It didn't take long for the ambulance to carry her away. Dallas came back inside. "I've called in the team to start processing this crime scene. They should all be here shortly, meanwhile I'm heading back to the station to book Howard." He looked at Benjamin. "You're free to head out to the hospital."

"Thanks," Benjamin replied. It was exactly where he wanted to be. He needed to make sure she was really okay, both physically and mentally. He couldn't imagine the horror she must have gone through. Her black eye and the blood on her face had enraged him. The fact that Howard had put hands on her made him want to rip Howard apart.

Before he left, he checked out the whole house. It was shocking, the amount of work that had been done inside, while outside it looked so deserted.

He stopped in the threshold of the master bedroom. His blood ran cold as he saw the ropes that were tied to the headboard. Had she been tied to the bed? Had Howard raped her?

Another rage slammed through him as he drew his hands into fists. Thank God that Dallas had already taken Howard away, otherwise it might have been Benjamin facing charges.

As he drove to the hospital, all he could think of was Bailey and the gratefulness that they had managed to find her before Howard hurt her any more than he already had.

The day had slipped away and night shadows had turned into darkness. Thank God she didn't have to spend another night in that horror of a house.

How sick was it that Howard had attempted to re-create Bailey's home in that house? It had been downright creepy. It was obvious Howard was mentally ill, but Benjamin didn't feel sorry for him.

Howard had certainly known the difference between right and wrong. He'd gone to great lengths to hide his guilt. He'd even met them at his apartment to throw them off him. Benjamin hoped like hell he went to prison for the rest of his life.

By the time he reached the hospital, his thoughts were all on Bailey. He knew she was a fighter and she would hopefully be okay in time. Right now, all he wanted was to be with her, to assure himself that she was really okay. He needed to see her with the blood cleaned off her face. However, he knew the black eye would take some time to heal.

Fatigue tugged at him as he wheeled into the hospital parking lot. It had been a hell of a long twenty-four hours or so. Now that the fear and anxiety were gone, his exhaustion was nearly overwhelming. He parked and got out and then walked toward the emergency entrance.

He went inside and to the desk, where Meri Whittaker, a young attractive woman, sat behind a plexiglass window. As soon as she saw him, she opened the window to greet him.

"Hey, Meri—Bailey Troy was brought in just a little while ago. Could you tell the doctor tending to her that I need to speak with him when he gets a chance?"

"I'll let him know," she replied. She closed the window and then went through a door. She was gone only a few minutes and then she returned to the desk. "He said he'll be out here shortly to speak with you."

"Thank you," he replied and then sat in one of the uncomfortable plastic chairs the room had to offer.

His head whirled with all kinds of thoughts as he waited for the doctor. Had Howard sexually assaulted her? Did she have wounds that hadn't been apparent? Did her body hold the signs of her being beaten? Dear God, he hoped not.

When they'd found her, she'd been wearing a shapeless gray dress that he knew wasn't one of her own. It had obviously been something unattractive that Howard had picked out for her.

It played in his mind that he still needed to end things with her. It was still past time for him to do so.

He was just going to have to pick the right time and it needed to be very soon. He couldn't go on loving her like he did. His heart was already going to be ripped out of his soul when he officially told her goodbye. At least now he knew she was safe. A deep gratefulness for that rushed through him.

He looked up as the outer door whooshed open and Angela came flying in. "Is she okay? Have you heard anything?" she asked frantically.

"No, nothing yet," he replied.

She sank down next to Benjamin and twisted a tissue between her fingers. "There are so many things I need to say to her, so many important things she needs to know. When I thought she was gone…" She let her words drift off.

At that moment Dr. Alexander Erickson entered the room. The doctor was younger than Benjamin, but he was known as a good physician who cared deeply about his patients. Benjamin and Angela both jumped out of their chairs to greet him.

"I've checked her over and other than the black eye and the bloody nose she sustained, she's going to be just fine," he said. "Still, I'm keeping her overnight. She'd been through quite a trauma and I think that's best for her."

"Can we see her?" Benjamin asked.

The doctor frowned. "I've sedated her to help her sleep. How about one of you can go in now and the other can wait until morning."

As much as Benjamin wanted to see her, he could feel Angela's desperate need to see her daughter. "Go on, Angela. I'll come back in the morning," he said.

Angela shot him a look of deep gratitude. "She's in room 107," Dr. Erickson said.

As Angela quickly disappeared down the hallway, Dr. Erickson looked at Benjamin. "I know Dallas is probably going to want to get a statement from her, but all that can wait until morning." He smiled. "She's going to be just fine. Bailey is a strong woman and she'll get through all this."

"Thanks. I'll be back here to see her first thing in the morning," Benjamin said.

He'd desperately wanted to see Bailey tonight, but he wouldn't go against doctor's orders and it was more important that Angela went in to see her daughter.

He checked in with Dallas, who told him they were at Howard's house still processing the scene. But he told Benjamin to go home and get some sleep and come in to the station around nine the next day.

By the time Benjamin got home, his exhaustion tugged on his shoulders and burned at his eyes. But a deep relief also flooded through him. He got out of his clothes, took a quick shower and then got into bed.

Thank God she was safe, but at some point soon he had to break things off with her. No matter how painful it was going to be, it had to be done.

That was his last thought before he fell asleep.

Chapter 15

Bailey relaxed into the hospital bed, just beginning to feel the effects of the sedative that flowed through her IV. A nurse had washed her face, removing all the blood that had been there from her bloody nose. She had an ice pack to use as needed on her black eye and she'd been checked out by the doctor.

They'd allowed her to take a quick shower before she pulled on a hospital gown. Right now, she didn't hurt anywhere too much. She was just grateful to be here and safe with all of Howard's touches on her scrubbed off her skin.

She still couldn't believe everything that had happened. She would have never believed Howard was capable of everything he had done to her. And all in the name of love. That hadn't been love at all. It had been something sick and twisted.

She'd just closed her eyes when she heard her door creak open. She opened her eyes and saw her mother. "Oh, Bailey," she said and hurried to the chair at Bailey's bedside.

Bailey raised the head of her bed and stared as her mother burst into tears. She grabbed Bailey's hand and held tight. "Oh, baby, look at your eye. Look what that animal did to you."

"It's okay now. It doesn't hurt too much," Bailey replied.

"I'm so sorry," Angela said. "Oh, Bailey, I've been so afraid for you."

"Don't cry, I'm safe now, Mom," Bailey said, shocked by her mother's display of emotion. Angela never got emotional about anything.

"I'm just so sorry about so many things. I—I wanted to raise you to be a strong woman. But I realized while you were missing that I never really showed you or told you how very much I love you."

Angela's words were as surprising as finding out Howard had been the one to kidnap her. "It's okay," she said.

"No, it's not okay. I've been too hard on you when I didn't need to be. I took out my bitterness at my life on you. You didn't even share with me about the important things that were going on in your life and I know that's because I didn't make myself available to you. I'm so sorry, Bailey. Can you ever forgive me?"

"Of course, I can… I do. I love you, Mom."

"And I love you, Bailey, and I don't care if you never have children. I just need you to be in my life." She released Bailey's hand, but remained leaning forward in the chair. "I swear things are going to be different from here on out."

"That would be nice," Bailey replied. "Can we talk some more tomorrow? I'm sorry, Mom, but I'm just so tired right now." She could barely keep her eyes open and she was floating on a cloud of well-being.

"Of course." Angela got up from the chair, leaned over and kissed Bailey on the cheek and then she left the room.

These were definitely strange days, when a man who was a respectable banker had kidnapped her in the name of love and her mother had suddenly seen the errors of her ways.

While Bailey was certain Howard would go to prison for a very long time, she wasn't so certain her mother would be able to sustain a new and different relationship with Bailey. Still, her mother's words of love had touched her to the core.

Thoughts of Benjamin filled her head, further warming her. She had hoped to see him, but if he came in now, she wouldn't even be able to have a real conversation with him. She was just too tired. Still, it was his vision that remained in her brain and made her smile with warmth and happiness as she quickly drifted off to sleep.

She awakened early the next morning, feeling surprisingly rested and refreshed. Her black eye throbbed a little, but it was nothing she couldn't handle. She was now eager to see the doctor and go home.

In the meantime, she raised the head of her bed and turned on the television, mostly for the white noise it would provide. Her mind was still filled with everything that had happened to her from the moment she had awakened in the thunderstorm and somebody—Howard—had been in her house. Her stalker had come for her in the storm and nobody had known. So much had happened and she was still trying to process it all.

It wasn't long before the smells of breakfast filled the air and she realized she was starving. All she'd really had to eat since being held against her will was a single taco and that had only been eaten in an effort to appease Howard.

Finally, an older woman she didn't know pushed in a cart to serve Bailey breakfast. There were scrambled eggs and bacon, a cup of fresh fruit, a side of toast, orange juice and coffee.

"Hmm, thank you," Bailey said. "This all looks delicious."

"Hope it tastes as good as it looks," the woman replied and then she was gone.

The first thing Bailey did was pop the top of her coffee so she could take a sip. She was almost finished with the meal when Dr. Erickson came in.

"How's my patient feeling today?" he asked. "I see your shiner is now a beautiful deep purple."

Bailey raised her hand and touched her black eye. "I guess I'm going to have to figure out how to accessorize around it, but other than that, I'm feeling fine and I'm ready to go home."

"I don't see a reason to keep you, so why don't you finish up your breakfast and meanwhile I'll have the nurse draw up your exit papers," he replied.

"Thanks, Dr. Erickson," she said.

"No problem," he replied and then left her room.

She had just finished eating when Dallas and Benjamin came into the room. Benjamin immediately ran to her side. "Bailey, how are you feeling?" His gaze was filled with unmistakable love and it both warmed her yet filled her with sadness, knowing it was a love she couldn't keep.

"I'd like to get an official statement from you," Dallas said. "Are you feeling up to doing that?"

"Absolutely, I'd just as soon put this all behind me as quickly as possible," she replied. Benjamin sat in the chair next to the bed and reached for her hand. She welcomed the warmth and strength that he offered her.

Dallas pulled up another chair and sat. "Tell me the events of the night you were taken from your house," he said. "Start at the very beginning of things."

Just that quickly she was back in it—back in the storm and fighting a masked man. Then she was in a kitchen that looked scarily, creepily like her own. She told Dallas everything that had happened.

"Did anything sexual happen?" he asked when she told him about being tied to the bed.

"Thankfully no, but I believe he would have raped me if I'd been there one more night," she said. She shivered at the very thought of what could have happened...what would have happened.

"How did you get the black eye and bloody nose?" Dallas asked.

"Yesterday morning at breakfast, I made the mistake of telling him I didn't care for sausage links. He punched me so hard and so fast, twice in the face, as he yelled about how ungrateful I was after he'd fixed the sausages for breakfast."

"I wish he was right here right now. I'd beat the hell out of him for hurting you," Benjamin said fiercely.

The interview went on for another twenty minutes or so and then Dallas left while Benjamin stayed behind. "Bailey, I've never been as scared as I was when you went missing," he said.

"Well, it's over now and the doctor is releasing me any minute."

"Do you have a ride home?" he asked.

"No, I was going to call Lizzy and see if she could come get me," Bailey replied.

"Now that I'm here, you don't have to do that. I'll gladly take you home."

Once again, she felt his love for her flooding through her and she knew that today was the day she would tell him goodbye. Within thirty minutes, they were in his car and headed to her house. She still wore the blue-flowered hospital gown as she refused to wear home the gray dress that Howard had her wear.

They didn't talk much on the drive. There would be plenty to say when she invited him in for a talk. Dread pressed tight against her chest with each mile that passed.

"Would you please come inside?" she asked once he pulled up in her driveway. "There's something serious I need to talk to you about."

"Yeah, I need to talk to you about something, too," he replied.

"Can I get you anything?" she asked once they were inside.

"No thanks, I'm fine." He sank down on the sofa.

"Can you excuse me for just a moment, I need to change out of this gown."

"Of course, take your time," he replied.

She ran up the stairs and into her bedroom where she grabbed a pair of jogging pants and a pink T-shirt from a drawer. She quickly changed and then went back downstairs and sat beside him on the sofa.

"Better?" he asked.

"Much better," she replied.

"Okay, you go first, what's on your mind?" His gaze was so soft, so warm on her, and to her surprise she began to cry. "Hey—hey, what's going on, Bailey? Please don't cry." He moved closer to her and began to put an arm around her, but she shrugged him away and cried even harder.

"Oh, Benjamin, I love you so much. I've never loved a man as much as I love you," she said through her tears. "But I've got to let you go. I've already let things go too far with you, but it's time for me to stop seeing you."

He gazed at her in what appeared to be both confusion

and an odd look of relief. Had he just been waiting for her to break it off with him? Had he wanted to stop seeing her, but didn't know how to tell her he no longer wanted to see her?

He frowned. "Can I ask you why?"

She gazed at him through her tears. "You're a good man, Benjamin and you deserve a woman who will love you and give you a family. I'm sure you probably want children, but the truth of the matter is I've kept a big secret from you."

"What secret?" he asked.

She drew in a deep breath. "I don't want kids," she blurted out.

He stared at her for several long moments and then he threw back his head and began to laugh. "Oh, this is so rich," he finally said, amusement lighting up his gorgeous eyes. "Fate definitely has a sense of humor."

She looked at him in utter confusion. "Want to fill me in on what is so funny?"

"I was going to break things off with you today because despite the fact that I love you madly and with all of my heart, I knew I had to let you go so you could have a family." He laughed once again. "Bailey, the truth of the matter is a bad case of mumps when I was twelve left me unable to have children. I can't make babies."

"For real?" she asked, an edge of excitement whirling around inside her as her heart beat a quickened pace.

"For real," he replied. "Is it for real that you don't want children?" He scooted closer to her on the sofa, bringing with him his wonderful scent.

"It's for real," she replied half-breathlessly. Was it possible that fate had brought them together because they truly belonged together? That she could love him and not tell him goodbye?

He reached out and stroked a finger down the side of her face. "Bailey, I love you so very much. I kept telling myself I needed to break things off with you and yet every time I was with you, I couldn't do it."

"Same," she replied. "But, Benjamin, don't you think I'm abnormal or selfish for not wanting children?" Tears once again blurred her vision.

"Of course not," he replied immediately. "I find it highly sexy that you're a strong woman and you know what you want. Bailey, I also know there isn't a selfish bone in your body. If you were abnormal or selfish, I wouldn't love you like I do."

He held her gaze for a long moment. Oh, she could get lost in his beautiful blue eyes. He slid off the sofa and to one knee. "I don't have a ring, but, Bailey, will you marry me? Will you marry me and make me the happiest man in the world?"

"Yes…oh, yes. I'll marry you and I'll be the happiest woman on earth." She bounced up from the sofa and he stood, as well. He pulled her into his arms and for a moment they simply gazed at each other. "Hi," she finally said.

"Hi yourself," he replied and then his lips took hers in a kiss that tasted of love and a deep commitment. It whispered of desire and a happily-ever-after with the man she'd always dreamed of. Finally, and forever, Officer Benjamin Cooper belonged to her.

Epilogue

Chief Dallas Calloway sat at the table in the workroom and stared at the board that held the photos of the murdered victims.

It was just after midnight and he was alone in the station except for one other officer who was manning dispatch and the front desk.

Still, despite the silence that surrounded him, his head wasn't quiet. Rather, the victims screamed in his brain, begging him for justice. They had been screaming in his head since the first victim had been found in Lucas's cornfield.

He now rubbed at his tired eyes. Sleep had been difficult with all the noise in his head and he knew he wasn't functioning at his very best.

What were they missing? Why couldn't they find this man who stabbed women and then trussed them up like scarecrows? What significance did the eyes have to him? Why did he take them and what in God's name did he do with them?

Dallas loved the small town he served and he couldn't stand it that a killer was using it as his personal killing field. And the worst part was he knew a clock was ticking down to another murder.

Somewhere in town, a madman was already plotting

and planning his next kill and there was absolutely nothing Dallas could do to prevent it.

The victims screamed again in his head and more than anything he wanted to give them the justice they deserved. Somehow, some way, he had to find this killer.

The Scarecrow Killer stood at his front window and watched as the sun went down. An excitement roared through his body at the same time the crows cawed in his head.

It was time for another scarecrow to be built. That was the only way he could make the crows go away. The best part was he'd decided whom he'd use as the next one.

Her blond hair and blue eyes were perfect. They were just like *hers*. He was hoping and praying she would be the one to finally stop the noise in his head. If he could just kill her for a final time then maybe it all would end. She'd be dead and wouldn't be able to haunt him anymore.

That was what he wanted and yet he had to admit he liked making the headlines. He liked that he had the whole town afraid. It was what they all deserved. They had never seen him, but they were seeing him now. He had to admit to himself that he liked stabbing his knife in their chests and feeling their warm blood. He liked sewing their mouths closed and taking their eyes out.

Now that he had his next victim picked out, it was just a matter of finding the right time and place to take her. In just a few days another scarecrow would appear. A new burst of excited adrenaline flooded through him as he thought about the fun to come.

* * * * *

Chapter 1

Sixteen months later...

Charlie Tillerman was a dead man—or he would be if the other hotshots were right...

If *he* was the saboteur.

Michaela Momber listened to her fellow hotshots' voices rumbling around the airplane cabin as they speculated over the identity of the saboteur who'd been messing with them for way too long. The incidents had been happening for over a year now. Stupid things at first that they hadn't even realized were intentional—like equipment that had been checked suddenly breaking. But because of the nature of their jobs, those things had been dangerous. Especially when the firehouse stove had exploded, sending Ethan Sommerly to the hospital with burns. Fortunately, his beard had saved him from any significant wounds, but once his beard was gone, all hell had broken loose. He wasn't just a hotshot firefighter, he was heir to some famous family.

That situation could have been worse, like when their vehicles had been tampered with, brake lines cuts. But now the attacks had become physical, with the saboteur striking Rory VanDam over the head so hard that he was in a coma for two weeks. *Saboteur* really wasn't a strong enough word for this person.

Rory had recovered from his traumatic head injury, which happened after the hotshot holiday party six months ago. He'd also recovered from a gunshot wound he suffered when a corrupt FBI agent had gone after him. Again.

Rory was flying the plane now, so his wasn't one of the voices Michaela heard from where she sat in the back of the plane. She'd boarded first, eager to take a seat and get some much-needed rest after the two weeks they'd spent battling a wildfire. But even though she tried to sleep, the majority of her twenty-member team kept talking. It wasn't just their voices keeping her awake, but also what they were talking about—or rather, whom.

"Charlie had access to my drinks," Luke Garrison remarked. "He could have been the one who drugged me. Maybe he was working with Marty Gingrich."

Marty Gingrich, a former state trooper, was the one who'd tried to kill Luke and his wife, though. Not Charlie.

But had Charlie helped? The thought had Michaela's stomach churning with dread, but she shook her head, rejecting the idea.

"It's more likely that Trooper Wells is helping Gingrich than Charlie," Michaela said, then stiffened with shock over the fact that she'd instinctively come to the bartender's defense.

"True," Hank said. "I could definitely see Wynona Wells being involved in this."

Henrietta "Hank" Rowlins was Michaela's best friend, so her quick agreement was no surprise. But did she suspect that Michaela had a reason for defending Charlie? Michaela felt a jab of guilt that she hadn't told her anything, but she'd hoped there would be nothing to tell. That it had just been a onetime thing on a night when she felt just too damn alone.

But it had been more than once.

"I don't trust Wells, either," Patrick "Trick" McRooney said. He might have just agreed with Hank because he was engaged to her. "But Charlie definitely has easier access to us."

Damn. Did Trick suspect?

He was the brother-in-law of the hotshot superintendent, Braden Zimmer. Braden had brought in his wife's brother to investigate the saboteur, figuring that he would be more objective than the superintendent could be about his team. But then Trick had fallen for Hank and lost all his objectivity.

Michaela hoped she hadn't done the same thing. Lost her objectivity.

Not falling for anyone. That was never going to happen, she would never risk her heart again. She couldn't trust anyone, most especially herself and her own damn judgment.

"Charlie's got more access at the bar," Ethan Sommerly said. "But at the firehouse?"

Carl Kozak, one of the older hotshots, snorted. "Thanks to Stanley, everyone has access to the firehouse. Sorry, Cody."

Cody Mallehan was Stanley's older foster brother and the reason Stanley was in Northern Lakes. He had moved the teenager here after Stanley aged out of the foster care system. Cody sighed. "We're working on it."

"We're also working hard on finding out who the saboteur is and on keeping the team safe," Braden added, as if trying to reassure them. With the dark circles beneath his eyes, he looked as exhausted as Michaela felt, he probably wasn't sleeping any more than she was.

"It's bad enough fighting a wildfire," Donovan Cunningham murmured. "But to have to worry about getting hurt at home, too…"

Apparently, Michaela wasn't the only one on edge right now. The stress had to be what was making her so sick. At least the wildfire they were returning from was in Ontario, so the plane ride would be short, which was good since Michaela's stomach went up and down with every bit of turbulence.

"That's why we have to investigate every possible suspect," Trick said. "Even Charlie."

"What's his motive?" Michaela found herself asking.

"You know," Cody said. "You were the one who was there when his bar burned down. You saved him."

Michaela smiled. "And he would want revenge on us for that?" He certainly hadn't seemed to want revenge on her, anyway, since he'd refused to let her pay for anything in his bar since the fire. And then they…

"He might want revenge because the arsonist who burned down his bar was really after us. He and the Filling Station were nearly collateral damage," Donovan said. He was an older hotshot, too, like Carl. Guys who'd been working as elite firefighters for a long time.

"The Filling Station is more than his bar," Braden said. "It's his home, and his family legacy."

So that did give him motive.

Even the superintendent who was usually loath to suspect anyone seemed to think Charlie had a motive. But…

If Charlie Tillerman was the saboteur, Michaela Momber had been sleeping with the enemy.

Had she done it again? Had she made a horrible mistake, trusting someone she shouldn't have? Not that she really trusted him. Not that she could really trust anyone...

Her stomach churned again, and she closed her eyes and arched her neck against the headrest of the airplane seat. She didn't usually get motion sickness, but lately everything had been making her queasy. For months now, she'd been feeling so damn nauseous and bloated. So bloated that she couldn't even button her pants anymore.

If she didn't know better, she might have thought she was pregnant. But that wasn't possible. She couldn't get pregnant. But it was good that she hadn't gotten pregnant with her ex. She shouldn't have trusted him to be a faithful husband, so she certainly wouldn't have trusted him to be a responsible father.

No. She wasn't pregnant. But with as sick as she'd been feeling, she probably had an ulcer. And no matter if he was the saboteur or not, Charlie Tillerman was partially responsible for that, too.

After her divorce, Michaela had no intention of ever getting involved with anyone again. Not that she and Charlie were *involved*.

But they were...

She wasn't sure what they were. But if anyone found out about them, they might think she was working with him, that she was complicit in the sabotage, too, just like so many people thought Trooper Wynona Wells might be complicit in all the horrible things her training sergeant Marty Gingrich had done to the hotshot team. Michaela really wished that it was her and not Charlie.

But she also had to be realistic and cautious, or she might wind up getting hurt, like Rory. She didn't want anyone else getting hurt, either, though. She desperately wanted the saboteur—whoever it was—caught and brought to justice.

Especially if that person was Charlie.

And if that person was Charlie, she wanted to be the one to catch him first. With the access she had to him, she might be the only person who could catch him.

The flames sputtered and cowered, shrinking away from the water blasting from the end of the hose Charlie Tillerman held tightly between his gloved hands. After the arson fire had destroyed his bar and nearly claimed his life over a year ago, Charlie had no interest in ever going near another one. But here he was, suited up in fire-retardant jacket and pants, battling a blaze.

Sweat rolled down his back and off his face. Despite it being June, the weather hadn't warmed up much yet this year, and this late at night, it was extra cool. But the fire burned hot, especially with as close as Charlie was standing to it, just inside the open garage door.

The flames flared up, trying to reach the wood rafters of the garage, but another blast of water sent them crashing back down…below the raised hood of the vehicle inside the garage. The hood and motor were black, and the windshield and headlights had shattered in the heat. It was too late to save the car, but the battle was now to save the structure, to stop the fire from spreading any farther.

From destroying anything more.

Like his livelihood and his home had been destroyed over a year ago. He'd rebuilt the Filling Station Bar and Grille within months of the fire, working alongside the contractors and the townspeople who'd volunteered to help. While the town in the Huron Forest, with its many inland lakes, was a seasonal tourist destination, it was the locals who had been his loyal patrons.

And it was those loyal patrons—even the hotshot firefighters whom some people held responsible for the fires in the first place—who'd helped him rebuild. The arsonist who'd torched his bar and started the forest fire that had trapped the Boy Scouts six months prior to the bar burning down had been holding a grudge against the hotshot team for not hiring him. But even though he had been apprehended and brought to justice, other tragic or near-tragic things kept happening in this town. And while the hotshots seemed to be at the heart of the threats, too many other people had been put in danger as well from the violence.

The most tragic of these incidents had been a murder. But people had also been nearly run down walking across the street or, while in their vehicles, had been run off the road. There had also been shootings and explosions and fires.

Like the one he was battling now, the hose from the rig between his gloved hands, blasting water onto the flames. If only he'd had the rig and this equipment the night his bar had burned down...

If only he'd had some control over the situation and hadn't felt so damn helpless and vulnerable...

But he'd learned long ago there was no controlling anything, sometimes not even himself. At least when it came to a certain female customer.

The flames died fast, extinguished by the water, which now dripped from the blackened shell of the vehicle. While the car was a total loss, they'd managed to limit the damage to the garage it was inside. This fire was probably just an accident, like the homeowner had claimed it was. He'd left the classic car running while he was working on it, and something must have sparked and started the engine on fire.

This wasn't like all those other things that had been happening in Northern Lakes. And this fire had nothing to do with the hotshots, since they weren't even in town. They were off somewhere battling another wildfire. There had been a lot of them lately, which had left the Northern Lakes Fire Department so short-staffed that they had put out an emergency call for volunteers.

Even though he'd had no intention of going near another fire, Charlie hadn't been able to ignore the call. Not after so many of his neighbors and the townspeople had helped him rebuild his business and his life. So he'd gone through training and had been out on—fortunately—just a few calls since he'd finished that training a month ago.

Maybe things were quiet because the hotshots had been gone so much. That quiet, from fires, also extended to other parts of Charlie's life. Professionally, the bar was quieter without the hotshots' business, and personally...

No. He could not risk having a personal life. He just... couldn't. After his divorce, he had decided relationships were too damn unpredictable, kind of like fires. There was just no way of knowing which way it would go, so the chances of getting burned were just too great to risk. And Charlie wasn't nearly a good enough judge of character to trust anyone with his heart again.

To trust *anyone* again. Even the angel who'd rescued him that night in his burning bar. He was actually the least likely to trust *her* because she was one of *them*. A Huron hotshot.

No. He definitely couldn't trust her. He had only seen her a few times since the night of the hotshot holiday party, which had been a private event at the Filling Station, six months ago.

Not that he wanted to see her again. It was easier if he didn't. Then he wasn't so damn tempted. But damn, he missed her, too.

"Hey, you awake?" Eric asked as he stared into the back of the rig, where Charlie was sitting alone.

He didn't even remember climbing inside the truck at the burned-out garage, much less riding back to the firehouse. But that was definitely where the rig was now, parked in one of the bays of the three-story concrete block building. That building, on the main street of Northern Lakes, was just down the road from his bar, which was too damn close, given some of what had been happening at the firehouse over the past year or so. The shootings, the explosions...

He shuddered at the memory of those things that had rattled the windows and the walls of the Filling Station, which wasn't just his business, but also his home since he lived in the apartment above it.

Charlie shook his head, trying to clear thoughts of those dangers and of *her* from his mind. But that hadn't been easy to do even before they...

He definitely couldn't let himself think about *that*. So he drew in a deep breath and nodded. "Yeah, I'm awake," he assured his fellow volunteer, who was also his brother-in-law.

Eric Veltema was a big guy with blond hair that turned reddish in his mustache and beard. He had a booming laugh and a big personality, just like Charlie's sister. Valerie was the one who should have followed their father into politics, not Charlie.

Charlie had always preferred tending the bar, like their grandfather had most of his life. Charlie looked like Grandpa Tillerman, too, with dark eyes and black hair, and now that he was getting close to forty, the stubble on his jaw was starting to come in gray.

"You're the night owl," Eric said, "staying up late and closing the bar. I didn't think you ever slept."

Charlie chuckled at the misconception. "I sleep. Unlike you, I don't have kids." A pang of regret struck him, along with a sense of loss for what might have been, what could have been. His ex-wife hadn't wanted any children, though, and after what had nearly happened to his nephew, Charlie had changed his mind, too. The world was entirely too dangerous to bring children into, especially in Northern Lakes.

Eric chuckled, too. "Is that the reason you're staying a bachelor now? Because you want to sleep?"

"That's one of them," Charlie admitted.

But he had other reasons, and his brother-in-law was well aware of them. He and Eric had been friends since they were kids. They'd gone to school together and grown up together. Eric had been like family even before he'd married Charlie's sister, who'd always thought her younger brother's friend was annoying. Despite falling in love with him, she claimed she still found him annoying.

"Seriously, though," Charlie continued, "is Nicholas sleeping through the night yet?"

Eric's grin slid away, and he sighed. "Most nights now, but he still has the occasional nightmare about the fire."

"He's not the only one," Charlie muttered.

He'd felt so damn helpless then, when those Boy Scouts

had been trapped in the burning forest and they'd had to rely on the hotshots to rescue them and put out the fire. He hoped to never feel that helpless again, but just a few months later, he'd been trapped in his own burning bar.

"That's why you have to win this election, man," Eric said. "With you as mayor, you'd have some clout to get this fire station away from the hotshot crew. Let them use someplace else as their headquarters, someplace where they don't put anyone else in danger with all their enemies and secret identities and crap."

Charlie's stomach churned with the thought of putting himself through another campaign. While he was a town council member, he hadn't had to campaign for that position because everybody had just written him into the open seat his grandfather had left behind when he died, like he'd left Charlie the bar.

But mayor was a position some other people wanted, like a local Realtor and the CEO of the lumber company that owned whatever forest wasn't state land. These two guys, Jason Cruise and Bentley Ford, had influence and money, like the people Charlie had run against before. And they would probably be just as cutthroat as his old opponents had been for that senate seat.

He took off his hat and pushed his hand through his hair. He was tempted to pull out some of the dark strands, that would probably be less painful than going into politics again. But his brother-in-law, sister and quite a few other locals had been putting the pressure on him to run. Even the incumbent mayor was offering to step down now and have Charlie assume his duties as an interim mayor, figuring that if he had the job before the election, he would have the advantage over his opponents. The deputy mayor had passed away from old age a few months earlier, so the mayor could appoint one of the town council members to take over for him.

Because Charlie wanted to protect his hometown—not just from the danger the hotshots posed, but also from the danger that ambitious real estate developers posed—he was going to have to take some action. And at the moment, he could think of only one.

He uttered a weary sigh and admitted, "I know something has to be done about them."

Every time there was a shooting or someone was nearly run down or there was an explosion or a fire, everyone in the vicinity was in danger, not just the hotshots.

"And I think you're the best man for the job, Charlie," Eric persisted, like he had been doing for the past few months. "Tillerman is the name that people in this town instinctively trust."

The election was six months away yet, but the current mayor had already publicly announced that he wasn't going to run again. Then he'd privately offered to step aside now if Charlie would agree to be interim mayor until the election. Being the "incumbent" would give him the advantage over any rival, all but guaranteeing him the win, especially if he did what the townspeople were lobbying for the mayor to do.

"You're just saying that because you want me to get rid of the hotshots," Charlie said.

"I'm not the only one who wants that," Eric reminded him. "And it's what *you* want, too."

But he didn't really want to get rid of all of them. At least, not one blue-eyed blonde beauty who made his pulse race just thinking about her.

When he finally stepped out of the back of the rig, his gaze met that blue one of hers. She was standing a little way behind Eric at the foot of the stairs that led up to the second and third stories of the building.

So the hotshots were back in town.

And from the angry expression on Michaela Momber's beautiful face, she had clearly overheard everything he and Eric had been talking about. Was she outraged for professional reasons, though, or for personal reasons?

The saboteur was feeling bold. They'd gone so long without being discovered that they felt invincible. It didn't matter who came after them or tried to find them—that person was going to fail, just like everyone else kept failing.

Braden Zimmer. The hotshot superintendent hadn't been able to figure it out. Nor had his assistant superintendents, Wyatt Andrews and Dawson Hess. Even his smart new wife, the arson investigator, hadn't been able to figure it out.

And then Braden had brought in his brother-in-law to help find the saboteur. But Trick McRooney had failed, just like Braden had.

They had no clue.

But if, by some chance, someone started getting close to figuring it out...

Started putting it all together...

Then that person was going to have to die. The saboteur hadn't actually considered murder before—not that someone couldn't have died during one of the *accidents*. Hell, a few nearly *had* died. And because of that, because of all the things that had happened and how many people had been hurt, the saboteur would definitely face jail time if they were discovered.

And if that happened, they would lose everything that they had, everything that they were. But none of that mattered as much as the saboteur's quest for justice.

For revenge…

Chapter 2

Charlie should have been used to Michaela walking away from him. That was what she'd been doing for the past several months. No. Longer than that. She'd walked away the night she'd rescued him from the fire at his bar.

Once she'd gotten him to safety, to an ambulance waiting outside, she'd walked away from him. She'd walked back into the fire. That was a little how Charlie felt as he rushed out after her—that he was walking back into a fire.

That was how he felt every time he got close to her, like he was going to get burned by the heat between them. The passion that ignited whenever they were alone or even just looked at each other. But they'd done more than just look. Eventually, after months of him flirting with her, of trying to get her to give him a chance...

She'd given him more than that. She'd given him more pleasure than he'd ever known.

Clearly nothing like that was going to happen tonight. He was more likely to get burned by her temper because she looked really mad about what she overheard them saying. But instead of unleashing her anger, she just walked away. And he realized that beneath her anger was the vulnerability he'd found beneath her toughness.

She wasn't as tough emotionally as she was physically.

And as angry as she was about what she'd heard, she probably felt equally betrayed. That sense of betrayal was something Charlie understood all too well from the things that had come out during his campaign.

The secrets he hadn't known about his ex, the secrets she'd purposely kept from him. Like her affairs and the money she'd taken from his campaign contributions.

At the time, he hadn't appreciated how much gratitude he owed his opponent for digging up that dirt. He'd just been angry at him for humiliating him and at her for her betrayal. He'd been angriest at himself, though, for being so damn blind.

But underneath his anger there had been pain. He hoped that wasn't the case with Michaela, he didn't want her hurting because of him, thinking that he'd betrayed her.

Needing to make sure that she was okay and to explain what she'd heard, he tried to break free of his brother-in-law's grasp. When he started after her, Eric grabbed his arm before he could get past him.

"Charlie, what's the deal with you and the lady hotshot?" Eric asked. "The way she looked at you…" He shivered, then chuckled.

Michaela had a reputation around Northern Lakes for being tough—icy, even. But while she was tough, there was nothing cold about her.

"You must realize that she'd be pissed about what she overheard us saying," Charlie pointed out.

"So." Eric shrugged. "The hotshots are going to know soon enough when you're the mayor of Northern Lakes and they're looking for a new place for their headquarters. They wore out their welcome here."

"I don't have time for this now." Charlie tugged his arm

free of his brother-in-law's big hand, and he rushed toward that side door.

The last thing Charlie wanted to talk about at the moment was running for mayor. Right now he just wanted to run for Michaela, to catch up to her so that he could explain what she'd heard.

And that wasn't just because of…what they'd both agreed was a bad idea. This attraction between them, this strange and secret arrangement they had…

He stepped outside, letting the door slam shut behind him. Once it closed, it was as if someone had extinguished all the light. It was alarmingly dark without the glow of the fluorescent lights from the garage chasing away the night. Clouds must have obscured the moon, but there should have been more light.

While the streetlamps didn't quite reach the side of the building, there were light poles in the parking lot next to the firehouse that illuminated the entire area. Usually…

What had happened to them?

And more importantly, what had happened to her?

"Michaela!" Charlie called out to her now, concern gripping him, making his muscles tense. "Michaela!"

"Shh…"

The whisper from the dark raised goose bumps along his skin, despite the heaviness of the firefighter gear he was still wearing. He would recognize that husky female voice anywhere. He heard it so often in his dreams, and then he would wake up to find himself reaching for her.

But she was never there.

She never stayed, as if what they'd done was some embarrassing secret she was determined to keep. And he wasn't sure why—except that, for some reason, he hadn't been any more eager to share than she had. After his last political campaign had exposed more about his personal life than even he had known, like his wife's affairs and overspending, he was doubly determined to keep his private life private. Which was another reason he was reluctant to accept even the interim mayor position, let alone run in another election.

Lowering his voice to match her whisper, he asked, "Where are you?" And why couldn't he see her? She was still wearing her yellow hotshot-firefighter gear when he'd seen her inside just moments ago. But it was so dark that he couldn't even see her uniform.

"Shh…" she hissed again from the darkness, but she sounded closer now, and there was a strange sense of urgency or caution in her voice.

She wasn't just trying to shut him up because she didn't want to hear his explanation. There was something else happening.

"What's going on?" he asked.

Then he heard what must have drawn her attention already: the sound of shoes or boots scraping across asphalt. They weren't alone. Someone else was out in the dark parking lot with them.

He opened his mouth to call out to them, but Michaela must have been close enough to see him now, because she whispered again, "Shh…"

What was going on?

Did she consider whoever else out there in the darkness a threat? And was that threat to their relationship she seemed so determined to keep secret? Or, given all the dangerous things that happened to and around the hotshots, was that threat to their lives?

* * *

Moments ago, when Michaela had stepped out into the darkness, she had already been reeling from what she'd just seen and heard in the firehouse. Charlie Tillerman, in the back of one of the rigs, in firefighter gear. Not yellow gear, like the hotshots wore, but black, like his thick, glossy hair and his dark eyes and apparently his soul.

He did want to get rid of the hotshots, and he and that other man had already been plotting how to do it. Her team was right to be suspicious of Charlie Tillerman. And she, once again, had been wrong about a person. On the plane ride into Northern Lakes, she'd decided to find out the truth about him, to find any evidence of him being the saboteur. She'd even intended to go over to his place tonight and look around. But maybe that had just been an excuse to see him again.

She hadn't even had to go to the Filling Station to find out the truth about him. But in that moment, she'd realized how badly she wanted him to not harbor any resentment toward the hotshots, to not want to hurt them.

But she was afraid that he had. At least, he'd hurt one of them...

So, feeling sick again, she'd rushed outside for some air, only to step into total darkness. Despite the darkness, she could feel someone else's presence. But she couldn't see who was out there. And she desperately wanted to see them.

Were they this close? The saboteur? It had to be the saboteur because she could hear the hiss of air, like tires deflating. A lot of trucks, like hers, were parked in the lot because many of the hotshots had been too tired to go home and were sleeping upstairs in the bunkroom right now. She hadn't wanted to make the drive home, either, since the firehouse in St. Paul—where she and Hank worked and lived when not out with the hotshots—was more than an hour away.

She'd intended instead to go to the Filling Station, despite the fact that the bar would have closed a couple of hours ago. Then she'd heard his voice rumbling out of the back of that rig, and after she'd heard him admit to wanting the hotshots gone, she just wanted to get away from him.

But he wasn't the one out here letting air out of tires. And if he wasn't…

Did that mean he wasn't the saboteur?

Charlie was here now, though. When he had opened the door seconds ago and light spilled into the parking lot, she glanced around the area, trying to find whoever else was out there.

But the door closed too quickly again, extinguishing that brief flicker of light and the flicker of hope Michaela had to see who was still hiding in the darkness. They must have shut off the lights somehow, or Michaela would have seen them already.

Had they seen her when she'd opened that door? And Charlie? Were the two of them in danger now, like Rory had been the night that the sound of all the engines running had lured him out into the hall?

She had no weapon, and she doubted Charlie had one, too. So what had she intended to do if she actually caught the saboteur in the act?

But she wanted to see who it was so damn badly that she hadn't considered how she would actually apprehend the person. She just wanted to know who'd been messing with them for so long, putting them in danger and also doing some petty, stupid stuff like this. Letting air out of tires.

For a second, when she'd heard Charlie talking, she thought it was him. And while she'd been angry, she'd also been...hurt. But now, knowing that it wasn't him but someone else—some *anonymous* someone else, who quite possibly was a member of her team...

Fury bubbled up inside her, and she wished she had a weapon. Or at least a flashlight. Her phone had died on the return trip from Ontario, and she hadn't had the chance to charge it yet. Or she would have used that to not just see the person, but take a picture of them in the act of sabotage.

Maybe Charlie had his phone on him. When he'd opened the door, she'd started back toward the building. Toward him, drawn to him, as she'd been for too damn long. She'd tried to resist the attraction, but he was just so good-looking and so charming. But those were the very reasons she should have resisted him, because she knew those traits were her weakness and made it as hard for her to see clearly as it was for her to see in the dark parking lot right now.

But as she moved closer to him, she could see him a bit in the faint light seeping out from under the door of the firehouse. She needed to find out if he had his phone on him, but she didn't want the sound of their voices to draw the saboteur's attention or to send the person running before they could see who it was.

So she moved even closer to him and whispered near his ear, "I need your cell."

His body moved in a slight shiver. And he nodded and pulled out his phone. "Call the police."

The police wouldn't get there in time to stop whoever

was out in the dark with them. And neither would anyone inside the building because she had no doubt that if the door opened again, the person would run off.

Why hadn't they done that already, though? When she'd walked out or when Charlie had?

What was the saboteur waiting for?

Did the person want to get caught?

Another sound emanated from the shadows, something that made Michaela gasp even before the flash of the flame. She'd heard the telltale flick of a lighter.

Then a bottle rolled toward them, right before footsteps pounded across the asphalt, running away from what they'd tossed: an explosive.

"Get down!" she yelled as that bottle, the rag inside burning brightly now, rolled right near them. They were close to the building, but not close enough to open the door and get inside before the glass exploded in a fireball from the accelerant inside the bottle.

Fragments of glass flew, and the blast, as close as it was, knocked Michaela back into Charlie, whose arms closed, almost reflexively, around her. But he fell back, too, into the steel door behind them.

And then, a moment later everything went black again when she lost consciousness.

Braden Zimmer was in his office on the second floor of the firehouse. He'd just intended to take care of a few things on his desk before heading home. Sam, his wife, wasn't home right now. She'd just wrapped up an arson investigation out west and was staying in Washington for a couple of days to spend time with two men who were both nicknamed Mack: her dad and her oldest brother. The younger

Mack had mysteriously shown up in Northern Lakes four months ago, just in the nick of time to save the life of another hotshot, one he'd known from their military service.

Mack Junior was back, but nobody really knew from where or what he'd been doing while he was there. Sam was determined to find out, but even as good as an investigator as she was, Braden wasn't sure she would get much information out of her oldest brother.

That wasn't all she was going to ask Mack, though. She wanted his help. Because even as good as an investigator as she was, she hadn't been able to figure out who the saboteur was either.

Mack had already helped out once, when he'd shown up in town all those months ago. If he hadn't, Braden would have wound up burying another member of his team. Rory VanDam or whatever his real name was. Like Ethan Sommerly, Rory insisted on keeping the name he'd assumed five years ago when he and Ethan, who was really Jonathan Canterbury, had survived a plane crash.

A member of your team isn't who you think they are...

Braden had received that anonymous—and ominous—note more than a year ago, but he was no closer to finding out who'd sent it or who they were referring to. At least two people on his team weren't who he'd thought they were.

They were even better. Really good guys, and Braden would have lost one if Mack hadn't shot the FBI agent trying to kill Rory VanDam. Mack knew who Rory really was from serving in the military together.

While neither Rory nor Ethan Sommerly was who they'd said they were, neither of them was the saboteur. They'd both been victims of the saboteur instead, as well as victims of the enemies from their own pasts. With the danger they'd been in, they were lucky to be alive.

The saboteur hadn't killed anyone yet, but Braden was worried that it was only a matter of time before one of the "accidents" that the saboteur kept staging caused fatal injuries for another hotshot.

And then Braden felt it.

The slight shudder of the building, as if something had struck it. He jumped up from his chair and rushed around his desk to pull open the door to the hall. He barely made it to the top of the stairs when he heard the yelling.

"Help! We need help!"

Braden didn't recognize the voice, but there were some new volunteers in the local fire department. The new crew had a rig out when he and his team had returned from Ontario earlier that evening. Maybe they'd struck the building trying to drive it back into the garage.

"Call an ambulance!" another voice shouted.

That voice, Braden recognized: Charlie, the bartender and owner of the Filling Station. He was one of the new volunteers, much to Braden's surprise. He hadn't shared that news with any of the other hotshots yet because they were already suspicious of Charlie. And he didn't want any of them trying to investigate on their own and getting hurt. It was bad enough that he'd put his brother-in-law Trick in danger by having him help investigate and protect the others.

But Braden would have to check out Charlie now. He'd known him and the Tillerman family for years, but he knew, after what Marty had done, that anyone was capable of being dangerous. And Braden couldn't deny that Charlie volunteering at the firehouse gave him easy access to it.

Of course, Carl had pointed out that, thanks to Stanley—the nineteen-year-old who helped out around the firehouse—frequently forgetting to lock the doors, pretty much anyone had access to the building. Maybe someone else—or some*thing* else—had caused that disturbance he'd just felt.

"What happened?" Braden asked, running down the stairs to the garage area. Once he hit the bottom step, he gasped, and he could see why there was such urgency in Charlie's voice because of what he held in his arms: Michaela's limp body. Her head lolled back, blood dripping from her temple, staining her pale blonde hair red. "Oh my God!" His hand shook as he pulled out his cell.

The other man, who'd yelled first for help, was on his phone, speaking to a 911 dispatcher from the call center.

But Braden called Owen. The paramedic was closer than the hospital since he was probably just a street over at his girlfriend's apartment. "What happened?" he asked Charlie again.

"Something blew up—a bottle. There's glass and something…gasoline…and fire," he said, his deep voice vibrating with concern and confusion.

It was clear that there had been another explosion of some kind and Michaela had been injured in it. Braden relayed those details to Owen, who assured him that he was already on his way. One of the paramedic rigs was parked in the garage, though, so Braden pulled open the doors to it. "There's a stretcher in here we can lay her on, and we can get something for her wound…"

And hopefully, Owen would be there as fast as he'd promised.

As Charlie carried Michaela toward the open doors of the rig, Braden stepped forward to help, but the bar owner's arms tightened around her as if he didn't want to let her go. "She's breathing. I think," he said, his voice gruff. "And she has a pulse but…"

He was scared.

And so was Braden.

Charlie was also hurt, blood running down the side of his face like it did from hers. Maybe that was why he seemed so confused. He could have a concussion.

"Help's on the way," the other man—the new volunteer— said, and he shuddered as he stared at Michaela, too. Then he looked at Charlie and gasped. "You're hurt, too, man!"

Ignoring him, Charlie jumped up into the back of the rig, and finally, he released Michaela's limp body onto the stretcher. The side door opened again, and Owen rushed inside and across the garage toward them.

"The asphalt's on fire," the paramedic said. "What the hell happened?"

"Some kind of explosive again," Braden said. "Michaela's still unconscious."

But then she moved slightly, shifting against the gurney as she started to regain consciousness. And her jacket fell open. Unlike the rest of the team, she hadn't changed out of all her gear yet. She wore the yellow pants, but they were unsnapped and straining over the slight swell of her belly.

And Braden, whose wife was expecting a baby within the next few weeks, realized that the female hotshot was pregnant, too. She'd never said anything to him. Hell, he hadn't even known she was seeing anyone.

But from the way Charlie was sticking so close to her side, even as Owen started treating her, Braden had another suspicion about the bar owner: that maybe he was the father of Michaela's unborn child.

But none of that mattered as much as making sure that Michaela and her baby survived the saboteur's latest attack. Or Braden's fear might be realized, he might be losing another hotshot.

Chapter 3

Charlie couldn't stop pacing the ER waiting room. If he stopped, his shaky legs might fold beneath him like they had that night the bar had been on fire. The explosion in the parking lot had literally knocked him off his feet, but that wasn't what was affecting him now.

He was scared, but not for himself. He was scared for Michaela.

"She has to be okay," he muttered beneath his breath. "She has to be."

She'd saved his life over a year ago when she pulled him out of the fire, but he hadn't been able to do anything tonight to protect her or to help her. He felt like he had when his nephew had been trapped in the forest fire and when he'd been trapped in his own burning bar—so helpless that he couldn't draw a deep breath because of the pressure, the panic, nearly crushing his chest.

He wasn't alone now like he'd been in that bar fire before Michaela found him. Most of the hotshots had shown up at the hospital, too, rolling in behind the ambulance that had transported Michaela here. He would have ridden with her, but he'd wanted Owen to focus on her and not on the stupid cut on his head.

His brother-in-law had insisted on driving Charlie. And

fortunately, Eric's truck had been one of the few in the lot that the tires hadn't been slashed. Maybe he and Michaela had prevented that from happening with their sudden interruption of the vandal's plan.

"You're bleeding, man," Eric said. "You need to get someone to look at you, too."

Maybe that was why he'd driven him to the hospital: he thought Charlie needed medical attention, too. But all Charlie needed was Michaela, to make sure that she was all right.

"He's right," Braden Zimmer, the hotshot superintendent, said. "You probably need stitches."

Charlie raised his hand to his face, to where the blood had slowly been trickling down from his forehead like a trail of sweat. His hand was already stained with blood, but that was probably Michaela's, from the wound on her temple.

She'd been bleeding more than he was. How bad was the injury to her head?

She'd lost consciousness. Even though she'd started moving in the back of the ambulance, she hadn't opened her eyes. She hadn't totally regained consciousness.

Yet.

"How is she?" he asked, his voice gruff.

Braden shook his head, his jaw tense, as if he was clenching it. "I haven't heard anything yet."

Charlie followed the trickle of blood on his face up to just above his left eyebrow, and he flinched from a sudden jab of pain. Then he jerked his hand back, and his fingers came away with fresh blood. He hadn't stopped bleeding yet.

"You need to see a doctor," Eric insisted. "You need stitches."

And the hotshot superintendent must have thought so,

too, because he rushed up to the waiting room desk clerk. Seconds later, the door opened to the interior of the ER, and a nurse came out for Charlie.

He didn't protest getting treatment now because this way, he would be closer to Michaela, to wherever she was being treated. And he would, hopefully, be able to find out how she was doing.

If she was going to be okay...

"We need to irrigate and stitch that wound," the nurse was saying as she led him down a short hall to an open area. She guided him toward one of the gurneys lined up between pulled-back curtains. All the beds were empty except for one, in which an older man was sleeping, his curtains open so the nurses could keep an eye on him.

Where was Michaela? Why wasn't she back here?

"Sit down," the nurse said.

"I..." He cleared his throat of the emotion rushing up on him. "I need to know how Michaela Momber is."

The nurse's brow furrowed a bit as she studied his black uniform. "Are you one of her coworkers? Were you hurt the same time she was?"

He nodded. Even though he technically wasn't a coworker, he had been hurt with her. Which was ironic, given that, for the past several months, he'd been more worried about getting hurt *by* her.

"She's in radiology," the nurse replied, "getting a head CT and an ultrasound."

He nodded again. "That's good. They'll be able to see if she has a concussion, then."

The woman nodded now and smiled. "And make sure that her baby is okay."

"Baby?" Finally, his shaky legs gave out, and he dropped down to sit on the edge of that stretcher.

The woman's mouth dropped open, and she shook her head. "Forget I said that. I assumed you knew..."

No. He'd had no idea that Michaela was pregnant.

Had she ever intended to tell him?

And was he the father?

"Pregnant?" Michaela snorted at the ridiculous claim. And they thought *she* was the one with a concussion? "I am not pregnant."

Or maybe she was still unconscious and she was just dreaming about the impossible, about something she had once wanted so damn badly. If so, this was a cruel dream, and tears stung her eyes. She shook her head again and winced at the pain that jolted her.

"You're definitely pregnant," the doctor said and pointed to the monitor of the machine pulled next to the bed in which Michaela was lying.

She blinked to clear the tears from her vision and focused on that screen. There were arms and legs and a head with the perfect little profile of a small nose and rosebud lips. She reached up to touch her aching head, and her fingers skimmed across a bandage. "I do have a concussion?"

That had to be what was going on, why she was seeing and hearing things.

When Rory VanDam had been struck over the head a couple of months ago, he spent two weeks in a coma because of the severity of the concussion. And when he'd finally woken up, he'd been so confused.

Like she was now. Because nothing was making any sense to her...

Like what she was seeing…

She had to be hallucinating…because that just wasn't possible.

"Your CT scan showed that you have a very mild concussion," the doctor said. "I think it was more likely you passed out because you were severely dehydrated and anemic. You must have horrible morning sickness."

Michaela shook her head. "I have an ulcer…" From all the stress. From the danger. From how gruesomely she'd lost one friend and how close she'd come to losing so many others, including her best friend.

Where was Hank? Probably with Trick McRooney. Ever since Hank had fallen for the new member of the hotshot team, Michaela had kind of lost her best friend. She'd felt so alone that she finally let Charlie's charm get to her and undermine her determination to stay single and uninvolved. Given her judgment, it was safest for her and for anyone she might get involved with.

Had Charlie gotten hurt, too? He'd been behind her, though, in the parking lot. So he had to be okay…since she was. But she really wasn't okay.

The doctor chuckled and pointed toward the screen. "That is not an ulcer."

"But I can't be pregnant," Michaela insisted.

"Why do you think that?" the doctor asked, her expression serious now as she met Michaela's gaze.

The woman, with her blond hair bound up in a high ponytail, looked very young. The name tag, with her photo, attached to her pocket proved that she was an MD. Dr. Brooke Smits. She had to be just a resident, maybe even an intern. That was probably why she didn't know what she was talking about, what she was seeing on that screen.

"I'm infertile," Michaela explained. "I don't even get periods."

"Well, you probably haven't had one for the last five months, but you must ovulate occasionally."

Michaela shook her head. "Ever since I was a teenager—from how hard I work out and how physically active I am—I stopped menstruating."

"Very low body fat, like you have, would affect your periods," Dr. Smits said. "But that doesn't mean that you're infertile. You would just have a little more difficulty getting pregnant."

"I tried for years with my ex-husband," Michaela said. "But his mistress had had no problem getting pregnant." She waited for the jab of pain she usually felt when she thought about him—about *them*—but she felt nothing now but for the throbbing in her temple. A sound echoed that throbbing, and she could see it on the monitor as a little flutter across the screen. A heartbeat.

"I am *really* pregnant?" she asked. Was it actually possible?

The doctor smiled brightly at her. "You really had no idea?"

Michaela shook her head, then tensed. "I had *no* idea. I've been working wildfires. The smoke…" Her voice cracked with fear for her child. "And I inhaled some carbon monoxide in the firehouse six months ago when all the trucks were started up. How much damage did I do?" .

She couldn't blink the tears away now as they streamed from her eyes, overcome with fear that she might have already harmed the dream that she'd thought for so long she would never realize. A child.

"The carbon monoxide incident probably happened

before you got pregnant. You look to be around twenty, maybe twenty-two weeks."

So, after the holiday party...

"And your baby's heart is strong and steady, and the lung development looks good. I would say the baby is healthy. Now, the mother—" the young doctor gave her a stern look "—needs to take better care of herself. You need prenatal vitamins and rest, or you're going to be passing out again, and you'll wind up on bed rest."

"I didn't pass out because I was tired," Michaela said, and she touched the bandage again.

Dr. Smits sighed. "I know there was another incident at the firehouse."

Another. Of course the doctor would be aware of how many people she'd treated in the ER had come from the firehouse. There had been way too many *incidents* involving the hotshots getting hurt.

"You're going to have to be extra careful," the doctor advised. "On your job and with your prenatal care. I'm going to give you a referral to an ob-gyn, and you should make an appointment as soon as possible."

Michaela sucked in a breath as a horrible thought occurred to her. "Am I going to be able to keep working?"

"The ob-gyn will be better able to answer your questions about restrictions and such," Dr. Smits replied.

Restrictions? There was no such thing as light duty as a hotshot. Michaela's job was so important to her—as her ex had said, maybe too important. It had taken her away from him so much, and it had taken away her chance of ever conceiving.

Or so she'd thought.

She hadn't been willing to give it up for her ex-husband.

She focused on the screen, on that perfect little profile, and warmth flooded her heart.

But for the baby…

She moved her hands to her stomach, running them over it, and she felt a little flutter inside her, a little movement, and on that screen, the baby kicked. She gasped. "That's what I've been feeling? I've been feeling her or him?"

"You want to know?" Dr. Smits asked.

"Yes," she answered. Not that it mattered. "Mostly I just want to know that he or she is healthy."

"I promise you that your baby really appears to be strong and healthy," the doctor reassured Michaela. "But you have to make sure *she* stays that way."

"She?"

The doctor smiled that bright, happy smile again. "Yes. You're having a daughter."

While Michaela wanted to know so that she could connect more fully with her child and that the baby would seem more real to her in what was such a surreal situation, she didn't really care what the gender of her child was. But she knew *who* would have cared: her father. Her daughter's grandfather would have been disappointed, like he'd been when his only child had been a daughter. But Michaela had no intention of telling her father about her pregnancy.

But the *baby's* father…

Charlie deserved to know, even though Michaela felt sick all over again at the thought of telling him. They had both agreed that this—whatever *this* was—was not going to be anything serious or lasting. Both had been burned before and had no intention of trying marriage again or even a relationship. What they had wasn't supposed to lead to anything.

But it had…

To a baby girl.

While Michaela was happy, would Charlie be? Or would he be like her father had been: resentful of her and her mother?

The dangers of her job weren't the only things that Michaela needed to protect her baby from…

Trick McRooney stood just outside the police tape, which had been strung around the firehouse parking lot right next to the building.

Another attack on their home turf.

By one of their own?

Trick nearly chuckled at the irony of him thinking that way, of being possessive of a place and of a team. For years, he'd avoided forming any sort of attachment to a job location and especially to people. His and his siblings' mom taking off when they were young had made it hard for him to trust people.

But that changed when he had joined the Huron Hotshots several months ago. Because he knew that he belonged here in Northern Lakes with his fiancée, Henrietta "Hank" Rowlins, and with his sister and brother-in-law.

But if these attacks kept happening, Braden was bound to lose his job. And Trick would probably lose his, too. But he cared less about the job than about someone losing their life. Michaela was in the hospital. He and Henrietta had been at the cottage she'd inherited from her grandfather when they got the call. Henrietta was on her way to the hospital, but had insisted that he come here to find out what he could about what had happened to her best friend and the only other female on the twenty-member team of hotshots.

But Trooper Wells had ordered him to stay outside the crime scene tape. On the outside of the firehouse. And out of her way.

As if he couldn't be trusted, when *she* was the one nobody trusted. She was the only suspect they had all agreed on when they discussed the saboteur on the plane ride home. Wynona Wells had worked too closely with the trooper who was in jail for trying to kill one of the hotshots and for his role in the death of another hotshot. Trick had taken Dirk Brown's place on the team, and it was his job to ensure that nobody else lost their life.

"C'mon, Trooper Wells," he called out to the officer again, as he had a few times prior, only to be ignored. "I need to know what happened here tonight." And if he could get inside the damn firehouse, he would be able to access the footage from the cameras Braden had had installed after Rory was hurt so badly. The cameras were mostly on the main level, though, to catch people going in and out the doors and up and down the stairs. There were none out in the parking lot. But maybe they would have some installed there, too.

She finally turned toward him. "You probably have a better idea what happened here than I do," she said. "None of you have been forthcoming with me about anything that has been going on with the hotshots."

Because they weren't sure they could trust her. Hell, they weren't sure they could trust each other. It almost had to be one of them. Didn't it?

Unless…

Trick had considered Charlie Tillerman a suspect.

There had been a couple of times when people—himself included—almost certainly had to have been drugged while they were at the bar. And who would have had the easiest access to do that other than the bartender?

But Charlie had been with Michaela when she got hurt tonight, and he had possibly been hurt, too. So that ruled him out as a suspect. Probably. Trick couldn't be sure, since he really had no idea what had happened tonight or how badly anyone had been hurt.

And the only light in the parking lot came from the ones the state police crime techs had set up. What had happened to the lights on the parking lot poles? And there was a motion light on the building by that side door that was supposed to automatically come on. But it was dark, too, even with Trooper Wells standing right in front of it.

Someone had obviously planned what had happened tonight. They'd extinguished all the lights so that they could slink around in the shadows like they'd been doing for over a year. That damn saboteur...

Some of the things they'd done were petty—messing with equipment, like the trucks that had flat tires sitting in the lot right now. There were a few of them. Braden's. And Donovan Cunningham's. He lived close enough that he probably should have gone home. But maybe he'd still been showering when the saboteur had struck.

Carl Kozak's truck tires were flat, too, and he lived close enough to have gone home, as well. Trick was glad that he and Henrietta had gone to her grandfather's cottage to shower and sleep instead of sticking around here.

There were a couple of other trucks in the lot that he didn't recognize. Maybe the new volunteer firefighter's rides. They'd had a call tonight and had one of the rigs out when the hotshots returned from Canada. And when he and the other hotshots had returned to the firehouse, the parking lot lights had been on then. All of them.

So whoever put them out could have been someone on their hotshot team who'd either thrown the breaker to shut them off or had somehow broken the bulbs. The only broken glass on the asphalt seemed to have come from that bottle, though—the one that had been rigged like a Molotov cocktail.

What had that been intended to do? Had it been meant for Michaela or for one of the vehicles? Or to start the firehouse itself aflame?

"We can't tell you what we don't know," Trick pointed out, his frustration overwhelming him.

Michaela better be okay. She was one of the toughest people he knew, though, so she had to be.

The trooper narrowed her eyes and studied his face. "But none of you will tell me what you do know, either."

"Have you tried talking to Michaela already?" he asked. If she had, then the hotshot was awake. When Braden had called them, he assured Henrietta that her best friend was already coming around, that she was going to be okay.

But Trick wondered if the hotshot superintendent had been speaking the truth or just saying what he wanted to be true. Braden desperately didn't want to lose another member of his team. Trick didn't want to, either.

"I was told she was unconscious still," Trooper Wells said. "But then, I've been told that before…"

"Rory was in a coma for two weeks," he said. But to protect the injured hotshot, Braden had held her off for the extra week that Rory had been kept in the hospital for observation and for his memory to return completely to him. He'd been so confused when he'd awakened.

And given his previous career as an undercover DEA officer, it was no wonder he'd been so disoriented. Trick hadn't lived the life Rory had, and he was confused.

Why did someone keep coming after them?

What the hell was the motive?

Don't miss
Hotshot's Dangerous Liaison
by Lisa Childs,
available July 2024 wherever
Harlequin® Romantic Suspense
books and ebooks are sold.

www.Harlequin.com